THE FLOWERS OF
BEDFORD
ELEMENTARY SCHOOL

Cover Art & Cover Wrap by Anze Ban Virant (abvatelier.com/contact)
Base Photograph by Shaun Hathaway
Interior Layout by Brady Moller

The Flowers of BEDFORD Elementary School

SHAUN HATHAWAY

Contents

An offering to:
God, Jesus, & the Holy Spirit

CHAPTER ONE
A PROLOGUE

Thin and daunting, the structure stood: A house.

A small house in the playground of an elementary school.

Chapter Two
A Walk-Through

The house was tall, dark grey, and compressed enough to hold a semi-rectangular shape. There were windows, two on the broadest sides, one of which faced the school, and one on each of the narrow ends. Small as it may be, it still had two levels. The gable roof with its generic dark shingling shone proudly in the basking sun and made the vinyl siding almost a cheery shade of grey in comparison.

*

The house appeared sometime during summer break. The principal never approved of it, the teachers knew nothing about the addition, and the school board never voted on it. The superintendent decided to explore the house by himself shortly after it had been spotted for the first time by one of the custodians.

Inside he found that the house was furnished and finished in a perfectly ordinary way. He opened the front door and stepped inside to the entryway. There on the left, he saw a rubber mat with grooves, designed to place one's shoes on top of and above that at a slightly above eye level, a row of hooks where you could hang your jackets, hats, scarves, etc. Without thinking, he took his shoes off and placed them on top of the rubber mat, and walked through the glass paneled door that separated the entryway from the rest of the house.

The house had an engineered hardwood floor with the plain horizontal striping you would expect to see in the most typical suburban home. To the left there was a staircase that led to the upstairs and underneath the staircase, a spandrel with a small door. In the center and extended to the wall on the right, was a miniature hallway, no more than eight feet wide. He decided to explore this small hallway first.

He walked down a space of what could not have been longer than twenty feet or so and saw that there were two doors spaced from one another, one to the left and one to the right. He opened the one on the left first and saw inside a laundry room. A white matching set of a washer and dryer, a shelf installed above it, and three hampers lined up against the wall opposite of the machines. They were a fitting grey color, considering the exterior of the house, and contrasted well against the white walls in the laundry room. The superintendent examined the back of the washer and dryer. He saw that the inlets on the washing machine, the dryer's blower, and both machines' respective power cords were all plugged in and equipped properly. He peeked inside both machines and saw nothing inside either of them, not quite sure what he imagined he was going to see anyways. He took a peek through the window centered in the back wall and could see the swingsets and grass. Certainly an odd reminder of where this house was located.

He stepped out of the laundry room and decided to enter the door on the right. It was a bathroom. There was a white vanity with a sink that had a matching white basin and a grey spout and handles. There were two long vertical cabinets on each side of the vanity and in the middle were three horizontal cabinets. Each had the same thin handle that consisted of a longish cylinder being attached to the door by two identical cylinders, that were installed lengthwise or widthwise depending on which was appropriate for each cabinet. He searched in each cabinet. The three in the middle were empty, but the two thin vertical cabinets each had three shelves inside that were being used to hold grey towels of varying sizes, larger in sizes as they ascended down the shelves.

He looked into the frameless rectangular mirror briefly and turned on the sink. Water ran with consistent pressure and he even went as far to satiate his curiosity by testing both the hot and the cold temperatures each handle was in charge of and they passed his objectiveless approval. He peered beside the vanity and saw the toilet. Ordinary shade of white that matched the vanity, walls, and even the sides of the shower he had only quickly seen in the reflection of the mirror. What made this one worthy of being considered fancy in his eyes, was the toilet lids themselves. Instead of the gravity driven, noisy, and often heavy porcelain seats that slammed on their own volition with such force that the violating sound could damage an ordinary man's eardrums, they were very thin and sleek plastic lids with hinges that did not allow a quick freefall, but instead a slow and steady descent into their respective places. He tested this out twice just to see if it was a fluke or design. Just like any ordinary person, he tested to see if it would flush by pressing the smooth, grey handle on its upper left quadrant. He peered at the toilet roll holder and even felt with the tips of his fingers the exceptionally soft toilet paper that had been placed there with the triangular fold in the front like the ones he saw at mid-priced hotels he stayed at when he had to go to out of state meetings.

The shower was his next point of investigation and he turned to see the hard plastic shower lining that seemed exceptionally flush with the wall for a shower with a plastic shell, only sticking out perhaps two inches away from the wall it was installed in. He rubbed his hand along the soothing comfort of the heavy grey linen shower curtain and peeled it back. There stuck out of the wall the grey handle with its circular backing, as per expected, and of course the matching grey showerhead. He was starting to detect a pattern with the colors. The handle was a very minimalist and smooth shape that had no defining edges, grooves, or textured feel to it whatsoever.

He was impressed with the minimalist functionality of the shell as a whole. There was an L-shaped shower niche that was an extension of the shell itself, instead of an addition and held a matching shampoo and conditioner set on the top of the L that rose to about chest level, or at least for a man of his stature at least, and the wide bottom of the shape was able to hold many more untouched bottles it came equipped with, including body wash, face moisturizer, exfoliating scrubs, and even lotion that was made to be applied after a final rinse in the shower. While the bottles of what he considered to be extras remained as a cute curiosity to his masculine senses, he was instantly a fan of the seat that was also an extension of the shell. It connected seamlessly and extended directly next to the end of the widthwise length of the L-shelving. It had a rectangular shape, but rounded at the end. He approximated the dimensions to be two feet wide and a foot and a half high. After his admiration period had ended, his rudimentary tests of the water pressure and temperatures of the shower also passed his test.

He exited the bathroom and closed the door behind him. Without thinking of where he was going to go next, his attention was brought to the kitchen to the right of the bathroom door. He walked the space of around fifteen feet or so in another narrow hallway and was standing on the linoleum that lined the kitchen floor. The color of the appliances and cabinets were certainly no surprise by now to the superintendent.

He first noticed the refrigerator, so plain and rectangular with its basic top door freezer and bottom drawer fridge design that was so practical it almost seemed vintage in comparison to the refrigerators he was used to nowadays. No ice maker, water dispenser, glass cut display in the front, touchscreen, or even so much as a special insignia on the front to indicate the brand. Just plain with its smooth rectangular handles that jutted out a neat finger's space away from the texture of their respective doors.

The freezer was nice, cold, shelfless and empty. The fridge portion had a classical hint of yellow illumination from the powerful lightbulb it had. There were three basic shelves, the top shelf being tall enough for gallons of milk and the like, the second shelf having a smaller height than the top and bottom, and the bottom shelf having perhaps a smidgen smaller of a height than the top shelf. They were all glass with those plastic bumpers at the end so when you wanted to take them out you weren't touching just glass. Underneath the final shelf were two identical sized drawers, the superintendent believed his mother taught him that at least one of those were called a crisper. All was cool to the touch and similarly empty. He closed the fridge and moved on to the rest of the kitchen.

The kitchen seemed exceptionally planned out, as the fridge was nicely flush against the wall and above it was the beginning of the cabinets which, the two above the fridge being rectangular twins in mirrored direction to one another. They connected to the entire cabinet system which hung over in a uniformity across the entire countertops, stopping right before the sink, and starting over again over more countertop, hitting a sharp corner, and starting over again perpendicular to the end of the last row, until it reached the oven. Well, it was time for him to inspect some more.

He ran his fingers along the countertop and felt an impressive smoothness that, in spite of it being just a rudimentary and rather cheap material such as laminate (unlike the very nice granite countertops which lined his kitchen), felt terrifically smooth and certainly sturdy enough to last a good fifteen years of use he estimated. He stopped to examine the sink with its medium depth basin, probably large enough to roughly fit a stock pot in with around a couple of inches poking out of the top. It was a nice stainless steel lining. The water coming from the sink also passed his tests. Directly above the sink was the window and he could see the large swathe of grass next to the end of the swingset and even some of the blacktop the house rested on. That view was not something he was going to get used to, he imagined.

Moving on, he worked his way to the oven, which to his pleasant surprise was electric. It wasn't that he was against open-flame gas ovens at home or anything, as a matter of fact it was a preference of his wife and himself, but he thought in the presence of children, that electric was probably a smart choice. It had four burners, so comically flush with the glass it was built into, and above that was a rather chimney bottom shaped exhaust fan. Well that seemed like an oddly expensive choice, he thought, in what was an otherwise cost efficient house thus far, but, he reasoned with himself, perhaps it was part of a set and was more economical in price than it would be to buy separately and outright. The oven portion was quite up to par with his expectations, three adjustable racks, but really who needed more than two while cooking, he thought. All turned on and seemed to get appropriately hot and he was satisfied.

Built nicely right against the space of the oven, was a long thin door with a cabinet above. He opened it to see a reasonably sized thirteen-gallon trash can with a new bag already placed inside and empty. Well, now that he had gotten to open that door, he found it to be the appropriate time to open the rest of the cabinets. He found nothing, yet again wondering exactly what he expected to find. Well, that was fine enough because his attention was turned to the right of him where he noticed the basic dining room setup that connected effortlessly to the kitchen.

It was a large oval table with that trademark shiny wood styling. It was placed horizontally to the wall instead of vertically, where it no doubt would have been near poking into the kitchen area were it to be placed that way. There were four wooden bow back chairs were placed around the table in a traditional style, one on each end and two across from one another on the width sides. A rather basic style with nothing much to critique or note, he wordlessly declared to himself. That being the extent of this side of the house, he figured it should be time that he turned back to examine the remainder of the downstairs.

He noticed a doorless doorjamb opening behind the chair on the farthest right and decided to walk through that way instead of retracing his path that led him here. He found himself standing right in front of the entryway door where he originally stood when he first entered and this time decided he wanted to check out that little spandrel underneath the staircase before moving on. He opened the little slanted wooden door and looked underneath the space below the stairs and saw nothing more than an empty area that decreased in size as the stairs descended. He briefly thought to himself how convenient one of these areas would be in his household for storing all of those seasonal decorations his wife overbought every year. With that uneventful conclusion to his peek under the stairs, he closed the spandrel door and turned around to walk towards the top of the hall.

He decided his journey should bring him to the next room the downstairs had to offer and went through the doorjamb on the left. He stepped in and saw a perfectly quaint living room. There was a long grey couch made to seat four people that sat flush against the wall with the windows to each side of it, a very swell looking rectangular coffee table that sat in front of the length of it, and of course flush against the wall was a wall mounted TV and an entertainment center underneath. Each end of the couch was also accompanied by little tables with lamps that took up approximately one-third of the table space it sat on. A few feet off of the right end table and cornered so it faced central to the living room was an overly plush recliner that looked like it was yet to be broken in by the stereotypical patriarchal figure that would be expected to sit there. He decided he wanted to test the couch's softness first before reaping the spoils of what was surely going to be a beautiful comfort provided by the recliner.

He sat down on the far left side of the couch and rubbed his hands along the linen(?) cushions. Was it linen? He asked himself. Either way, when he rubbed his hands against the grain on the cushion, it moved the fabric in a way where it looked like it revealed a secret darker fabric beneath. He played with the changing hues for a few moments and decided it was probably best to try to make it look like how he found it and did a few cautious adjusting swipes before getting up.

He moved along to the recliner with a little more zest in his step than he would probably like to be caught with and plopped himself down dramatically in the recliner chair, like a child left to wander in a discount furniture store, mimicking their father. He tested the reclining function, and sat back into the seat, pushing his back against the support to feel and experience the full range of motion offered by this plush seating. He was more than satisfied and practically had to remind himself that what he was doing was still technically work and pressed the recliner in with his feet and got back up.

As he got to his feet he noticed that there was a nice, sturdy wooden shelving on the far side of the wall to the left with broad spacing and lengthy boards that would be very ideal for a blossoming family's board game collection. The shelves were like most in this house: empty. Nevertheless, he turned around and decided that the entertainment center would be his next object of interest. He opened the little cabinets underneath and there was of course nothing material besides the shelves in there. Now that what felt like his common courtesy check was over, he found the TV's remote sitting atop the entertainment center and decided to try turning it on.

The very simple maneuver of pointing and pressing the power button had proved successful as the TV began to turn on, announcing with a smooth shaped box centric on the screen, that it was searching for a signal. When the television had evidently decided it searched hard enough for one to be found, it gave up and went to a blank screen with a rich blue color that more seriously told the viewer that there was no signal in all capital letters. Half-expecting to at least watch the Public Access Channels of the surrounding area or even a news station or two, he resigned the effort and turned off the TV and carefully rested the remote back in an even fashion that pressed itself against the wall.

It had seemed as though his examination of the living room was complete, except the superficial testing of the lamps. In what could be described as a layman's OCD fashion, he hurriedly pulled the strings on each lamp on and off to make sure, to no one but himself, that the light-bulbs indeed worked. Stimulated plenty by this downstairs, he now wanted to proceed out of the living room. He saw that there was an opening past the recliner that would bring him back to that now familiar, miniature hall.

He walked through the opening, turned to the right, made his way beside the laundry room door and turned towards the entryway door. He continued walking until he found himself placing his hand alongside the railing of the stairs and standing at the bottom of the steps. Plenty stimulated by all of what the downstairs had to offer, he now wondered what would await him upstairs.

*

The stairs were made of a wood of nice solidity, but overlaying it was a fuzzy runner carpet. It covered around three quarters of each step leaving only the edges exposed. On one hand, he felt that the choice of a fuzzy carpet may have been slightly impractical for a house clearly designed to be a 'shoes-off' sort of residence as there was not a solid amount of grip to be had underfoot. On the other hand however, he could only imagine the heightened excitement a child might have sliding down the stairs, propelling themselves with increasing speed using their feet and hands to drag farther and farther down until the momentum was plenty enough to help move their weight naturally without assistance.

Just thinking of the fun a child might have with this runner, he himself was almost tempted to climb to the very top of the stairs just so he may turn around to face the descending steps, sit down on the top step, and let his naturally heavier stature carry his weight to the bottom in a controlled freefall slide. This however, was work, he had to remind himself even once more, but still, who was around to see him? Surely no other staff or students would be around to make sure their superintendent was keeping up his professional rapport and even more certainly he knew that God would not tally this act of playfulness as a sin against oneself, but merely as an expression of joy he allows his children to have in his Holy presence. Still, though, he let his own self-imposed argument win that 'work was work' and appearances had to be maintained, at least until he retired in another five to seven years or so.

Now it began to bother him, was he to be so caring of what men of the flesh really had to think about him? Surely he loved his coworkers and staff, even when they were at their most judging. Such as the numerous times he tried to introduce more lackadaisical dress codes into the district offices. He had been met with such resistance from secretaries and financial administrators who far surpassed him in years both in age and time in the district, that he found himself somehow at the mercy of their discretion rather than his own. So here he stood, now on the top of the stairs, wearing a two piece suit that fifteen years ago would have only been reserved for weddings or the far too often funerals that occurred on his mother's side of the family.

Now with his mind still in full adrift from reality, he felt his hand reach the end of the railing and was shifted back to his present moment: the upstairs. The landing was spacious enough and he saw what could have been expected from the ordinariness the rest of the house offered; one door on the left wall, one door on the right wall, and one door in front of him. Seeing the immediate closeness of the door in front of him, he decided that he may as well begin with the door in the center.

Another bathroom, and while the vanity was nearly identical to the one that existed downstairs, except perhaps a tad smaller to accommodate the slightly smaller size of this room, there was a noticeable difference, no shower. In place of that shower that impressed him so much earlier, there instead was a grey freestanding tub in its place. It was an oval-esque shape with high-rising ends that made it look ideal for a longer soak in the tub that he knew his wife was fond of taking after a long day. It always seemed so relaxing, being able to just sit there in a hot tub of water with the smell of the lavender 'sea soak' she liberally poured in there in addition to some sort of salt that was supposed to help with aches and pains. He wanted desperately to try it some time, but was too sheepish to ask his wife, knowing how expensive and difficult she says the sea soak is to find and given the amount that she says is needed to necessitate a fully relaxing environment, she would certainly notice the portion missing, was he to try to sneak in a bath while she was out.

His hand longingly rubbed along the smooth acrylic side of the tub and decided it was time to try out the rather fancy spout. Instead of being naturally extended out of an opening on one side of the tub, it instead rose from beside the bath and lurked over the side closest to the wall. It was a very long, thin, grey spout with two accompanying handles that were operated by pulling directly down from its upright position instead of pulling it from its side to inwards. It passed with flying colors. Though the water came out in a much thinner stream than one of the wider mouth spouts traditional to a tub, it came out with impressive force and temperatures appropriate to the operation of its spouts. It even drained effortlessly. Had there been a brand name for him to find on the smooth surface, he would have surely made a mental note of it to himself so he may consider an upgrade from the older style, oversized porcelain tub that dominated his own upstairs bathroom.

Perhaps less excitingly, but still important, the sink also worked to a proficient standard. He quickly peeked through the cabinets in the vanity and saw the same matching sets of different sized grey towels and moved on. Peeking out the window swiftly, he saw a view of the playground not dissimilar to the view that would be seen from a classroom on the second floor of the school. Still, a very strange sight from the inside of a house designed for residential purposes. However, it was time to move on past this bathroom and its exceptional tub so that he could evaluate the remaining rooms upstairs.

He exited the bathroom and closed the door behind him and noted how softly and effortlessly the door closed, completely without squeaking, awkward stutters caused by the hinges, or an abnormal amount of strength needed to succinctly fit the door inside its jamb. There really was a romanticism to exploring a new house, he thought. It was untouched by the wear of homeowners and its virginal beauty shone through and beyond its seeming plainness.

Without straining his thoughts on a decision, he found himself gravitating towards the door on the right and turned its circular knob with ease. While it made sense given the furnished completion that the rest of the house had, it still struck him as odd seeing the twin sized bed pushed right against the wall underneath the window. It was obviously a bedroom, most likely designed for a child or teen or at the very least not the head of the household, he imagined. The bed was complete with two pillows that lay flat with some cushioned elevation at the head of the mattress, followed underneath by a tightly made set of sheets and a rather plump looking comforter, perhaps even weighted. He settled with brushing and patting his hands along the bed to feel the comforts that it may offer, no matter how badly he may have wanted to lie down upon it.

He noticed that at the end of the room there was a large dresser that was pressed flush against the walls. It was a typical design, six equally sized rectangular drawers with a thin, flat top that would be able to support plenty of youthful decorations and accessories. He opened the drawers with an air of what felt very well could have been the beginnings of the feeling of guilt. As though he was intruding upon the privacy that an in-use bedroom would typically carry. He tried to shake the nonsensical thought from his mind as he found there was nothing to be found in the dresser anyhow.

He backed away from the dresser and took a longer look around the square shaped room and couldn't help but notice its emptiness. Perhaps the immediate mental calculations he did to decide to himself that it was a room for a youth was wrong. After all it was entirely barren besides the dresser and well-made bed. Was it a guest room, maybe? But why the four chairs downstairs for the dining room. It seemed as though it was more fitting for a family living situation. It was almost as though the house was made and furnished by the familiarity one might gather from browsing through homemaker magazines and gleaned interior design from various family oriented sitcoms, but lacked the forethought of what living arrangement was actually necessary to be able to support the family its downstairs accommodated. Maybe he was overthinking, he thought. A quick peek out the window to see the growing grass fields of the play-ground that will be trimmed soon enough once the landscaping company the district has a contract with decides it is close enough to the beginning of the school year to tidy up its appearance.

He exited the bedroom of sorts and walked directly across to the door on the left of the landing and entered. Inside was a complete furnishing that seemed exceptionally fit for the type of master bedroom he was acquainted with. Directly in the center of the wall it was placed against, headboard first, was what looked like a king-sized bed. It had a grey velvet headboard with a cushion button directly in its center that undoubtedly had been placed there for aesthetic reasons more than necessary ones. It must have been around two and a half feet tall and was as wide as the mattress, but with the absence of adults leaning their backs against the headboard, it looked like it was towering over the bed. He pressed his knuckles in a loosely held fist against the velvet and felt its wonderfully firm presence bounce back against his force.

While that was certainly the most eye-catching attribute to the bed, or at least to himself anyways, there was a nice assortment of pillows that rested below, two double stacked large pillows and one of those funny little circular pillows he never quite understood the purpose of, in between the stacks. The sheets were tightly pressed and the comforter made with such precision that despite its very plush appearance, he was almost certain he would have been able to bounce a quarter off of it, had he any in his pocket. He wanted more so than the other bed, to lie down upon this beautiful presence of a bed and spread his arms and legs out in a fashion one would repeat lying in the snow to make an angelic caricature of their body's shape. He settled once more for a patting of the hands and a few long brushes of the palm in a lengthwise manner.

On each side of the bed, he saw two identical stool shaped end tables without drawers, but similar to the pair downstairs in the living room, each had their own lamps. The rudimentary tests of their lightbulbs passed. A nice touch to this room was the walk-in closet that was to the left side of the room. He slowly opened the wooden shutter doors and saw the long rod that extended the entire width of the closet. He ran his fingertips along the valet rod and felt the smooth wooden exterior without any fear of splinters. It was a wonderfully simple design, but he couldn't help but admire its craftsmanship, even if it was realistically cut down, shaped, and sanded by a machine.

He stepped out and carefully closed the closet doors. While the rest of the room may have a bit of empty space, the beautifully presented bed, the bedside tables, and the nicely crafted closet made it feel much more welcoming, at least in an immediate sense, opposed to the other bedroom across the hallway. With a young married couple, this room could be used to its fullest potential. But it wouldn't become home to a young married couple or any couple as a matter of fact, because it was here. Located on top of the far right end of a blacktop for the playground of an elementary school. He peeked outside the window on the left wall and saw the swingset perfectly centered in the window at the intersection of the four panes and without any further thought, left the room.

He made his way down the stairs, through the entryway, retrieved his shoes from the rubber mat, placed them back on his feet, and exited through the front door, minding to shut the door tightly so the natural debris of the woodchips, grass, and dirt from the playground couldn't invade the tidiness of the new house. He wasn't really sure what to make of the house, but he knew it was safe, well-furnished, and rather livable. Still, what to do with it.

He knew it would cost a small fortune to tear it down or relocate it and would most certainly cause a public uproar with a likely chance of the local media getting involved if the district had to come forward and admit that they don't know where the house came from or why it was at their local elementary school. So he decided to save face and he decided he would call together a private meeting with the school board and the principal to discuss their plan. The school board was made up of retirees from the town who no longer had any children in the district anymore, but probably stayed on because they no longer knew what else they should do with their time, so they could be easily convinced enough if he told them it came from a new grant and although it should've been brought to their attention first, he could plead the defense of it being easier to ask for forgiveness than to ask for permission in the highly bureaucratic world of school politics. The principal was even closer to retirement than he was and prided himself on exploring alternative methods of education, so he was sure this would be easy for him to accept and if not so immediately, an additional padding to his holiday bonus would probably be enough persuasion.

*

His mind was made and he walked to his car, connected his cellphone to the giant touchscreen display that he still hadn't quite got the hang of, and started to make the phone calls necessary to accomplish his plan.

*

Never once did he stop to wonder how there was running water, functional plumbing, and running electricity. Never once did he stop to wonder how the window centered on the left wall in the upstairs bedroom could have the same view as the window centered on the back wall in the downstairs laundry room.

Chapter Three
Inception

To say that it was built would not be completely accurate.

To say that it was born would not be completely inaccurate.

It was a manifestation.

Christian theologians differ on the subject, even Catholics from Orthodox, but a general consensus across all submits to the fact that the only being capable of creating something from true nothingness is God. Any other creator, no matter how supernatural, has to come from a source. This house came from a source.

There are typically tell-tale signs that an object is an apport. When it first appears, it is typically warm and sometimes damp to the touch, but when the house had been left to sit out to dry in the sun and naturally come to a temperature only regulated by the sun's warmth, who was to know? Another sign would be noticeable imperfections that its ordinary counterpart would not have. In this case: a window with an impossible view.

CHAPTER FOUR
CONCEPTION PT. I

A sacrificial womb created by an invitation.

Chapter Five
A Foundation for Temptation (Mia)

It was a shade of blue dark enough to be mistaken for black in mediocre lighting but lacked the subtlety or distinctive depth to be described as navy. The handles on each door were thin, rectangular bars overstretched a black basin shape that had the depth of a ramekin, where one could easily rest their four fingers inside of and gain the momentum necessary to pull back the handle forcefully when either the winter or the rust have gotten the best of the door's internal mechanics. Its tires live a good five inches below its metal frame, rugged, but only months away from failing the penny test new drivers inherit from their parents. The oversized window deflectors on the driver and passenger side windows that add to the bulked appearance of the SUV have begun to outlive their adhesives and sag with lethargy that is only fixed in an aesthetical way by closing the respective windows flush. The car and its driver sat in a parking lot outside of the entrance to one of the state's trails. Heavy and large was the SUV's body, heavier was the burden to be left behind.

Her pale skin was flush, her blood vessels filled with an influx of blood so drastic it felt as though her flooded capillaries were going to erupt beneath the surfaces of her skin and leak beneath her cheeks, pouring down the traces of her face, following the curve of her chin, and ending to pool at the build of her jutting collarbones. She almost wished for it to happen, letting herself be painted by her anger and violent sadness. The tears streamed down her face, digging tunnels into the layer of foundation she applied to make herself feel pretty now reduced to a path for her crying to be directed. Tears gliding across the infinitesimal cracks in her makeup, like a flood devastating the desert's arid surface. The tears continued to come out hot and made the pains of her grotesquely bruised eye far more sharp.

The sobs long past being caught in her throat turned to hoarse screams and ripped into the flesh of her larynx in a way that could remain as a permanence. It felt like waves of serrated lining in her throat were being blown against by the forced air erupting from each scream her body let out. The saliva that splashed against the top of her mouth felt as thick as blood, the blood that crashed against the back of her teeth felt as thin as water.

She clenched her teeth together as she screamed, her slight overbite reminded her of the imperfection of her front left tooth which stood out in appearance among the uniformity of her otherwise straight teeth because of its size. It hung past where the right tooth ended and it made her feel deformed. A mouth designed to rip, tear, and hurt the things it encountered and not pretty, welcoming, or motherly enough to speak the sweet things that she wanted to flow from her lips. Her lips were cracked and split, the dried chaps only catching sparse hydration from tears. At only sixteen years old, Mia wanted to die.

*

Abby and Mia were not childhood friends raised together and inseparable. They were not generational family friends ushered into a bond who called one another cousins. They were friends that only began to mesh their time together drastically at the end of sophomore year and now two and a half months before their junior year started, the friendship had become a staple in their lives. It was a horrible undoing.

The first domino was tipped when they went out to eat at a pizzeria close to Abby's home in town. Mia had the car, a well-used blue Tahoe manufactured a few years before she was even born, and drove them wherever they wanted to go. They sat down in the red pleather booth, accompanied by an endless amount of cracks connecting one to another as a sign of its age, and planned ahead to order a pizza to split. Their waiter approached their table.

He smiled wide with a mouthwash-rinsed tobacco smile. A small, but heavy bead piercing dangled from his bottom lip; the miniature weight caused his lower lip to dangle ever so slightly to give the illusion of being fuller than it actually was. His receding hairline shaped downwards across his skull into a nearly tidy V-shape, but he kept it buzzed low so it seemed like his hairstyle was still under his control. Just long enough to brush it with his palm, but too short to accentuate its full extent.

He smelled of years old Calvin Klein cologne that had far passed its expiration date sitting in its seventy-five cent vending machine in the men's restroom, a novelty that was only still kept there as a reminder of a bygone era that the owner convinced himself was worthy to be fond of. It used to be stocked with condoms and Spanish Fly and it wasn't until last year when one of the barely fifteen year old hostesses painted the ugliness of it by asking the owner how he would feel about some guy trying to use it on his daughter. Now all that was left in there was expired cologne and breath spray that came in eye-dropper bottles so far past their freshness that the sugar contents began to crystallize.

Visible on his right arm were several color tattoos of cheaply stenciled dragons breathing fire that had been faded by at least seven years since the low-quality ink was pressed into his naive skin. He wore the company uniform shirt that had the typical three buttons and collar combo by the throat and purposely unbottoned the top two to make visible the imitation amethyst pendant that hung by a fraying hemp rope around his neck. He felt it was good timing that he shaved down his beard to a pencil thin jawline wrap around this morning.

His eyes narrowed as he saw the two girls walk through the door and had he not been the only one waiting tables in the shop that slow Tuesday afternoon, the hostess would have no doubt made sure he wasn't able to wait on them. He pocketed his nametag. Even if he couldn't express it in words, he knew the plastic reminder that he was company property while he was there would be a faux-pas at best and a turn-off at worst when trying to present himself.

He saw the girl on the left, subtle makeup, small earrings that didn't dangle further than a centimeter from the bottom of her ear, dark green t-shirt with those wavy sleeves he didn't understand the point of, a pair of high-waisted jeans, and a pair of Converse with an embroidered flower patch on the ankle side shoe facing him. However, across from her was one who looked more 'fun' to him. She accentuated her eyes with thick black eyeliner and practically electric blue eyeshadow, her lips glowed with thick pink lipstick, her left ear had a row of four piercings increasing in size in descending order ending with a large Native American-adjacent style feather earring swinging loosely, she wore a loose sweatshirt that was rough-edged with a crude scissor cut across the front to be manipulated into a liberally revealing crop-top fashion, denim shorts cut so high that it made her smartphone look enormous as it stuck out the half-torn pocket that peeked out the underside of where the shorts ended on her thigh, and a pair of white Adidas slides. As he looked closer at what interested him, he could see on her upper thigh she either had a small cluster of self-harming scars or stretch marks, but in either case, he knew he could use it as a way to lean on an insecurity of hers.

He made sure to lean himself down with a slight bend in his body that showed favor to the girl he felt most likely to ensnare in his shattered perception of intimacy. He laid down a thick layer of his best false-self: a man capable of charm. He shared his name with a confidence that the girl on the right would remember. Austin. She remembered.

*

Mia and Abby had eaten down their pizza until they both were left with one slice each. The check had been paid for and their dutiful waiter Austin had brought back the cardboard box made for children's pizzas as their take-out box. Austin even went the extra mile to wrap their individual pieces in foil sheets so that they could reheat it easily in the oven because when it was microwaved, he told them, it just didn't taste right.

Mia had been feeling bloated since before they even sat down at the booth and couldn't tell if it was just confused signals from her stomach letting her know she was hungry, but after eating, it still felt the same. She had worked herself into a silent panic wondering why the bloating felt so constant and had become convinced that she could feel a faint trickle of wetness pressed into herself from the inner side of her underwear and told Abby she needed to use the restroom before they left. Abby said that she would meet her outside by the car and took their to-go box in tow.

*

Seeing that she had been separated from her friend, Austin quickly tossed his waist-folded apron onto the hostess' countertop and told her he was going on his smoke break. He caught up with Abby at the door and made sure to keep his body close to hers and spoke softer so they would have to lean in to one another to hear. The comments lacked substance and were sexual in nature, but so was the type of attention that Abby had been craving. Enthralled by the idea of being with an older guy for the exciting stories she would have with him, she played into his stupid flirtations and made sure to initiate the first barrier-breaking touch of placing her hand gently on the lower end of his bicep.

*

Mia had worked herself into a privatized frenzy over nothing, but now more than ever she was convinced that her period would at the very least be starting soon. She composed herself first in the stall, then stepping out in front of one of the evenly spaced sinks and their awkwardly placed oval mirrors, she adjusted her clothing once more, washed her hands with extra diligence after being reminded of the slightly unsavory condition of the restroom she had speed-walked into out of a self-inflicted rush, and exited. She did a last look around the restaurant as a visual confirmation that Abby had indeed beat her outside and proceeded through the exit door, unaware the first gear had shifted into what would ultimately alter her life.

Abby's back was pressed with a voluntary amount of force against the passenger side door of Mia's car while her right arm wrapped around the upper portion of Austin's back and her right hand was repeatedly grabbing at the back of his neck with weak grips. Austin was leaning his frame over to match Abby's height so that they could exchange their mismatched tongues into each other's mouths. His life-worn face of over-consumption pressed tightly into the face of a girl who just became eligible for her license four months prior. His non-dominant hand continuously palmed the small of her back while his preferred hand began to grope crudely at the backside of her shorts.

Mia's heart skipped a beat and was instantly reminded of her parents' nine year age gap and the grief of her life caused by such immature parents and she boiled with anger and anxiety. She could feel her face getting hot and the strength in her shoulders go out, but the need to stop this horrible sight overshadowed her growing weakness. She yelled Abby's name and she looked past his shoulder with smeared lipstick and a stupid smile that suggested she was proud of herself and felt like showing her the prize she thought she had won. Her smile quickly turned to a frown and tremendous anger when Mia began to shout.

She told Austin that Abby was only sixteen, and Austin having to at least play the part in such a public place, pretended to act surprised and placed his hands in the air as if to suggest that they were never on her to begin with or that he had simply surrendered his prey for the moment, and walked back into the pizzeria.

The verbal fight had begun in the parking lot, continued in the car, and only had been reduced to a seething disdain for one another by the time Abby had been dropped off. It was out of nothing more than sincere concern on Mia's end that she felt she needed to speak so strongly. It was out of nothing more than enraged hormones and confusion sparked by the unsubtle erotic poems and images that she flooded her Twitter feed with. The tear had become irreparable over the course of one night. Mia would cry on her way home and continue her mourning in her room. Abby's rage would blind her and she would find a way to embarrass Mia as she had embarrassed her today.

*

Abby knew what would be enough to devastate Mia, or at least bring her down to the level Abby thought Mia viewed Abby on when she was willfully letting her body be heavily pet by Austin. A key schism between Abby and Mia had been their view on sex. Mia had what Abby believed to be a far more sheltered idea that it really was something to be saved for marriage or at the very least with someone you love. Abby thought it was a romanticized view on something that had been far 'disproven' in purpose by the modern world, but in reality it was a belief Mia had been able to come to after living in the household where the unwanted results of a meaningless sexual bond tied resentful strangers to one another. Strangers who would make the same mistake a second time that gave Mia a little sister.

Abby knew that virginity was just a social construct; a phrase that she had heard enough times in sentences to determine that she had understood the meaning and could now use in her own thoughts and ideas. Her own beliefs were far more nuanced and modern because she was old enough to know what the world was really made of, after all, she wasn't ten years old anymore. No, as a matter of fact she wasn't ten years old anymore. She could never have gone back to that level of innocence or her old perspectives anymore.

*

When Abby was eleven years old, she was gifted her very own laptop to use. Her parents saw that technology was quickly progressing far past their needed usage or at least understanding, of course the exception being the newest and largest televisions they were most assuredly going to keep wise on, and saw that their daughter could be left behind if they didn't act fast. Yes, of course Abby was very well versed in using the shared family PC in the living room where they still had the overly large (and far heavier than what seemed reasonable) CRT monitor and bulky, yellowing shell that held their now ancient computer in, and she navigated her way around those Putt-Putt and Freddi Fish games with such ease now, so the upgrade seemed logical enough. It wasn't their expertise, Dad ran a sandwich shop out of one of the town's convenience stores and Mom ran a ceramics class at the community center. They mostly just remembered the internet as a place where they could print out recipes or send funny emails to relatives. They didn't know.

She knew how to look things up online, she had done it for projects at school when they gave them those sort of flat and square laptops that had a funny red rubber button they could use to move the cursor. Naturally, she wanted to look things up. Her parents cable subscription came with an internet bundle and they dutifully let them upgrade their cables and equipment, so now Abby had the wi-fi all to herself, after some assistance from her parents and the support team of exhausted specialists, and she could hardly believe how fast it was. She ran back to her room to use her new gift. It was even faster than the computers at school.

She had a song stuck in her head. It was from some dance she had seen last week. Her parents had brought her to go see The Harlem Globetrotters live. It was amazing. She had only seen basketball from scenes in movies and what the PE teacher made them practice in third grade, but this game had been way better than that. There were all sorts of tricks they did with the ball, one of them disguised themselves as a grandma in the audience, and they pranked the team by stopping and doing a dance. They danced to a song she had never heard before. It was like her head could remember the words of the song, but when she tried to sing it out loud or type it in, she could only remember the first word 'Jump' followed by a humming melody that sounded like "huh-mon-ing".

She wanted to find that song. She decided she would start with the word 'Jump' and start typing in words that sounded like the ending melody. She went onto Google and started with 'jump calming'. Videos and links to articles about exercises for elementary teachers to practice with their students. That wasn't it. Next she tried 'jump call me" and the music video for 'Jump' by Kriss Kross came up. She listened to it and realized it was that song her Dad sometimes played in the car and sang along to; she liked it, but it certainly was not the song she was looking for.

Maybe the second word didn't start with a C. She half-sang the melody out loud again and decided to try H sounds next. She started typing in 'jump holly' but she definitely knew it couldn't have been a Christmas song, it would've sounded different if it was. She hit backspace until 'holly' had been erased and thought harder. Maybe it was just a word she hadn't heard of yet and didn't know how to spell it yet. She typed in 'jump hommy' and nothing but nonsense links came up and an auto-suggestion to search for 'jump mommy' instead, which she knew it could not have been. She was getting slightly irritated but decided if she wanted to find the song and hear it faster, she should switch over to the Google Videos search tab.

She switched over and ignored the mixed results of gibberish titles and kid videos that had the word mommy in it and began to type in her next attempt: 'jump homny'. It looked like a ridiculous word on the screen and began to doubt herself. However, when she started saying it out loud, it made her feel like she was at least getting close to it. So she decided to hit Enter. Google offered an immediate suggestion: Did you mean: jump horny?

She had never seen that word before. She started to whisper it out loud to herself and inadvertently began mis-enunciating the word so that she could sell herself on it being this mystery word. She repeated it again and again 'horn-A' 'jump horn-A'. That was it, she had now convinced herself. She hit the italicized blue suggestion and allowed the results to load.

All the videos had either a black screen over them or were super blurry so she couldn't even see what was actually going on in the thumbnail. All the links next to the videos were to websites she had never heard of before. She was confused why everything was either blurred out or blacked out and she resigned to clicking on the first result that was simply titled 'jump horny.mov'. The video expanded in size until it had taken up a lion's portion of her screen and the circle in the middle made of dots began to spin against the backdrop of a black screen.

Before the video had fully loaded, the oppressive ambient hum of the sound of a fan's blades spinning being caught by a webcamera's microphone began to play loudly. The sudden noise scared Abby and not just because of its suddenness: the sound felt thick with anticipation. She immediately cranked down the volume of her laptop, frightened that her parents would hear, but still, why did it scare her that her parents might hear? She was just clicking on a song, at least she thought. The video had begun to load and it was a mosaic of compression. The details began to come as the person off camera adjusted a light so the setting would be more immediately visible to the camera.

The biggest sight that made an immediate impression upon her was the dirty orange tint of light that illuminated the room the video took place in. It was a room, its sparseness and grimy feel made it feel like an immediately masculine space. She could see tan walls, a door to the left that was closed and had a red hoodie hanging off of it. There were posters that featured a grainy bunny symbol on the bottom of them and what looked like women covering their chests with their arms, but the pixelation made it hard to tell with exactness. She felt uncomfortable seeing a potentially naked woman, even at that removed of a distance. There was a dresser, an unmade bed in the background, some clothes strewn about the room, but her attention was pulled toward the mesh backing of the computer chair that sat in the direct center of the screen.

She could hear sounds of heavy footsteps and the general sounds of someone trying to set up the shot and then she saw the chair start to get pushed aside by a thick caucasian arm, with noticeable arm hair visible even through the digital distortion. Soon a body had stepped into view, only visible from the top of the knees to the top of a stomach. It was a man's body, he seemed to be an average weight, with perhaps some minor chubbiness, like he was only a couple years removed from the thinness of his college youth. He was clothed in a white tank top and a yellow pair of Nike track pants with a pointed bulge sticking out towards the camera. It made Abby's heart skip a beat. She wasn't entirely sure what about the video was making her so nervous, but she couldn't help it, her body was being flooded with adrenaline.

The man's body shifted to turn to a profile view facing the right, making the large indent against his pants take on a longer length. He rubbed his hands along the top of the bulge and pulled back the fabric of his track pants to make the silhouette of his erection more graphic. Though she had a vague understanding of what she thought she was seeing, the graphic detail of the imprint no longer left any doubt in her mind as to what she was seeing. She had never seen one like this before.

When she was just six or seven years old, she remembered her younger cousin Tommy running around after taking his pants and diaper off, but despite the impression it may have left on her, the extent of her thoughts started and ended at the noticeable difference between what she had underneath her pants and what he had. She asked Mom what it was and when they got home she pulled out an anatomy book filled with paper collage illustrations of the human anatomy and her mother explained its basic functions and purpose. She was told what it was, so she was no longer curious and moved on, not having many thoughts about 'it' until now.

The man in the video firmly gripped the outline hard, trying his best to show the length in proportion to the size of his hand and then let go.

He moved his hands to each side of his hips while still standing in the profile pose and slowly began to pull his pants down slowly, making sure the fabric movements were emphatically struggling against the resistance caused by evident arousal. The pants had moved down far enough where the beginning of his pubic hair reached above the drawstrings and now more than ever Abby realized that she was watching something she wasn't supposed to, but the butterflies in her stomach began fluttering against her insides in frenzied patterns and she was almost paralyzed with fear and curiosity. Her heart began to sound in her ears with intensely growing speed.

The pants had now slipped down completely and lay level with the top of his knees. She watched as his sex moved in an almost spring like fashion in response to the friction of his pants being pulled against it. The video whirred with a flair of unsteady pixels until the video was able to show 'it' with as much clarity as the webcam could offer. As soon as he was fully exposed, Abby could feel the back of her ears run intensely hot and the flush of her face rise with such quick heat she could feel it in the lower lids of her eyes. He began to grab hold and moved his hand along its length a few times before turning back to face the camera.

He grabbed ahold of himself and began to masturbate himself with enough force to cause the sound of his palm catching against the flesh of his crotch to be heard through the webcam's microphone in distorted, often out of sync claps. The intensity only continued to rise until the video became a blur reminiscent of the cloudiness in a cup of water used to clean her watercolor brushes when she painted. He started to make grunting noises that were loud enough to be heard through the thick buzzing ambience and the sounds of his masturbation. They were deep, gruff sounds that came and went in short bursts. She turned the volume down even more on her laptop, but leaned herself closer to hear it better without knowing why. She could feel a pressure go against her bladder and her whole pelvic region began to feel uneasy.

She was in this hunched position, eyes and ears inches away from the cause of her heart's unsteady beating, for what must have been five or so minutes until the man's grunts became more frequent and intense. She moved herself back so that she would be able to fully view what was going on in the video and saw as the man's legs looked like they twitched in wide motions and his body shuffled back and forth off of his now rocking feet. She could feel a catch in her throat and the beginnings of tears form in her eyes because she knew she was doing something wrong, but she was so anxious and she didn't understand and wanted to know what was happening. She could see the muscles in his thigh flex with involuntary force and several small spurts of white shot forth from the end of his glans. The intensity of his reaction had begun to die down and now she watched as the ejaculate dribbled over his knuckles and made minute pittering sounds as it hit what must have been his desk below.

She closed the browser and closed her laptop as quickly as she could without making a noise loud enough to alert her parents and ran from her bed and into the bathroom connected to her room. She sat down on the tiled floor, curling herself on the ground between the sink and the door and began to cry. She ripped the bath sheet from off of the hanger and used half of it as a makeshift pillow for her head and the ends of it to bite onto so that her sobs, which were pouring over in waves now, would be muffled. She felt so ashamed, she felt disgusted, but her stomach felt light and jittery and it felt almost like she was going to pee. The new sensations made her feel even more scared and she cried until she had drained the remaining energy out of her to cry anymore and she got back onto her feet and slinked her way back to bed until her body forced a deep sleep on her in an attempt to recover.

She slept deep enough to regain some control over her emotions to be able to adequately hide her thoughts in front of her parents. Gradually her thoughts and feelings of shame over the next few weeks began to subside and the desire to try getting that funny feeling again grew stronger. She would end up revisiting that video several times over the following months and eventually clicked on the website it came from and started exploring from there until it became a daily habit by the time she had turned fifteen. The tastes had grown more niche and degrading as time went on. When she had turned sixteen she felt like her body had developed enough to look like some of the girls in the videos and now she wanted to be used like them too.

*

She knew Mia was repulsed by Abby's fantasies when she talked about them and now Mia's disapproval and Abby's desires culminated into this schism. Abby decided Mia should be the object of repulsion instead.

Abby, still hyper with anger, grabbed her laptop and went to a lower caliber porn site dedicated to amateur materials and started searching by new uploads for POV material. She found one that fit her needs. It had a young girl, no older than nineteen years old, performing fellatio on a man whose skin on his legs identified him as someone realistically in their mid-to-late-forties. The girl had the same semi-skinny build as Mia and had the same length brunette hair as her too. What she decided to do would take a few steps, so she downloaded the video.

She took the video and went through all of the photos and videos of Mia she could find and searched until she found one that had the most similar angle and lighting to the video. She took the root file and searched online for one of those free 'deepfake' tools people liked to use to do things like place their face on Bruce Willis' character during a scene in Die Hard. After sorting through different options, she finally found one that allowed her to make one free video without an email and uploaded the root video and her close-up video of Mia. She didn't need the whole thing to look perfect, just enough.

The website took a liberal amount of time to generate the video so it could show her reminders that her wait time could be cut in half if she wanted to subscribe for a monthly fee, but she waited patiently. All the time that passed offered her a chance to rethink her decision and instead was wasted on bated breath for the result. It had finally loaded and she was prompted to preview it before downloading, but she skipped to down-loading it as an .MP4 immediately. Opening it up with her media player, she began to skim through it feverishly trying to make sure the digital mask of her best friend's face had not slipped off the actress reduced to these paid actions on camera.

She found a three second segment that looked real past a shadow of a doubt and recorded it on her phone so that the digital on digital recording could eliminate any of the imperfections that might have been able to be detected from a crisp source image. To further add to the effect, she cropped the video down further on her phone to make it look like it was recorded vertically by a smartphone. Abby was able to create her own reality, one where Mia could be the dejected harlot, playing submissive to an older man's hand tangled in her hair on camera with his body in her mouth.

She posted the video on a private story on Snapchat the next morning. That three second loop of her friend's digital fake with a caption that read "Who knew she wasn't so innocent after all?" followed by Mia's phone number and waited.

*

Predictably Mia's phone began to blow up. Predictably her father's phone with the monitoring app began to blow up. It allowed him to see all notifications, texts, images, posts and messages on social media and apps, and even deleted photos and hidden albums in the camera roll. He didn't need all of those features to see boys from her school sending the video to her and asking all manners of questions. Some messages called her the usual names one might expect after a video of that nature was posted, some crude jokes asking how much she charges, others sent unsolicited nude pictures, and even the occasional few boys who tried to find the most polite way they could word the disgusting fantasy they wanted to share with her.

Mia only had less than an hour to react to this onslaught. She turned off her phone and began to cry. Her little sister Sadie walked in on Mia's coming apart. Mia couldn't even begin to peel her face off of the pillow she laid her head upon nor muster the energy to angrily shew her Sadie away and certainly not enough understanding to be able to explain her distress to Sadie who was barely going to be entering fifth grade in a few weeks. Her father had seen enough of what he needed to see before abruptly leaving his on-call job as an industrial equipment cleaner. A move that was going to cost him a three hundred dollar shift that could've gone to the prescriptions he convinced himself he still needed for his back pain.

It was an explosive violence from the moment he had kicked in the wood grain front door. Mia's mother instinctively ran to find Sadie to grab and hide in her bedroom without a second thought for her oldest daughter who was in distress far before her father had even prematurely left his job. Mia knew that it was an ugly distress she had to be further victim to and in preparation grabbed her purse with her car keys, phone, and wallet to clutch close to her.

He grabbed her by the hair directly through her part so it became entangled as soon as his hand was able to form a grip. He dragged her off of the bed and let her knees skid across the floor until they reached the kitchen. He kicked her in the stomach while holding tight her hair he was ripping without concern. He began to scream at her, asking her questions that no answers could ever be sufficient for and even cruel comparisons to her own mother's behavior at that age. It was impossible to argue against the evidence that had been doctored against her, even if she was able to form words out of her bleats of requests for mercy to her father. The argument was pointless, he would have used anything as an excuse to beat Mia. Ever since her body began to develop it disgusted him to know what it could be used for.

Several hard slaps went across her face before he ended the streak with a punch directly to the thinnest part of her left eye's socket. Her screams were horrible. It was as if she was a wild animal pleading even for help from the hunter who shot her. She forced herself to gain footing and ripped herself away from his grip, leaving behind a fistful of hair, and ran through the front door and into her car as he chased behind her until she had managed to escape the driveway. His fury wasn't satisfied until a chunk of cement from the driveway he took in his hand cracked one of her back seat windows, causing her to temporarily swerve in shock before regaining her path on the road.

*

Mia punched at the top of her steering wheel until she could feel and hear an audible pop in her middle finger's knuckle from the last violent strike against the leather wrap-around. Her remaining screams she could muster out shifted to a high whining sound as she wrapped her non-dominant hand around her broken knuckle and surrounding area. Her hand wrapped around her injury tightly, like a distorted bandage of bruised skin and splintered fingernails sharp as glass shards and arranged like uneven stalks.

As far as she could see, with her limited view and tunneling perception, her life was over. There was nothing more she could imagine to do. This small clique of students of a class of over one hundred fifty students, in a school of over one thousand teens, in a town with over sixty thousand people, and her abusive father, one of only seven billion people, had ended her world.

She would miss Sadie, but hoped this would finally make her father stray from his abusive patterns. She wished she would miss her mother more than she did. Her part-time job was nothing but a means to an end for car maintenance, her car was nothing but a medium of transportation, and now her body was viewed as nothing more than a tool for boys' pleasure. She saved herself to be a virginal bride only for the world to view her as the whore.

She took the seat belt and began tugging on it, first hitting frustration when meeting with the resistance of the safety feature of the belt, automatically locking when detecting force at a certain speed, and eventually was able to pull out its full length. She began wrapping it around her neck, tightly until the latch plate dangled in front of her throat like a decorative choker. She took its remaining length that reached above her head and removed her headrest, wrapping it once in between the metal prongs and snapping it back into its place.

Her eyes were blurry with the remnant of her tears, her head was forcefully jerked back tight against the headrest into an angle where she had to stare downwards to even look through her windshield. The seat belt was choking her uncomfortably, even despite her desire for the death, the body still reacted to discomfort and wanted to fight against it, but her will to die overtook her instinct to survive. She backed the car up until it had reached the back end of the parking lot she was in, and she lined her car up to be in a straight shot to the pole mounted lights with the tall concrete base at the bottom and drove as fast as the speed of her car would pick up.

She crashed and her neck snapped with horrible force. She survived for around three minutes after the crash until the crushed airflow in her throat caused her to succumb to a grotesque asphyxiation. In her final moments, she sent forth a prayer of repentance and an asking of mercy and the father heard.

CHAPTER SIX
A FOUNDATION FOR TEMPTATION (SADIE)

Sadie could hear Mia's screaming through the muffling filter of her mother's hands cupped around her ears. The sharp percussive slap of her father striking her older sister across the face became a dull thudding sound, it reminded her of the sound the rocks would make when she smashed them together underwater when Mom brought her to the beach. She could hear her start her car, followed by the sound of glass being struck that was so sharp that it felt like the sound was right in her ears. The door was kicked inwards again by her father and Mom flinched with her hands still around her daughter's face, causing Sadie's face to quickly turn and return to its beginning position.

Her father continued to stomp through the kitchen, smashing his steel-toed boots into the cabinets until they concaved and shattered inwards. Mom curled herself closer to Sadie and began to rest her cheek against the top of Sadie's head, wetting the part in her well-combed hair with the hot tears that rolled down Mom's face. They stayed like that and listened in suffering silence for what must have been half an hour. Eventually his rage had begun to subside and he turned his attention from destroying any more of their kitchen, to getting back in his car and speeding out of the driveway. Sadie's emotions were confused and rose inside of her without direction.

Sadie asked Mom questions about Mia, not knowing what happened or why or where she went or what was going to happen. She was scared and hurt. Mom didn't respond and just kept hushing reassuring words that lacked specificity or direction. She handed Sadie her phone, told her to watch some YouTube, and exited the room so that she could clean the mess in the kitchen while taking hidden sips of plastic bottle vodka. Sadie tried to watch something to help keep her focus, but she couldn't manage to keep her mind in two places at once.

She squirmed with wild discomfort trying to lay down on her stomach to watch the videos that were supposed to ease her mind and she began to make audible groans and started to bite her lip and release it over and over again until she couldn't handle the building tension in her body any longer. She stood up and tried lifting herself up onto her toes and placing herself back flat on her foot in repetition, she shook her arms, waved her hands, and even tried holding her breath until the pressure in her cheeks felt like they were going to explode the flesh from off of her mouth. Anything she could try just to expel the energy from her. Nothing worked and she kicked the box spring of her bed until her toe bent back and started to pulse with pain. She didn't know what to do with her body and so she laid down and screamed with the weight of her body consciously unsupported by her body pressing her face down into the gap between her pillows. She couldn't stand the tightness of everything around her and she had to leave.

Sadie lifted her beet red face from off her bed and started to leave the room. She walked out to the kitchen to see her mother, body slumping in a diagonal direction from the kitchen floor and into the sink. She turned around and looked at Sadie, mouth full of blood. She told Sadie that Mommy had slipped and hurt her mouth off of the sink. She slurred her words with the thickness of blood washing out the crispness of her enunciation and her drunkenness sabotaging the intention of her message. Sadie looked at her Mom's hair that started to cling to the front of her mouth and felt the anxiety within her rise higher and hotter until she couldn't stare any longer and walked through the front door.

She walked first and then started to run. She ran until she found herself outside of the long driveway which led to her school. She continued to run, panting far more than breathing, and started to cry. She continued until she was in the playground, already clear across the blacktop and stood in place, trying to interpret her surroundings. Everything seemed too blurry to understand but she was turning her head too fast and it didn't allow anything to come into focus. She felt a wetness running down her leg and she saw that she had been peeing herself and she wasn't aware for how long. Her tears turned to wailing and she fell to the ground scraping her knee brutishly across the blacktop, and wailed until her screaming cries had choked her airways too tightly and she passed out, squarely on the right end of the blacktop.

*

The shattering news came to the already broken family in their various, horrible states. Police found Mia's mom collapsing her balance continuously against the kitchen countertop. Drunken, shirt lifted up to be tucked inside of her mouth as a makeshift bandaging to absorb her gums' bleeding. She spit out her improvised wound care and began sobbing when they told her the news. It was impossible to tell if it was because of the tragedy of Mia or because she was caught in her drunkenness by someone other than her immediate family. They told her they tried calling her but she said Sadie had her phone and was in her own bedroom. They asked where the father was and she didn't know, so they focused on talking to Mia's younger sister instead. They figured it was best to try to tell Sadie themselves given her mother's embarrassing state.

They walked past the disastrous kitchen and saw a door slightly ajar with what looked like pink bedding and they assumed it safe to be the younger daughter in question. They opened the door to its extent and saw no one in there, but they did see her phone lying face down by the foot of the bed. They checked the other rooms and there was nobody else they could find in the house.

Quickly the cops turned and came back to ask the mother where Sadie was. She didn't know she wasn't in her room anymore. The visual evidence the mother had of watching Sadie leave the front door had been erased by the volatile amount of alcohol she choked down too fast and too often. They tried asking her further questions, but they knew it was pointless and began to search the immediate area.

Time had elapsed faster than the officers wanted to admit, but after assistance from four additional cops, they were able to locate her on the playground. Blood had been dried across her knee and the scent of urine had been soaked into her clothes. They were able to wake her up and called the EMTs to examine Sadie in case there were any abnormalities besides how and where she had been found.

Her airways had been clear, there were no physical injuries to report besides the rough scrape on her knee which they were able to clean and bandage without problem besides some minor wincing from the young girl. They evaluated her consciousness and she was able to tell them basic information such as her name and where she lived, but she was visibly confused and needed help catching her up to her present surroundings and circumstance. It took them several minutes before they felt confident she had returned to an adequate state of understanding.

The worst day of her life had begun when the officers who found her, had to tell her Mia was dead. The day only got worse when they introduced her to a social worker named Jennifer who had to explain that she wasn't going to be able to go back home to her mom or dad. Jennifer tried to comfort Sadie and tried to hold Sadie's hand in solidarity until her Aunt had arrived. The officers could only stare, wondering how one little girl would be able to carry all this grief.

*

Erin was cycling between chores in the apartment she shared with her husband when she received a phone call. They had told her only that Sadie was taken in by Child Protective Services without mention of what had happened to Mia. Erin had only lived half a mile away from her sister and her kids, but was entirely cut from their lives after threatening to call the cops on her nieces' father for trying to forge checks in Erin's name. She was told that she didn't understand and he was going through a rough time since he hurt his back at work.

Christmas and birthday cards were searched for cash and thrown away and the father told Sadie that Erin didn't like children who still slept with a nightlight on and that's why she stopped coming over. It wasn't fair, Sadie worked so hard on being brave since Dad told her that but she still didn't come back. She knew she was already getting too old for one and she already felt embarrassed, so every night she would turn it off right when she felt like she was going to sleep so she didn't have to stay up in the darkness too long, but long enough so that she could get used to it and grow up enough and tell Auntie Erin all about it. No matter how scary it was she never turned the nightlight back on. No matter how scary.

*

Three months prior, Sadie had been on her nightly routine of conquering her fear of the dark and had even gotten so good about it, that she hadn't even been plugging it in for the past week. She only used her lamp now when she wanted it to be light or dark in her room when it was close to bedtime and now she felt comfortable turning the lamp off before she was even super tired. She had been closing her eyes and slowly lulling her body to sleep with her usual tight cuddle of blankets pulled right to the under-side of her lip. She was staring without focus towards her door when it began to open.

It didn't open subtly but it wasn't forced with a slam, it merely was pushed until it was open to its fullest. The jagged saunter of her father in silhouette reached the inside of the door jamb and stood there crooked and disheveled. The ring of his shirt that surrounded his neck looked like it sunk down nearly to his chest, like he had been tearing at it and stretching it past a reasonable length. His pants were sagging slowly down his legs but he wasn't trying to pull them back up, his dominant arm was too busy supporting his weight against the jamb and his other arm seemed to be pawing at his face without a semblance of steady or even intervals. He twitched his neck around as if he was trying to find a position his neck would allow him to speak with.

It was like an airless speech that fell horribly out of his mouth. He sputtered out her name through extended stops and starts several times. He told her he was dying. He sounded like he was trying to say his heart was stopping but everything that came out of his mouth sounded like he was speaking backwards letters. His zombie stature struggled to stay still and through the shadow presence of him in the doorframe, she could see thick strings of saliva fall from off his chin onto the floor.

The blackness of his outline only seemed to deepen with darkening shades but still it felt like Sadie could still feel the pinpointed vision of his eyes and the desperate emotions they were trying to convey. His speech continued to slur as he tried to recite his daughter's name while she was left helpless and paralyzed watching what she thought was a dead version of her father walking through her house. It was as if he gave up and he turned his body, twitch by twitch, until he was facing the left and began dragging his foot as if it no longer was attached to him. She could hear the slow drag and thump of his new gait until it sounded like he had reached the dining room table, her only indicator being the sound of a chair falling and his body slamming down on the floor shortly after.

*

Erin always expected to get this phone call, but the words coming through the speaker of her phone pressed against her ear still made her pause with surprise. She asked if Sadie was okay and was told that her assessment cleared her of any physical injuries but that she was in a lot of emotional distress. Erin asked them to elaborate but she was told it was best for her to come down and see her as soon as she could. Erin wondered why Sadie was at the school in the summertime.

She drove her way down to the school with her husband Travis on the speakerphone while she tried to explain the best she could what was happening. Travis was at work, but he knew his wife always texted, so phone calls were reserved for highly urgent matters, so he answered. He knew this day would come as well, but was less shocked by the news that they were going to take Sadie in and was thankful that they kept the guest bedroom in their apartment instead of converting it into something that would have been useless and expensive. But Travis asked his wife about Mia. Where was she?

Erin, in all of her stress, entirely forgot to ask about Mia. She had no idea where she was. She couldn't give her husband a clear answer and said that she would ask when she arrived at the school. Now her anxiety began to rise, why was she suddenly so scared? Where was Mia?

*

The first responders came to the scene knowing they would find a tragedy. Her body was discovered when a young couple were driving down the road when they could hear the ominous and endless drone of a car's horn continuously sounding off and when the young wife, Nicole, craned her neck towards her window, she was able to see over the banking underneath where the parking lot was and saw a car crumpled into itself against one of the lights. She stuttered out her yell to her husband and told him that they needed to stop immediately and see if the owner was okay. Her husband, Blake, caught off guard by the level of panic in his wife's voice, agreed, and quickly turned onto the road that led to the parking lot.

There were no other cars in the parking lot and the scale of mess caused by the vehicle's purposeful destruction left a blown out half-circle by the front of the car that spread across at least five parking spaces each way. Blake stopped the car cautiously, but quickly, as soon as they saw the ruin. Nicole was fully in a panic and began to whip off her own seat belt with a swiftness that almost caused the latch plate to smash against her teeth. She opened the car door with force and kept her arm out to keep the door's bounce, from the door hitting its fullest extent, to stop from colliding with her as she was stepping out with urgency. Blake wanted to follow right behind her, but couldn't stop staring, he kept thinking of the old adventure films his dad used to show him when he was a kid and his father still could be there, but he didn't know why? Until the split seconds that felt like millenia in the slower moving march of time adrenaline forces you to experience reminded him. He kept staring at the front of the car, its impact caused the front to blow out on the sides, somehow far longer on each side than seemed even possible. It looked like a neatly folded map, being grabbed in the center, tight and recklessly, by the hands of an eager explorer.

She ran towards the car and when she had reached the passenger side window and stopped before she was going to place her hands on the handle to rip it open in an attempt of rescue. She screamed. She couldn't stop screaming. The young wife, four weeks pregnant and unaware that she was carrying a beautiful life that could end up in the same devastation that was before her now if she let the world in too much, stood there and screamed. Blake finally was able to snap out of his stupefied horror and got out of the car to run towards her to see what had happened.

He took his wife in his arms and turned her face towards her chest, trying to shield her from further looking at the consequences of this fallen world. He looked for himself now while his wife screamed and turned to sobs against his chest and stared. He felt adrenaline flood through his veins with terrible quickness and he continued to stare. The sounds of his heart beating drowned out the environmental noises around him and even his wife's cries into his body and he continued to stare. The world felt like it had collapsed on this blacktop cement. He continued to stare.

They knew they didn't have to stay there after the preliminary questions were asked by all of the first responders, but it felt like they were glued in place, unable to move until this unknown evil had shown them its victim. One of them leaned into the shattered window of the driver's side after they had cleared away the remaining, shattered glass, and cut the top of the seat belt. With a sickening autonomy, he watched the belt slither its serpentine body from off her neck. They inched her body out of the car, and as an act of spite that the evil had lost her soul, decided to damage her flesh further for his audience, and caused the paramedic lifting the weight of her shoulders and upwards to slip on debris that was not under his foot until that second, and let the weight of herself bring her neck to a freefall against the hard plastic siding of the stretcher. It was the only remnant of force needed to cause her head to fling backwards in a dead weight, now entirely unsupported by any bones in her neck, her head, heavy and obedient to the law of its gravity, pointed downwards towards the ground while her chin pointed skywards. Nicole and Blake saw and felt an unnatural disgust rise inside their chests.

*

Erin arrived in the parking lot and was able to see from the road before she pulled in, that there was a small crowd of first responders and her niece, Sadie, on the playground. She walked as quickly as she could without running, afraid that it would cause even more alarm to her already nervous niece. She had finally reached the blacktop and could see her now. Sadie saw her and, for the first time today, had felt joy. She ran with a child's understanding of a limp from the big scrape on her knee, and hugged her Auntie Erin for the first time since she was in third grade. She immediately wanted to cry. Embracing the joy of all of Sadie's love that had been restricted from her for so long now, Erin felt the maternal bond strike her in a glowing warmth. This was a moment that was to become, assigned by a plan beyond either of their knowledge.

As the embrace continued, Sadie began to cry. Erin could only have imagined what traumatic event had happened to this beautiful child that led her to being finally taken away by her parents and held her even tighter. Sadie began to muffle out words into Auntie Erin's embrace but Auntie couldn't hear her. So she began to gently push her back against her arms to signal that she wanted to step out from the embrace so she could talk. Her tears and sniffles interrupted what Sadie wanted to say, but she was able to collect herself enough to tell Erin that Mia was dead.

She didn't need Sadie to repeat herself, the dull pain had immediately clenched her throat closed. Sadie now back into her distress needed her Auntie's hugs more than ever, and ran back to Erin's arms. Erin held her tightly as she could feel the heaviness of tears well up under her eyelids and begin to be pushed out by the ones yet to come. She kneeled down further and rested her cheek on the top of Sadie's head and let her tears fall upon the now messy part in Sadie's hair.

The police filled her in quietly away from Sadie's earshot explaining that all the evidence they were able to gather determined that it was a suicide and just left it at it being a car crash that took her from her place here on Earth instead of adding descriptions that weren't necessary for the crushing weight of grief already placed upon this new family dynamic's shoulders. The social worker expressed her condolences and asked if there were any basic necessities that Erin needed for Sadie before she brought her home. Erin visually mapped her apartment and nodded her head no, they would be fine. Tears wiped on sleeves, she knew she had to be stronger for Sadie right now, until Travis got home, so he could be strong for Erin.

*

Two months had passed by. Painfully day by day Erin and Sadie's backs were broken with sadness and confusion as they navigated what was now their lives. Abby had been let out on bail pending an investigation into her involvement with Mia's suicide, the extreme nature of Mia's suicide had been enough to bring the cyberbullying charge to a federal charge of harassment. Mia's father had been in jail. Battery, domestic violence, possession of a controlled substance, and child neglect. He tried hanging himself twice while being held in the county jail before being transferred. It wasn't out of regret or sadness. He was afraid of what would become of him in prison. Erin's sister was charged with child neglect and would be facing her sentencing soon.

Though, in spite of all the deafening wails of grief that closed upon the Aunt and Niece, their bond had now become tighter than ever before. Travis loved playing the role of father too, but the closeness that had formed between Erin and Sadie was irrefutable. For the first two weeks Erin slept in the guest bedroom with Sadie. Once Sadie felt at home enough to be left alone in her room at night, equipped with a ceramic nightlight in the shape of a robot, complete with the square head, antenna, and a rectangular mouth that displayed a squiggly soundwave. She needed the light now more than ever. She saw Mia in her room at night.

The room was a simple four wall and square shaped set-up. Sadie's bed was tucked into the top left corner of the room, a large circular rug lay flat on the ground around a foot away from the legs of the bed frame. She had a small nightstand by her bed, opposite to her bed at the top right corner of the room was a simple plastic bin used to store her slowly growing toy collection, and in between the toy bin and her nightstand was a simple two plug outlet that was approximately four inches off the ground and that was where her nightlight was plugged in.

Sadie thought she could see the silhouette of her sister and quickly as she saw it, it went away, on her first night alone, that is. Gradually the shadow stayed longer to look at Sadie each night and had even begun moving after a week. Sadie thought if she could just stay really brave and not look away from it, maybe Mia would stay. Unknowingly, she acknowledged its existence in a way it needed in order to survive.

The apparition grew stronger and had begun talking to her. It started as soft whispers of Sadie's name, until it was able to replicate the voice and tone Sadie would recognize as the way Mia talked to her. Sadie talked back and now it could begin temptation.

It knew how badly Sadie wanted to be brave and it tested her willingness. It stood right on the edge of where her nightlight's radius ended and talked to her. It finally asked her if she wanted to see her up close. Sadie hadn't seen her sister since she had died and nodded her head yes. It creeped closer to the light until Sadie could make out the details of what she was seeing. It was Mia's face in agony, head tilted back with her eyes pointed downwards, and a horrific imprint of the seat belt that wrapped across her unnaturally long neck. A perverse caricature of Mia's death mask. Sadie panicked and moved the sheets quickly to cover half of her face and it quickly retreated to the shadows again.

It whispered to Sadie that she must hate her now that she looks different. Sadie tried to be brave again and she shook her head no over and over again so her response could be seen clearly. Sadie wanted to see Mia, she wanted her to live here with Auntie Erin and Uncle Travis. It told her it would, but she had to do something first. Sadie promised to help.

Although Sadie would not be able to see, now that it had retracted back into the darkness, but it was smiling. It contorted the muscles of its grotesque disguise, and it smiled widely. The tapetum lucidum glow of its eyes stared back at Sadie through the darkness, wide and filled with pleasure, knowing that Sadie would listen to its instructions.

*

Erin had a meeting with Sadie's principal, homeroom teacher, and the school's counselor so that they could discuss the changes that had taken place and how best they could create a support system that would help her re-adjust to the school year. They sat on the lower level of the school in a room that looked out to the playground so that Sadie could be free to play while their meeting took place. Mia told her that she needed to do something special today when she got to the playground and that she needed to listen really closely when she got there.

Sadie ran around on the grass, up the play structures, and along the side of the swingset with her head slightly upturned, her right ear facing upwards so that she could be ready to hear whatever was to be told to her today so she could help Mia live with her again. It all had to be done secretly and if she told Auntie Erin or Uncle Travis, none of it would work. Even though she didn't know what she had to do or why she couldn't at least tell Auntie Erin about it, she trusted her older sister. Inside the adults talked about her inability to mature emotionally over the past few years as a result of the trauma and neglect at home and while she still acted like she was only in first or second grade, by the end of the school year, the counselor thought she would be able to help her get back to an appropriate age-level maturity. Sadie continued to wander outside waiting for her big sister.

Sadie heard the voice telling her to look under the twisty slide that ran down from the big play structure and she excitedly ran to her task. She saw a baby raccoon. It was tiny and furry, it really looked like a miniature version of the adult raccoons she saw sometimes, but with softer features and shorter fur. Its demeanor looked gentle and the perfect curves of its snout gave her the impression that it might not even have teeth yet. It pawed around on the ground walking, but without the confidence of a direction. It was skinny and Sadie thought it must have been abandoned by her mother.

The voice told her to pick it up and Sadie was happy to oblige because she wanted to pet the soft creature. Her next instruction was to go to the end of the blacktop and sit down with it. Sadie went about to do so and was only temporarily frozen with the reminder of when she had passed out on the same spot, but moved past the feeling and sat down with the baby in her hands. What the voice told her to do made Sadie cry.

The counselor suggested tasks that lacked actual weight or meaning to Erin who had experienced some of these same traumas alongside her niece. Doing mindfulness practices at home with Sadie wasn't going to help her understand why her parents are in jail and why her sister isn't coming home. The principal nodded in agreement, coming from a life of relatively little hardship, he imagined that this was a reasonable way to help the child.

Sadie's upper lip was covered with what came from her running nose and the hot tears that splashed down from her eyes. She had to hold the little raccoon still with the palm of her left hand against its neck, pressed firmly against the ground. She didn't know why Mia would ask her to do this, but she threatened to never come back to visit her room if she didn't do it, so Sadie had to, otherwise she would have to say goodbye to the sister she never had the chance to when she was alive. So she held the lost baby animal down and balled her right fist up and swung it down onto its snout. Once wasn't good enough, she was told and she had to keep striking. Again. It wasn't good enough. Again.

She was egged on by the voice until she could no longer reasonably keep her sobs down to a hidden volume and started bringing her fist up and down upon the animal repeatedly, harder and harder, unable to look at the violence she was being asked to create. The raccoon squirmed with all of its might, legs splaying forth in different directions, trying to grab the traction of the ground beneath it so that it could escape this horrible torture it would never be able to understand its position of victim in. Sadie could feel the horrible pulsing and wriggling of the baby raccoons developing and limber spine try to slip out of her hands and it made her cry even harder as she had to continuously strike down on this innocent animal.

She continued until she could no longer feel it moving. Its airways had been blocked long enough by the palm against its neck and the collapsing of its snout and it must have died from the lack of oxygen. Before she could realize that its lack of motion indicated its death, she slammed her fist down one last time until the bone splintered upwards and cut her hand open. Her wailing could be heard inside and at once, Erin and the homeroom teacher immediately got out of their chairs to run and see what had happened. Sadie's blood intermingled with the innocent animal's and all of it fed that dreadful spot on the blacktop. The opening was made and it could now be occupied.

*

Sadie was taken to the hospital and never came back to school that year. She had gotten leptospirosis from the raccoon. Despite the aggressive antibiotics and frequent doctor appointments, the disease had eaten away at her with an unnatural progression. Her kidneys had begun failing and she risked falling into a coma without constant monitoring. She had fallen into its oppression.

CHAPTER SEVEN
CONCEPTION PT. II

So it was, an egg unfit for life, unnaturally created and forcefully inseminated by evil. Like all creatures, it started as a cluster of cells.

*

It quickly transformed from its fertilized egg state to a blastocyst within the span of two hours. Being born entirely from outside of a mammal, the womb was exposed to the natural air of the environment and was hidden by its entities behind the faux rock climbing wall. The scale of the blastocyst was large in proportion to what a human might host, but still miniscule to the enormity of its hiding place, measuring just around one centimeter. It moved with small rocking motions against the paper thin womb it was encased in as it continued to develop.

*

Sadie was rushed to the hospital by her Aunt Erin and the principal told the teacher and counselor to both go home after sternly reminding them of their HIPAA oath and said he was going to write a report about the incident and even went so far as to send them emails asking for statements that evening, knowing they were merely formalities for their comfort. He waited until they had left and cleaned the mess himself to avoid any word of this event being brought out into the open for gawking parents and the easily frightened staff. First he gathered the smashed corpse into a trash bag using those comically elastic yellow kitchen gloves, doing his best to pick up all remaining solids that remained of the poor animal's face. He then went and grabbed the power washer from the custodian's room, soaking the area with generous amounts of liquid soap, and sprayed away the remaining, flat gore, unaware of what was growing in the playground.

The principal quickly returned the power washer to the custodian's disorganized menagerie of tools, grabbed his laptop, and swiftly proceeded to leave the school, not knowing what to think, but knowing what he had to do to make sure no one else caught wind of this horror. Although horrific, grisly, and certainly psychologically alarming, he wanted more than anything to protect Sadie and her Aunt from any further stress and trauma the ignorance of the community would undoubtedly cause.

*

By the fourth hour of its fertilization, it had developed into its beginning fetal state. A swirl of grey matter, practically viscous more than an actualized solidity, floating in its transparent womb, By hour six it became more discernible, the fetus had more physicality to it, and with nobody around to endanger the birth, the entities brought the womb to where its hosted creation would remain: on the blacktop. The night had arrived late as it did during the summer day, sun setting by the eighth hour.

The tenth hour had arrived and it reached a more complete state as a fetus. It was a mass, a giant, gnarled mess of unstructured planks of wood, sheets of glass, and plastic, loosely fused together by thin, artifice tissue. It floated in the amniotic fluid of the ever expanding womb, connecting to a singular point inside the womb, by a large, impenetrably black umbilical cord. The thin coating that was the womb which the abomination was kept in began to tear, and in the peak darkness of the night, it was taken from its comfort and shaped.

CHAPTER EIGHT
A MEETING TO DISCUSS THE HOUSE

The superintendent had successfully been able to convince the board that it was a project entirely done with grant money and despite their initial upset not being contacted first, convincing them it was done entirely with grant money lessened the blow, as he had expected it would. The principal was initially in a private outrage after ending his original phone call with the superintendent, wondering what sort of horrible authority his boss, who very rarely even stepped foot into his school, always double downing his focus on the district's high school instead, was imposing upon the school he had been dutifully caring for. However, once he agreed to meet with the superintendent in private before a presentation to the school board, his cowardice took hold of his demeanor and forced him to agree with what his boss was saying and now after openly expressing his approval to his boss, he now had to privately lie to himself until he was able to convince himself of the validity of this house project.

Now that the legally painful part of the elaborate cover-up was done, it was now time to address the staff and somehow get them on board with this enigma. The superintendent decided he himself should stand alongside the principal to address the staff and continue the lie on his own terms. It was only a short time now before school was to start and it wasn't something they were going to be able to easily ignore.

The meeting was a bit sudden. Not every staff member had been available as they had been out of state or simply just told them they had prior engagements on that day, most likely so they could avoid what they assumed was going to be an hours long meeting discussing monotonous tasks that could be summed up by a firsthand account of one of their coworkers over a lunch break. That however was not the case, and those that did show up, certainly never would have been able to guess at what they were to be presented.

So they began to arrive. Teachers, paras, secretary, nurse, and the custodian who first noticed the structure and notified the superintendent, knowing that the principal had been away and visiting family (a quick lie told only to the custodian to avoid the constant calls about the increasing list of repairs the building needed). Surprisingly the superintendent managed to keep his cool on that call. He wanted to immediately jump at the custodian, asking him what kind of an insane story was he trying to make up or asking how he didn't notice a whole building being built behind the school, but he thought to himself the same exact questions. How did he not notice an entire building being assembled behind one of the schools he oversaw? So he played it off saying simply that he would be there in a couple hours and that the custodian was free to take the rest of the day off.

The staff all stood around the cafeteria tables that were set up with an assortment of basic breakfast items like bagels, danishes, a coffee cake, and of course the most sought after: the three dozen assorted donuts from Dunkin. They grazed and chatted away over the assortments until the time had come where they were supposed to at least be seated in the 'science' room (their usual meeting room given its spacious design and plentiful tables). The majority of the staff walked in together and there standing by the pulled down screen stood the principal and superintendent facing towards one another and chatting, finalizing their story.

They all sat down and after the span of around five minutes, the room finally fell into a collected silence. The superintendent opened the meeting by thanking everyone present for attending and made some stale joke about summer vacation going by too fast. However, it was time to get down to business.

Over the course of the past few days, the superintendent had made a simple, yet quite professional looking PowerPoint presentation, thanks to a website dedicated to free slideshow templates, for this house. He outlined the project as a private grant that's intentions were to help expose students to reduced-stress home environments, where they would be able to freely explore a domestic living situation without the threat of verbal, physical, or emotional abuse. The foundation's name was ChildHaven. It was a non-profit foundation that was founded only three years prior in Oregon. The lie was elaborate, but despite the initially confused looks he saw on the staff's faces, he could not detect any suspicion from their reactions.

He continued on saying that they were the only school in the northeastern United States. He explained, telling that this school was selected by a lottery of sorts, where they had to meet certain statistical requirements that related to poverty levels, illiteracy rates, and the percentage of school-aged children in foster care. They were one of over four thousand schools that were entered. He couldn't tell if those details were too much, if it was too much of an over-explanation. He paused and gauged their reactions. They all were quiet and simple gestures of positive acknowledgment. Slow head nods, lips plumped out with an exaggerated look of being impressed, and slightly widened eyes that peered around the room as if to indicate whoever they may make eye contact with was in agreement with their minor amazement. This was going well.

He wanted to overstate his apologies over the last minute nature of this whole plan, especially with school so close to starting, but he told them that he was at the mercy of their response rate and didn't expect to hear the results until at least after the first quarter of the school year, but once the results were drawn, they drove over the prefab home in just under five days from their main office. He made a joke about how confusing it must have been for the poor custodian who came to work and saw this strange grey building in their playground and they all laughed a short laugh together, including the custodian who found it, playing coyly along with the joke by shrugging his shoulders for the staff to see. The superintendent was soaring with confidence now, and almost felt like ad-libbing additional ideas and details for the story, seeing how well it was going, but he restrained himself.

He positioned his arm to broadly gesture towards the window as he invited everyone to join him to come look at the house together. They were on the second floor and because of the distance between floors in the school, at their direct eye level was the roof of the house. With some minor craning of the necks, they were able to make out the details of the front of the house and even the sides. It was certainly amusing for all of the staff. It was like looking at a new restaurant in town they were probably never going to eat at, but what an excitement to see its newness shine nonetheless.

Once a couple of moments had passed, the principal chimed in on the superintendent's behalf and commented on what a solid looking build it was. The murmurings of all the staff agreed. While they stood by the window staring, the superintendent began to list off all of its rooms, features, and amenities. Their approval grew each time he listed something new, after all, it had a living room, kitchen, dining room, two bathrooms, two bedrooms, and even a laundry room with all sorts of simple appliances and furniture pieces to accompany each room. The superintendent was quite happy he started with the spiel about the grant and foundation because he could only imagine the whispers about the money it would have cost the school to build, especially when every teacher had their own list of things that they thought was necessary for their school that was lacking.

The superintendent guided with a suggestion that everyone go back to their seats so that they could get to the latter half of this meeting. They all filed their way back to their spots and the two showrunners made their way to be in front of the projector screen. The superintendent whispered into the principal's ear as everyone was situating themselves in their seats. It was the principal's time to be the principal of the school and be the trusted intermediate between administration and the internal operations of the school. He could address its use at their school and how they would be using it.

He started by explaining to them that there were certain reports, in the form of pre-formatted paperwork, of course, and that it was expected to be filled out. Each staff member (sans the custodian, secretary, lunch aides, and the bus drivers) was to be assigned a certain amount of students, of course homeroom teachers and their respective paras would be most immediately matched with the students they have in class, and the rest would be assigned as logically as possible (counselors with 'troubled' students they're frequently in contact with, the nurse with kids that require daily medications, and so forth). It would be a five-minute questionnaire where the staff member was to record the students answers, followed by a paper that had a spreadsheet of statements and a scale from one to five marking strongly agree to strongly disagree and a paragraphs worth of lined space where they may add additional comments.

The questions for the children related to how they felt in relation to the house, how safe did it feel to be in the house, what are the differences that this house may have versus what their house may have, has it made them think about ways they could help around their own home, and other related questions to ask them. The teacher's paper would be statements in relation to the students and various behaviors. The staff were all visibly looking around the room, some even silently mouthing words to their colleagues, to express their confusion and groaning over the additional workload.

This was where his vague diplomatic charm of the principal that helped him gain his slightly above neutral reputation among the staff came in. He stated, however, with it being so close to the beginning of the school year, he was not expecting them to be able to pull this feat out of their hat nor were they expected to work double or triple-time to make the first report in October. No, it was a very new program and ChildHaven would not expect them to be able to pull off such a difficult task. The realistic goal the principal laid out for them is that they would be able to begin the questionnaires by the beginning of the second quarter of the year, allowing the whole first quarter of the year to be used for their usual pains of adjusting the students to the new year.

The superintendent started to even marvel at the impressiveness of his own lie, knowing that the paperwork would be coming back to only him and furthermore, most likely getting lost in his filing cabinet. He thought that maybe he actually would take some of his free time to read through the reports. Maybe he would even go so far as to send letters of correspondence to the principal from the foundation's behest. He didn't know, but he started exciting himself with the prospects of this imaginary grant.

Before he got himself too excited, it was now time to face the staff's questions. This would be the test that determined if his elaborate lie would crumble under the weight. The superintendent decided to at least get on with it.

He stepped up to where the principal was standing to talk, thanked the principal for his help and support with this project, and opened the floor for questions. He couldn't tell if the sparse amount of hands was simply due to the apathy of the more tenured employees or if his explanations were satisfactory. Either way, it was at least a partial relief for now.

The first question taken was from one of the first grade teachers, Mrs. Younie, started with a simple enough question, asking when they were expecting to bring the students into the house and for how long. Why this had not been something the superintendent took into account eluded him for the moment and he bought a microscopic chomp of time by telling her that it was a good question. He replied by telling them all that it was at the teacher's discretion and like any use of a spare classroom, they should communicate with one another to ensure no two schedules of usage were overlapping. In reference to the question of time duration he would like the kids to spend in there, he said a goal would ideally be one hour a week. It could be done in spurts of fifteen minutes, two half hour 'trips', or even just one long hour class spent in there.

He was impressed with himself for this answer, but simultaneously nervous that his failure to mention this in the formal presentation would raise concerns. Thankfully, this was not the case. Mrs. Younie was satisfied with the answer and he was able to move onto the next question.

A third grade teacher, Mrs. Balmaseda, raised her hand, with a slight lack of confidence, not being sure if the question was a bit silly or not, and asked what exactly it is they want them to do with the students in the house. She felt more reassured after seeing several of her colleagues nod their heads agreeing, quite relieved to hear someone ask. The superintendent, feeling pretty confident himself now, was able to come up with an answer quite swiftly. He started by saying the ideal situation would be to allow the students to play a sort of supervised 'game of house' where they were all able to emulate their normal day living in the house. However, the exposure to a safe and welcoming environment in a home setting would be sufficient enough as well if the teachers were not able to spare their schedule and used the house to teach a subject in, to at least let them experience the setting.

A bit inconvenient, they all thought, but plausible if they were allowed to simply continue or start a required lesson there. Another question, this time from Ms. Xie, a kindergarten teacher. She asked about safety concerns, especially for her little ones, asking if there were any exceptionally dangerous areas they should know, did it have a gas stove, a basement, any small areas a child might hide in, any loose nails or wires? The superintendent was happy to talk about how he personally inspected the house himself and the only possible concern he might have would be the possibility of a child trying to hide away in the spandrel under the stairs, but they would easily be able to place a lock over that if it were to be a major concern for Ms. Xie. However, as far as any loose nails or wires, the electrical is new and the carpentry was solid, and the last comforting thought he added was that the stovetop and oven were electric. He reassured her once more before she began to speak, saying that he would happily order some stove knob cover locks for the appliance were it to be troubling to her. She was happy with that response and mentioned that she would like that.

A final question, this time from the school nurse, Ms. Abebe. It was a simple couple of questions, but kind of odd coming from someone that didn't have to directly deal with the answer to the question. She asked would it interfere with the way recess operates and would the kids be allowed to use the house during recess. The superintendent was a little stumped as to how to answer that. He said that it would be at the discretion of the principal. The principal, perfectly fine with taking the burden of such a simple question, said that it would be a decision that could be made at their preliminary meetings the week directly before school.

With no further questions from the audience of staff members, the principal continued to mention that with them are printouts that will be sent home to parents explaining the new project and its purpose. It was written by the superintendent and had the mark of approval that was the school's letterhead at the top. It was important that any questions about the project be directly forwarded to the superintendent for him to be able to answer directly. The principal and the staff were quite happy to see him take the burden of the responsibility of answering what were certainly going to be hundreds of redundant questions from parents who didn't bother actually reading the paper they sent out. The superintendent was just happy that this meeting went well.

So it began.

CHAPTER NINE
MRS. BRIXEY

Sandra Gardenia Brixey was one of the two fifth grade teachers at the school. She had been working at the elementary school for a total of seven years now and was a stern believer in the necessity of life skills as a necessary complement to the basic educational blocks the school was intended to provide. She had sharpened her teaching skills as a Home Economics teacher at an adult education center and found herself gravitating towards the world of youth education as a preventative measure against the adult inadequacy she saw on the rise.

Seeing an entire finished house with basic amenities seemed like an incredible way to ingrain these ideas in her children. With only a week before school was to begin, she pleaded with the principal to let her set her classroom in the house instead. Between him and herself, the principal really saw no other legitimate use for the house besides perhaps a teacher's lounge or a surreal play structure for the children and told her that she should at least examine it first to make sure she can set up a central classroom that would be able to fit all of the children at one time in the house. She agreed and went about preparations that would ultimately foster her eventual plummet.

*

She was eager to investigate the strange grant project the principal had described and hoped that the other teachers wouldn't mind if she was to claim it as her own, at least for now, but as soon as she stood in its shadow, it was as if all at once, her excitement had been dissipated and replaced with a feeling of emptiness. It was terribly uncanny, the feeling. It was painfully similar to the beginning onsets of her seasonal affective disorder and she could almost feel the coldness of winter brush against her exposed skin even as the summer's warmth had enveloped the playground. The sadness began to penetrate her very being as she entered the front door.

That entryway with the rubber mat and hooks for hanging extra layers did manage to temporarily distract her momentary depression that was threatening to swallow her whole at a rapid pace. She thought it was a wonderful touch to be able to add structure, routine, and common manners to the children's lives. So like any good house guest, she took off her shoes before entering the rest of the home.

It was as though it were a perfect answer to all of her wants and desires she had at her previous position. Instead of overly equipped sets and ridiculous out of date equipment that resembled a line cook's diner fantasy rather than an average home's kitchen, this was a perfectly ordinary house with practicality. It reminded her of a sparsely loved miniature and viewed herself as the doll who was to bring character to its plain existence, but, as with most dolls, she was to be subject to the desires of the house's true owner.

She started her tour with the kitchen, naturally. Everything continued to live up to her highest hopes of plainness. Smooth, featureless refrigerator, inexpensive countertops, tidy shelving, mid-sized oven, a flat electric stove-top, and even the classic standard of a thirteen-gallon trash bin. More to her pleasant surprise, when she had finished her basic observational sweep, she turned to see the dining room setup. She would be able to teach them how to set a table and place a meal for guests. A bit of an 'extra' in the realm of life skills, yes, but a wonderful knowledge to possess.

She ran her hand along one of the bow backed chairs, allowing the thick finish to glide her hand around the curve until coming to a stop on the slope. An abrupt flash of nostalgia caused her to stay in place.

*

She was in her Nana's apartment. She had recently moved into an apartment complex designated for elderly citizens on fixed incomes, but because of her Nana's wonderful nature of only holding onto what she deemed to be useful and worth being treasured, it was an easy move from her house that was 'just too big' now that it was just her. The valuables were small in nature, mostly jewelry, trinkets of various natures, and of course, her clothing. One of the first things she did to make her 'furnished' apartment feel more furnished, was to buy a bigger dining room table and some nice bow backed chairs she found while her and Sandra's mom went to a consignment shop. They rented a little U-Haul and determined not to let their increasing ages get the best of them, loaded and unloaded the set, piece by piece, assisted by a sturdy elevator and the kindness of passersby who would hold the door open for them as they shimmied through the carelessly narrow glass doors of the entryway.

Once they had finished the makeover of the dining room in her apartment, Nana felt so much more at home. They took the dining room table that came with the apartment and politely asked the apartment's supervisor to retrieve the old set. Finally, Nana could prepare a welcoming dinner party for her family.

Coil burners ripped hot with a bright red hue, stainless steel pots and saucepans were filled with the beginning steps of their multi-dish meal. Loyally together in close quarters, were Nana, Sandra's mother, and Sandra herself, three generations of women preparing and hosting. Sandra was only fifteen, but already quickly found herself highly talented in all things house-making. Sandra turned around to finish setting the table and felt the very first kick in her stomach and smiled a private smile for herself. Her body was thin and she found herself easily able to hide the subtle beginnings of growth by wearing high waisted jeans and some flower patterned empire blouses she had sewn herself.

She hid the comforting caress she gave her growing stomach and excused herself to the restroom after feeling a sudden pressure on her bladder. She walked down the tiny hallway that was next to the dining room, opened the door to the bathroom, and saw Nana's corpse face down in the tub.

*

That wasn't right. That wasn't the right memory. She didn't die until at least a few months after that dinner. She wasn't even the one who found her body. Besides, she didn't die in the tub, Sandra's mother told her that Nana's heart stopped in her sleep. Why would she imagine something so grotesque as that? She ripped her hand off of the bow backed chair as if the chair itself was what had poisoned her nostalgia.

Mrs. Brixey was here for her students. So she composed herself and needed desperately to move on to another room. She ducked out back to the main hallway and decided to go past the stairs and explore the door on the right first. It was a bathroom. She thought how nice it would be to have a restroom just for her classroom instead of the awful shared restrooms in the hallways that would become victim to the horrific layered stench of the industrial 'unscented' cleaner that was thrown on every surface without conservative measure by the custodian. Plus, that is definitely a skill her students could learn that would reap immediate rewards, learning how to properly care for a bathroom and all.

She poked through with less observational sharpness than she had with the kitchen, partially because there was far less to be noted for classroom use in an environment such as this. She noted the shower and thought that it was a novel addition to the setup, but hoped there wouldn't be many occasions where it would be of necessary usage. She walked up to the vanity to idly poke around its appearance to see if there was anything worth noting. Casually opening the cabinets, she was curious to see if any of the cabinets may have some helpful contents. She opened first the long, vertical cabinets on the sides of the vanity and saw the well-folded and pristine grey towels and admired the symmetry. It reminded her of staying at a hotel.

Almost excited to see if there were any other hidden amenities, she began to open the horizontal drawers in the middle. She felt very mild disappointment when she opened the first two cabinets and saw nothing but the bottoms of the drawers staring back at her, but then she opened the third drawer to find a curious sight: a pregnancy test.

It was a simple, white rectangular stick with the cap off to the side. The thin end was sticking out and it was visibly used, as she leaned closer she could see the simple control window. It had one blue line going across the height of the window. Inappropriate as it may be, she was more curious than ever and didn't know if that singular line meant positive or negative, and she knew it was really wrong to even try to figure out the answer, but why was there a pregnancy test left here anyways? She pulled the drawer out to its fullest and saw that pressed against the back was the box it must have belonged to.

She saw it was face down and picked it up so she could read the directions more clearly. There it was, stating clearly that a blue line will appear if you are pregnant, if no line appears then you are not pregnant. Without thinking she began to move the box around in her hand and when she saw the front of the box, she stopped. There on the front in big letters were the words CLEARBLUE EASY and underneath, its corresponding subtitle ONE-STEP PREGNANCY TEST and its small copyright that read © 1993 WHITEHALL LABORATORIES, NY., N.Y.

She remembered walking into the drug store, confidently. She was wearing her navy blue button-front dress that drifted just above her knees and let her red on white polka dot shoulder bag hang to her side in between her waist and her right hand that hovered around the side of it for security. Thick rimmed sunglasses that added extra coverage around her face and a slightly oversized newsboy cap in an unassuming shade of blue that she tucked her tight hair bun inside of. She was giddy. Far too giddy for a girl her age scoping out what she was there to purchase. Despite her inward thrill, she had to use her mature height and appearance to her advantage and carry herself in a more reserved, 'adult' fashion that wouldn't arouse suspicion.

She walked over to the all too familiar aisle which she always walked a little slower past, peeking at all of the first steps of maternity she longed for, and now she could finally be that girl, no, that young woman, in the aisle with purpose. She went through all of her choices with an excitement that was almost hard to control. Finally, she saw the postcard sized ad that boasted: THE FIRST ONE-STEP, ONE PIECE PREGNANCY TEST: CLEARBLUE EASY. She read on the back that it only took three minutes to get the results and immediately grabbed it.

She went to the clerk, looking slightly off to the right to avoid a direct glance with him, and pulled her wallet out, used the money she had made from working part-time at Jordan Marsh, and bought her test. She walked home and went right to the bathroom to take her test, and with a bottom lip bitten with anticipation, she waited, counting nearly every second of the countdown in her head, and looked down to see that beautiful, single blue line.

*

She noticed that she was rubbing her stomach without even realizing, snapped out of it, and placed the box back into the drawer and slammed it shut. It was just a coincidence or alternatively, wasn't even real at all. She was shaken up by the gruesome image of her Nana's corpse that flashed in her head and it was just bringing up memories from around that time and mixed with the weird sense of melancholy she had been feeling since she got here was just coming together and making her see things. Maybe it was just claustrophobia? The bathroom was slightly smaller than the kitchen and dining room, so maybe it was just the subtle reduction of space that had been making her feel anxious. Whatever it was, she just wanted to get out of the room.

She closed the bathroom door harder than what she would courteously do, had she the calm necessary to operate normally. She enjoyed the larger openness of not being confined into a room for a few moments. One extended breath, a tight close of the eyes, and a readjusted balance and she was ready to move on. So she moved to the door on the left and walked inside.

It was a laundry room. The orderly and tidiness of her own laundry room at home always made her feel at ease. Something about the naturally sanitary nature of the environment and taking what was once filthy made clean, a process done in the secrecy of the closed doors of each machine.

She was allowed this moment of calm for herself before she decided to do any sort of examination of her immediate surroundings. Relief. Relief.

She looked around and saw the set of hampers, perfectly empty and clean. She decided to take a peek outside of the window, as she hadn't bothered in any of the other rooms and more than ever she really could use the grounding exercise of placing herself physically in the world. She saw the swingset and grass with such a clear view it made her laugh. It was such a nonsense sight that the absurdity of it helped alleviate her anxiety.

She moved around the small room for a little bit with general aimlessness before focusing on the washer and dryer set.

She opened the top loader washing machine and saw that the inside was entirely untouched. It was wonderful. A machine like this would easily be able to last at least five years of frequent usage. It was such a practical skill that yes, while some of her students may already know how to use a washer or dryer, she wasn't necessarily doing it for the children with healthy structure and abundant knowledge available at home, she was doing it for the ones without.

Especially for those children. Especially for the ones who came to school everyday wearing the same combination of three outfits that evidently were being washed from week to week. They would be able to feel clean. Even despite her earlier comment to herself, maybe even be able to take regular showers here. This could be a huge change for those kids, it could help their confidence, which in turn could help them put more effort into their academics so they could reach back to grade level and that could help them be more social with more than just the other kids that were forced to join their lower level reading and math groups and they would no longer be shunned off by the other kids for having their own extra time with different teachers during the day. Sandra was practically beaming with the positive outcomes that would be a direct result of this new arrangement and decided to open the dryer next.

The dryer had a large door in the center of it opposed to being a top-loader, so she bent down and opened the door with a slightly hard tug that wasn't uncommon when breaking in a new machine. She looked inside and although the lighting was a little funnier down at this level with her body practically eclipsing the opening, it was almost like she could see something in the back. For the sake of her own relief, she decided to reach in to paw around the metal surface and its equidistant ridges until she felt a thin crumple of fabric. She reached her back quickly out of instinct, feeling something when you were expecting nothing. Feeling foolish and decidedly too skittish, she reached her hand back in and grabbed the mysterious fabric out of the dryer.

She held the balled clothing in her hands and stood back upright. She let the majority of the material fall from her hands while maintaining a grip on what appeared to be an opening within the item. It rolled out in a freefall and revealed itself as clothing. A dress.

It was a three-tier pattern dress with thin straps. The first tier that covered the chest to stomach was a pattern of a top-view of cartoonishly proportioned dandelions, clustered together amongst a dark purple background, their thin, light green stems occasionally poking from behind their bulbous heads. The second pattern covered from the stomach to the thighs and had roses. Roses on extraordinarily long stems that looped inside of the roses that were aligned to the left of them, all falling together amongst an airy, light blue background. The third and final tier flowed more openly and was to cover the thighs to slightly above the knee it looked like, based on the length. It had a strong presence of yellow, red, and white flowers amongst a thickly layered background making it look like a highly clustered flower garden of sorts.

It wasn't from a store or thrift shop, but it was hers. She had sewn it.

*

It was after school and Sandra had needed to do something with her time, so she decided it was as good a time as any to grab some jute twine to try out her hand at some fun ideas she saw in her mom's Crafts magazine. She grabbed her shoulder bag, put on her string necklace with a felt pendant in the shape of a cluster of grapes, and headed down to the Ben Franklin store about half a mile away from her house wearing a beautiful three-tier dress she had just finished sewing a week prior. The clean and freshly crafted fabric felt wonderful against her body, she thought. Its lightness brushed against her with an almost ticklish playfulness and it made her feel so good about herself knowing she could make something as functional and pretty. It reminded her of a homemade version of a dress she might find at the Charlotte Russe in the mall.

She walked cheerfully the entire walk and took every stranger's glance at her as an unspoken compliment to first her appearance and second her craftsmanship. All of the attention she imagined she was getting was almost enough to make her blush, and she had felt quite certain of her attractiveness and talents by the time she had reached her destination. She had opened the door to a place of comfort where she knew she would find herself spending a fair stretch of time perusing the aisles in, mentally noting the various new hobbies she might find herself drawn to.

It was when she was walking down one of these aisles she saw him. He was a few inches shy of six feet tall, but he wore a plain, olive green t-shirt that allowed a good portion of his bicep to show out of, where she could see the tracing lines of muscles throughout his arm with enough visual clarity to tell he worked with his hands a lot. He was reading the contents on various packages of clay with a small red basket on the floor filled with small coils of metal wiring and various tubes of paint. His hair was a dark brown that teetered on being black and was a slicked-over cut she thought she might see on an older, but handsome celebrity. His jeans were covered in stains that would only look subtle in a movie perhaps, but looking at them in person, it did look like more of a cry for attention. It didn't quite matter enough to her, though.

He had strong features that were apparent even just by seeing his profile view. A forward and broad chin, a strong Greek-adjacent nose, and a smoothed complexion just a shade lighter than a farmer's tan. She wanted to see his front-facing view before she made her final decisions. So, in her very forward manner, walked closer to him and asked if he was an artist.

His attention was caught and he did turn his body to face her and in that moment she was able to notice his unusually light brown eyes. He must have been at least twenty nine years old. He was slightly caught off guard by her question and then began to answer with a false humbleness stating that he enjoyed sculpting in his free time and that he was actually a painter and general laborer full time. She wanted to hear him talk more, to see if his voice was adequately full enough to her standard of measure. He continued the conversation by padding out his small successes in local contests with creative processes he was making up on the spot in an appearance to sound far more intelligent than he knew he was. He reached his hand behind his head in an unsubtle attempt to flex without forcibly doing so to impress her.

She stood there and continued to look over his being, mentally calculating. She had the belief that the more outwards masculinity that was present in a man, the more likely he was to be fruitful. In her case, she thought his ruggish appearance was a direct result of the amount of testosterone present in his body, making him more able to produce children. She didn't want his life, his love, or his time, she only wanted to have a cute baby. He had enough unique physical attributes that she thought would blend well with her perfectly pretty and typical caucasian features. Blinded by aspirations of being a mother, now knowing she could proficiently cook, clean, decorate, and even sew her own clothes now. Despite her worryingly young age, she continued in her pursuit.

She asked him if he lived nearby. He explained that he lived over three hours away, but he was out here for a job that his boss brought the crew in to work on for a couple of weeks. He said that they put him up in a local motel, but it wasn't anything fancy. Certainly nothing fancy enough to impress a girl like her. She played coy enough and joked that it was quite an assumption thinking she would be interested in seeing it in the first place.

He nervously began talking himself back in circles hoping to find an exit point to the next subject in the conversation. She giggled at him and told him that he was just going to have to let her see for herself, now that he made her all curious and what not. He knew he had to keep telling himself she at least looked like she was nineteen or so in order to be able to continue in his pervert fantasy being actualized in front of him and she knew she had to keep playing the part of the young, but freshly adult woman, at least in public, to be able to convince him that he was no longer guilty of the public's accusing eye. Arthur extended his hand and name as an invitation. She replied with a smile and a welcoming grip upon his hand that she hoped was playful enough to distract him from asking for her name.

It wasn't a motel fancy enough to impress her, but she didn't need to be impressed, she just wanted him to do his share. So, unromantically she faked her way through enjoying his practical mauling of her neck and breasts with his half-biting kisses and brutish hands. He kept her back flat against the bed while she stared at the ceiling, smiling, knowing she was finally going to get her wish. He struggled stupidly with his jeans and ripped them down to his ankles and hobbled with a hand on the end of the bed while he ripped the rolled up denim from off of his ankles. She looked up and was caught with the pathetic sight of his erection pressing sideways against a pair of loose fitting 'tighty-whities' and looked back at the ceiling as to not let her body physically reject what was necessary for the conception.

She focused on the oncoming joys of pregnancy to let her body relax enough to be stimulated by his fumbling hands, pressing against her private flesh and rubbing it in twitched and scattered motions before lifting her dress to her stomach and rolling her underwear down her thighs attempting to be sensuous while she did her best not to cringe. He brought himself up in front of her while she spread her legs to try to give him enough space to situate himself in position. He grabbed onto himself and finally inserted himself.

She closed her eyes and bit her lip in an attempt to suffer his rough entry and he took it upon himself to view it as a sign of pleasure and doubled his effort into slamming into her pelvis without a set rhythm. He groaned loudly and beads of sweat dripped onto her collarbones and caused her to temporarily lose her illusion of pleasure. He didn't notice.

He continued to indulge himself in what he knew to be more of a rape or at the most a virgin's quick scheme to lose her virginity, than an act of shared love. All of this he was doing to a girl that he knew couldn't have been any older than sixteen. He continued to pleasure himself with her body and leaned closer to her face to tell her that he was going to finish and wanted to finish on her chest. He had been spending his past few days in this motel watching rented porn from the 'adult bookstore' he found while driving around town and he thought this girl was naive enough to let him enact his fantasy of degrading ownership of her body. He wanted to let her know that her body was now nothing more than a toy for him to use. He wanted to feel he had a claim to this minor's body.

She broke her own imagined character of calm and pleasure for a moment and sternly told him no, that he needed to finish inside of her. He tried to play it off saying that he didn't want to have any kids and that he thought she would look so pretty with his spill across her. She told him no again and moved her legs to press his pelvis against her and caused him to unceremoniously finish inside her as she had wanted.

She had let her legs lose their grip on him and let him move from off of her. He was panicking. He wanted to use her body for a thrill and now he might have gotten her pregnant. How would he explain this to his family, her family that knew her real age, and how could he go back home to face his fiancée? He started yelling.

He gathered his clothes with force and started redressing his nakedness with his underwear and jeans, asking her if she knew what she just did and how crazy she must be. In his anger he even let out a slip by calling her a real stupid kid, acknowledging his understanding of the true age gap. He started hissing with anger asking if she just wanted him for child support or enough money to get an abortion.

When she heard that last word, it upset her deeply and she began yelling back. She told him that she only wanted him to get her pregnant and that she would under no circumstances get an abortion. He got furious and leaned in real close to her face as she was sitting up from the bed and told her she wasn't going to get anything from him, no matter what any court says, hoping she would be young enough to not know the actual legal proceedings that followed a child support claim. She told him she didn't want his money or his disgusting personality in her life. She just wanted to have a baby.

He crumpled her underwear into a ball from off of the floor and threw them at her, calling her derogatory names, demanding she leave the motel. She slid them on and walked out, upset by his remarks, but happy with her result, and started to walk back downtown until she was familiar enough with where she was to walk back home. She felt gross because of his body inside hers, but kept telling herself it was the price to be paid and she could shower herself off to feel clean once more.

*

Sandra clutched the dress and pressed it to her chest as she unclenched the muscles raging in her throat and face and allowed air and tears to flow forth into the fabric of the dress. She let the front of her body press against the dryer and let the weight of her upper body keep her upright. She tried her best to forget about the cheap conception.

She didn't know any better when she was young, she simply thought sex was nothing but a means to an end and for women she was told it was for pregnancy and for men it was for pleasure. At least that's how she heard it discussed, even in health class. There wasn't mention of the sacred nature of the act, only that it could lead to pregnancy or STDs. That was the only time she had allowed herself to be intimate until twelve years later when she was married.

When she found out that the act was a way to express love and a union. How it was supposed to feel good for the woman too and that it wasn't supposed to make her feel dirty after the act was finished. It was a bonding of flesh, one that could facilitate life, yes, but just as importantly, expressed devotion.

She had let herself be used by a man too full of himself to admit to what he was, willingly letting a fifteen year old child's attempt at seduction work. Allowing himself to play victim to some sort of a trick plotted by her as if he wasn't aware of the consequences of an action like that. How sick she felt to her stomach on her wedding night.

She spent the first several hours after their consummation crying, realizing what she had let her body be reduced to for the sake of a goal she wasn't ready to handle the success of. She confessed to her groom the horrible nature of her first experience and he sat by her, allowing her to cover herself with as many sheets as she felt was necessary to feel safe and secure and listened. He had only continued to love her and that was partially what made her cry even harder, knowing that this was the bond she wished that she had fully reserved herself for. He held no scorn against her and she fell deeper in love with Christopher Brixey.

She allowed the comforting memories of her husband to help her regain the balance she needed in her feet and stood, face hot with shame. She removed herself from the laundry room and slammed the door behind her. She ran to the living room, not sure of where she was even going first, and sat down on the couch. She forgot she was clutching the dress and it wrought more distress in her body, like she could smell the stains of his sweat that had fallen into the fabric that day.

She threw the dress away from her, not caring where it may have landed. She tried unsuccessfully to steady her stuttered breathing. She instinctively pulled out her phone and started playing a simple mini-golf game she downloaded on her phone. She had used handheld games as a sort of grounding technique for her whenever she felt overwhelmed.

She remembered when she was eleven years old and she started the onset of puberty and it was causing her to have really bad moments of

ADHD where she could not bring herself to be focused on any singular event happening and causing her to feel self-conscious over her inability to focus, and she would panic until everything became an overwhelming blur to her.

Her mother told her to try to focus on something menial and repetitive when she was feeling overwhelmed, like playing a small game of thumb war against herself, but it wasn't stimulating enough. Her mother was now becoming overwhelmed with her own daughter's shrinking attention span, so she stopped off at a Kay-Bee Toy & Hobby shop and bought a small handheld game without bothering to look at any more than the price tag. She brought it home to Sandra and watched as she became instantly transfixed.

Sandra loved her little handheld game. It was a longish, green case that looked like a smoothed out rectangle with a curve on the very bottom that turned inwards and made it look as if the game had little plastic legs and that its small, square screen was its face. It had a large, vibrant logo that said TEENAGE MUTANT NINJA and underneath in its own separate font and color the word TURTLES. Above it were four turtles with long arms, ninja weapons, and angry looking faces with matching red masks tied with exaggerated knots. There was a giant white logo above the turtles that said KONAMI. She had only vaguely heard of the Teenage Mutant Ninja Turtles, but everything else was a mystery, but an exciting mystery.

She took it out of its plastic shell and began to play with the textures of it all. The plastic was smooth with ridges only necessary to add definition to the shape. She saw two large green buttons on each side of the game and saw the one on the left had four raised button shapes going in all four directions, and the other big green button on the right only had two raised button shapes, one on the left and one on the right. She played around just moving her thumb around them, taking in all of the different feelings her thumb was processing. Each button felt slightly loose, as if it was held on to a tightly coiled spring by mere suggestion, but still, it stayed in place through all of her aggressive movements.

She eyed the four grey, horizontal buttons that were lined up underneath the screen and read their corresponding labels: OFF, SOUND, GAME SELECT, ON/START, and a label underneath a very tiny opening that read ALL CLEAR. She immersed herself in the faint colored background that was a brick wall and some water spilling from giant pipes. She turned on the game and a flash of black shapes and characters filled the screen before the official game screen had been shown. It made very compressed and distorted beeping sounds of various pitches and on the screen came a turtle holding a ninja sword and in the corner a lady tied up with a chain in some weird circular chamber.

She didn't know what she was doing at first but started to detect which raised buttons moved the turtle or made him jump and which ones made him punch or swing the sword. All sorts of little robot looking things jumped at him and what she thought must have been mines or something were being thrown around the screen. When her character died the first time, she had noticed the score counter on the bottom.

She had finally been able to focus on something. Not only that, but intense focus with motivation. When she lifted her head from the game after a few rounds, suddenly the world wasn't so blurry and noisy and she could pinpoint what was needed of her attention. She loved that game and played it for a good two years before all of the black shapes and character cels were burned into the LCD screen. She was sad when it finally died, but did save up her money and eventually switch which game she would play. She found out it was from a brand called Tiger Electronics and would cautiously pick up a new one each time another died.

Her mindless playing of the game on her phone was able to level her thinking until she could bring herself to look around the room once more and find that the dress was no longer there. She brought about all this stress on herself because of one memory that went sour earlier and she felt so silly that she even laughed a little followed by some clearing sniffles that had ended her nasal congestion that was brought about by her intense crying.

She got herself back up once more to just calmly get through the tour of this house, it was for her students benefit and not her own that determined why she needed to make this work. She stood up, wiping the remaining dampness around her eyes with the sides of her hands, and walked over to the entertainment center underneath the television and saw the remote sitting there. She grabbed the remote, thinking how funny it would be if this house had cable.

She held the remote in her hand, but before she could bring herself to hit the power button, she could feel herself freezing up. She couldn't help but feel as though it was going to be a mistake to turn on the TV. It was a feeling of impending doom. She felt like she was leaning herself in closer to kiss the lips of disaster by even trying to find the will to go on in exploring the amenities of this house. She denied her senses that told her not to continue in an effort to prove to herself that she was in no danger, besides the one she had imagined. With her hubris, she pressed down on the power button and the TV's black screen displayed black before cutting to the images that made Mrs. Brixey run away.

She stood in anticipation staring at the screen. She felt half relieved in the very short moments of the projected blackness of a screen loading its image, but continued biting her tongue with sharp pressure in the secrecy of her tightly pressed lips. Then she saw it.

It was a video. It was an impossible recording of a memory that never found its shame in the presence of a camera. The angle was as though it were recorded from beside Sandra's chin, her ear occasionally making its way into frame. She looked out of the backseat of a car's window as her mother held Sandra's swaddled baby in one arm and a basket in another and walked to the front of a church they had driven two hours away from home to go to, so that no one in their hometown would know. It was an hour before the first Sunday service would begin and she had climbed halfway up the large stone steps.

She centered the basket in the steps so that it was impossible to miss, and placed the peaceful child, unaware of her surrender from her natural mother, into the basket and walked back to the car. Sandra's mother sat silently in the car as they waited for deacons to arrive and take the child, in her jute twine basket, into the building.

Mrs. Brixey left the house in tears, running away to her car where she sat and thought about suicide for the first time since her mother forced her to give up her child.

Chapter Ten
A Prelude to the Final Staff Meeting

It was Saturday night, two nights prior to the last staff meeting before the school year was to officially begin and the principal was sitting at his dining room table working through all of the requested days off that were already put in by the teachers at his school. He browsed through them and made quiet comments to himself about his opinions on the validity of the explanations behind some of the requests. Did someone really need three days off to go to their nephew's wedding? It didn't necessarily bother him that the time off was being requested, but he supposed that these miniature reactionary comments were probably going to be the only thing keeping him sane as he trudged through the mud of countless menial tasks that were required as an 'administrative staff member'. He had just read the fourth request citing 'vet appointment' when his phone rang. It was Mrs. Brixey calling.

He remembered having a conversation with her shortly after the last meeting in regards to her interest in turning the house into an alternative classroom for her students, so he thought maybe this was in reference to that. But why call him now? Late on a Saturday night and insisting upon a phone call rather than a simple email was enough to irk the principal into having a pre-suggested irritability when he answered the phone. The pretense of anger was dropped as soon as he was able to hear her distressed voice.

She told him that she could not work at the school any longer, she had made too many mistakes to be a role model for the children. She asked how she could possibly teach them responsibility after losing her own child, not wanting to hear an actual answer. The principal was confused and tried to get a proverbial foot in the door for the conversation so that she wasn't just sitting there alone in her morbid thoughts. He didn't know what any of it really meant or where any of it was coming from, but as he stuttered through trying to get a word in, she hung up and immediately turned off her phone.

He panicked and tried calling her over and over only to be instantly sent to voicemail. His stomach had plummeted and before he could articulate what he was doing or why, he found himself accessing the school's security cameras through the online portal he had. He filled the screen with the checkerboard pattern of all the cameras of the school until he saw motion in the camera pointing towards the kitchen and began hurriedly clicking on it until it filled the screen.

Sandra Brixey stood in the entryway to the kitchen, right behind the serving table where the children would grab their lunches, with a plastic student's chair behind her, and placed a large, plastic bag over her head. The cameras had high enough resolution to tell it was her, but not enough to tell the principal the specifics of what she was doing and the labels on the tank that stood about chin height on her, with a small tube that ran up the length of her body and into the bag. She sat down and began to turn the nozzle on the tank. Her audience member had vomited into his hand.

He picked up his cell phone and called his local police station to let them know what was currently happening. All he could do was sit and wait for first responders to arrive while her body twitched against falling into her death. The lagging frames of the live video painted a solid color over her face as her movements became too quick to capture accurately, and he stared at the featureless face begin to slump like a scarecrow's head which had been loosed from its rope.

*

She had failed her attempt. Since her death was prevented, so was the news coverage. The principal took the advice of one of the police officers and removed all helium tanks that were present in the school, brought them outside, bled them dry, and placed them in the back of his car to recycle them. His heart was sick with sadness and disgust. Why did it have to happen here? He worked himself to practically a fit of rage against her actions, not knowing where to accurately place all of his confused emotions and eventually resigned to crying.

He needed to pull himself together. Today was Sunday and tomorrow there was a staff meeting. He called the superintendent to let him know what had occurred last night. Unsurprisingly, he wanted to keep the incident as hush-hush as possible and said he would personally see to selecting a long-term substitute for Mrs. Brixey and would call him back this afternoon with a proper candidate.

Panic can become a tightening noose, the principal told himself, and knew that he had to first steady himself before he could even imagine instilling confidence into the rest of the staff. He spent the next several hours in his office, slowly looking through the rest of the requested days off and browsing through emails, making sure to make them repetitive and meaningless enough tasks to quiet his racing thoughts. It was nighttime, it was time to go home and he felt exhausted, but in a good way, one that made him feel normal. He could feel his eyes heavy and tired from hours of staring at the screen, not from crying. His energy level was depleted, but from accomplishing part of his to-do list, and not because his heart was slamming itself so hard against his chest that he thought it would bruise and cause him to die. He slid himself into the driver's seat of the car and avoided looking at the helium tanks in his backseat before driving home.

*

Monday morning had come and his unsuccessful attempts at sleep had him dressed and ready for the day by four-thirty in the morning. He sat around in his house until he had argued and won against himself the debate of whether or not Dunkin' Donuts had already opened, and headed out to them. The morning was bright. Brighter than he thought it should be, at least, this terribly close to one side of midnight. He knew he had far too much time to waste before the meeting that wasn't slated to start for over five hours from the time he pulled into the parking lot that all but swallowed whole three quarters of the square, white, brown, orange, and pink colored building. He first parked to the spot closest to the handicap parking space and thought better of it, asking himself if he really needed to be in that close proximity to the building if he were only going to sit in there and collect his cobweb covered thoughts for an undecided amount of time. So he pulled backwards from his spot and parked at the far left end of the lot and walked himself to the front door, allowing the slight breeze of morning to consume the area of his face and slide down into his lungs.

He opened the front door and saw a mixed staff of five individuals of highly varying age ranges, working in a chaotic harmony to prep the store adequately for the influx they were bound to be faced with by six that morning. One of the youngest crew members had just turned from filling a slot with large plastic cups and pressed herself right close to the counter and smiled at the principal, asking with swiftness, but not with a burden of urgency to be placed upon him, and asked how she could help him this morning. Though he had been awake for over an hour by this point, he still had yet to find a source of energy as potent as the one that allowed this teenager to greet him this morning and decided to start his order with a large, black coffee, hot not iced, before proceeding with a request for four dozen variety donuts and two fifty count packages of the munchkins, making sure to state that it was absolutely no rush on the extravagant amount of baked goods he needed and that he would just be sitting at one of their tables with his laptop.

His insistent additions of guilt-infused reminders for them to take their time made all of the welling annoyance inside the teenage cashier to be put to ease and she assured that it would now be done in no time for him, because it was rare, she told herself, for someone to at least be this courteous to her in the morning here. So he opened up his laptop, struggled his way through connecting and signing in(?) to the free wi-fi offered there, and started at the front page of Yahoo! News to tell him what should be of high importance in this conscious moment. As soon as he had arrived on the home screen however, his coffee was called out to him to take. He felt the hotness of it warm his hand as though he had gripped the small leg of an overheating radiator and allowed it to continue warming his skin until it felt like he felt as if the redness swelling to the surface of his skin was an indication of his internal muscles being cooked and placed it on the table.

He didn't like black coffee and that was all the more reason he ordered it. He didn't expect to actually drink all of it, nor did he want to, but the bitterness and strength in each sip it punched was what was necessary to knock him from his half-somnambulist state of being awake, but without necessary awarenesses. He took the first sip and it made his face move and twist with far more motion than it had experienced since he had self-declared himself as up this morning. It was exactly what he needed, to his minor dismay.

He had received the phone call at around four in the afternoon yesterday when the superintendent declared to him that the best long-term substitute available on such notice would be a para from the middle school. Yes, they were wanted and needed there as well, but the classroom which Ms. Ramos was previously assigned to at least had a teacher in the room. He would need to introduce her and explain that Mrs. Brixey had taken a leave of absence from the school following personal circumstances. He briefed over her accreditations listed on the resume she originally applied with, which had been now forwarded to himself. An associate's degree in special education, that was really all he needed to skim from that. Enough of the teachers there would find themselves agreeable to someone who would dedicate their time in college to finding ways to benefit children in special education.

He took another sip and swallowed hard to get the bitter drink down. He was starting to really feel like he was waking up. He felt at ease with how he was going to introduce the new sub. It was going to be an upset for a lot of the staff as many of them found her plenty agreeable, but the circumstances demanded a change. Plus, Hortensia Ramos was young, and most certainly was to be excited by an opportunity to run her very own classroom. She would be a new energy that could help counter the overwhelming events that have been eclipsing the oncoming school year.

He had returned to Yahoo! News to be able to scour for some daily dose of news he would be able to use as a point of conversation for no one in particular, maybe his wife, had she nothing of major note she wanted to discuss from her day. He skimmed through the what seemed like endless page of political coverage by holding the down arrow on his keyboard, hoping almost desperately for something that didn't hang on the topic of politics to read. As he scrolled he saw an ad for Reynolds Oven Bags and Slow Cooker Liners and the image of Sandra's twitching body flashed several moving frames across his eyelids during his extended blink and by the time his eyes had opened again, he could feel the tears forming surface tension. They threatened to fall over the bags under his eyes until his concentration was interrupted by the cashier projecting her voice across the restaurant to let him know that his order was ready. He took two trips to grab them all and fit them in his backseat before heading to school.

He found himself padding out his time once he had arrived, placing the donut boxes in particular symmetries in accordance to one another along a cafeteria table. He was trying to pass the nearly three and a half hours left before the staff were going to arrive. He decided to go into his office after he could no longer conceivably pretend he was organizing the donuts or munchkins in any way that mattered. He connected his laptop to his larger monitor and quickly clicked off of his open tabs once he saw the dreaded ad once more.

His heart felt heavy and he felt like he was going to fall into a sleep of death if he couldn't somehow alleviate himself of the trauma he was failing to suppress. He called Chris, Sandra's husband. After four long rings and the guilt of even calling this man who is going through so much obvious distress beginning to set in, Chris, with a weak voice and a tired inflection, answered. The principal was nearly at a loss for words and even began to internally doubt his own reasons for calling him, but he marched on nonetheless, and asked how Sandra was doing. There was a slight pause before Chris answered, holding back tears that would not come out despite best efforts because of his drying and burning tear ducts, overworked from a night of a life-shattering horror. He said that she was currently in a coma and they are assessing the estimated length of time she may remain in one and what the long-term effects will be if she is able to pull through as they are hoping. His heavy heart felt empty now, as though part of his ability to express emotions had been ripped from him and he could feel the chill of a void swirl around his internal being.

He expressed his condolences with a quiet and somber tone, pleading with Chris that should there be anything at all that he may contribute to her recovery efforts or his own support system, that he be contacted. Chris thanked him with as much sincerity as he was able to muster and they ended their phone call with an extended silence. Both men sat in silence holding their depressive states at bay as best they could, combatting its consuming nature with their exhaustion.

The principal stared off to the ends of his office and caught the time. Still at least two and a half hours before anyone would arrive and three hours total before the meeting was to start. Any effectiveness the coffee had on him was now nil and he badly wanted to sleep away this ongoing nightmare he had found himself in the midst of. He grabbed his phone, set an alarm for an hour and forty five minutes from his present time, and headed to the nurse's office to take a nap on the twin sized emergency bed she had for kids who needed to lay down.

He walked down the hallway to his destination and on his way passed by a classroom with its windows wide open, allowing him to partially see the house. His quickly evaporating energy made him almost entirely forget about it, the real center to the discussion for the meeting. He turned his head to face forward and walked on until he was able to reach the nurse's office and laid his body flat on the plastic feeling mattress and thought back on the memory of him sitting in the nurse's room when he was in kindergarten after he had peed his pants during recess and had needed to be cleaned up by the nurse.

He remembered having to strip down from below the waist and be aggressively wiped down with a rag freshly wrung of hot water. He remembered how she scolded him repeatedly while he stood vulnerable in her care and how the fabrics of the rag felt as though they were going to rip into his fragile and naked body. He remembered being scared by her pointed words and her frequent reminder that she was going to have to call home. She made him stand there, hands covering his crying eyes while his nakedness was exposed, as she called his mother and refused to give him the oversized spare shorts she kept in the wooden chest by the door until she had finished the phone call.

He thought of this memory as he drifted into an unpleasant sleep; his attempt of passing time before having to explain a tragedy in vague terms.

CHAPTER ELEVEN
THE FINAL STAFF MEETING BEFORE BEGINNING

The principal's alarm went off and he woke up, comfortable with the amount of rest he was able to absorb from such a short nap, pushed the thin and scratchy grey blanket off of his body, making a mental note to personally buy a better blanket for these kids, and moved his body until he was sitting upright. He felt like he had woken up in his doctor's office and while it felt oddly comfortable, he certainly did not like the idea of waking up there. So he got on up and walked back to his office where he grabbed his laptop and went his way to the cafeteria where he would be able to greet his staff as they should start trickling in over the next forty or so minutes. He thought better of taking the first donut, citing nothing but himself in thinking that would appear too taboo.

He passed his time with a meaningless effort by checking through his spam inbox for his email, wondering how even though it was in the spam folder, some of these even managed to bypass their security. He also noticed how often he decided to mark plenty of reputable companies as spam instead of just unsubscribing from their email lists and almost thought about going back to some of them seeing the deals he had apparently missed out on. He hesitated and then decided it wasn't worth the effort and just continued to browse the other emails without targeted intention.

Soon the first teachers began to arrive, large purses in tow, some even with some cardboard boxes filled with decorations for their classrooms that they no doubt were looking to get a jump start on today after the meeting. This was another reason for him to try to make this meeting as brisk as possible. He wanted them to be able to begin setting up early. Let them finally bring some normalcy back into this increasing onslaught of strange happenings in this school. He smiled widely and it occurred to him just how long it had been since he last spoke this morning as his dry voice began to crack as he greeted the beginning wave of staff members.

Soon enough everyone that needed to be in attendance, even Hortensia Ramos had arrived, were there and all of them had their chance to snag a donut and a munchkin or two. It was time to move onto the meeting. So he got the general attendees to listen for his directions and they all followed suit to the science room.

He started off by saying that unfortunately Sandra Brixey was taking an extended leave of absence due to medical issues that he could not publicly disclose to them at this time. The pockets of the room that hadn't fallen completely silent were noisy with gasps and nervous, sympathetic whispers. He regretted deeply even mentioning the medical side of her distresses, but had the news eventually been fed to the pipeline that she had passed away or would no longer be able to return due to long-term complications from her attempted suicide, it would not be so shocking of a reveal to the body of teachers. He showed more emotion than was intentional as he spoke, leaving the staff only to assume the worst in their minds.

*

He tried to cushion the hard blow of this news to his next transition by saying that all of the staff should keep her in their prayers and thoughts. He then said, while she will be dearly missed for the time being, that there was a new long-term substitute who would be taking her place. He introduced Hortensia Ramos and invited her to stand as he briefed them on her experience as a para at the local middle school and her Associate's Degree. She warmly introduced herself, understandably nervous around the collected tenure of such experienced staff, but she had a large smile and a sincere voice so her charm made her instantly agreeable to them.

The introduction had gone well and now it was time to discuss the purpose of the house once more. He went over an abbreviated version of what they had discussed at their previous meeting in relation to the various aspects of the house and what it was to be used for. Now as they mentioned at the last meeting, they didn't realistically expect to be able to even get progress done until at least the end of the first quarter or very beginning of the second quarter of the school year, so they needed to figure out what to do with it until then. The principal assured the staff that he wanted it to be a decision made entirely by the individuals who were going to be directly interacting with the structure: all of them. So he opened the floor for ideas.

*

Suggestions came and went but the only two that seemed to have had any bearing of weight or reasonable plausibility to the attendees were as follows: lock the door until guaranteed usage or send a specials teacher (such as art, library, technology, etc.) outside during each recess to monitor the house and let it be a limited use addition to the playground. However with that second option, the team that monitored the two recess periods would have to come together to set a list of ground rules for the house that followed school guidelines and principles as well as kept in mind the future intentional use of the building.

The teachers said it would be a wonderful addition to the playground and the options the kids could have during recess. The individuals who all had to actually watch the children during recess all silently disagreed, but understood the unspoken authority that the teachers had over their opinions and that no matter what they voiced, it would ultimately not matter. So they kept their quiet, knowing they have been at the mercy of decisions that have never been theirs to make during their entire careers at the school. What comforted them, however, was the willingness to step up that the librarian and art teacher in particular displayed. If they were to bear the brunt of the new building's responsibilities, then so it shall be, that would be fine by them. So it was decided.

*

The meeting was disbanded and the principal mentioned that he would see them all tomorrow as their last official prep day before school started Wednesday. The recess team all stayed back while the teachers chatted their ways out of the door and to their respective classrooms. Though all of them who helped monitor the two recess periods each day were there to discuss the matter, unsurprisingly the conversation was dominated by the additional art teacher and librarian as they began writing an impossibly long list of rules and guidelines they insisted the kids would be able to follow without issue. They held their silence once more and allowed them to write their list of expectations to be dashed to pieces upon the first student's entry. They assured them it would be easy and they would go over all of the rules during the morning assembly on Wednesday.

Had it been their way to begin with, they would have voted to lock the door shut on the house, but now that another group would have it theirs, they decided to let them sink on their own. Or so they thought to themselves and agreed later on with one another as they were leaving the building. Why they had grown to harness such pessimism over simple matters like this never was more than a passing thought to any of them, so they continued on, not knowing how to live any better than what they knew now.

CHAPTER TWELVE
A NIGHT MORE TO WAIT

The last teachers had left for the evening, after over-tidying their classrooms for the inevitable mess that was to come tomorrow. The first day of the new school year was to kick off on a Wednesday, starting the year off with only a three day week to get the kids adjusted and ready. The three day week never really helped any of the kids adjust, it could have been any number between one and five and the results would be nearly identical, but at the core of it, was it really for the students or the teachers? Yes, the students are thrilled at the prospect of less school, but it was not their hairs that have been turned grey from the last minute curriculum expectations being handed down to them by bureaucrats who go by macroscopic statistics and data rather than an individual child's needs. So they half-heartedly anticipate the soon to come Friday as they leave the parking lot.

*

None of this affected the house which sat in this elementary school's playground. Regardless of any number of stressors that may affect the human occupants of this school, the house sat there, patiently waiting to consume. Its intentions, its foundation, and its will was entirely of its foul creators. Born into this world a horribly unnatural birth, it was an accuser, a sower of doubt, or even a boogeyman.

CHAPTER THIRTEEN
PAISLEY PT. I

The cross was made out of twigs, stuck around two inches inside of the ground above the mound of dirt. Paisley's father had dug the grave only about two and a half feet deep and padded the soft dirt on top of it with proper enough attention to make sure that it would not crumble apart, stamping the dirt down with a shovel. There was a large stone that spread almost across the entire width of the dirt. On it was messy, green acrylic paint writing that said the word Noodle.

Inside the shallow grave lay the small, curled body of an orange and white English cocker spaniel puppy. Noodle was wrapped inside of a pink background, white paw-print pattern blanket made of fleece. Paisley had picked it out specially for Noodle to cuddle in her little brown square dog bed. She insisted that her puppy be buried in it.

Noodle had caught distemper. They first noticed when Paisley told her parents that it looked like Noodle had a lot of sleepy seeds in her eyes. Not thinking anything major about it, the parents were quick to just wipe the puppy's eyes once or twice a day and move on from that. It wasn't until Noodle stopped eating her meals that they took notice of anything being wrong. They brought her to the vets and began treating him with antibiotics and paying extra attention to his state.

There was a time where it seemed like Noodle was finally able to pull back through the struggle of it all, like a cancer patient experiencing remission, showing strength, resilience and an even balance of mood. This lasted for around three days before the final stage of disease had caught on to the small pup. Noodle would lay in bed, body twitching in stilted leap-like movements with his legs and drooling. At first they thought Noodle was just experiencing very vivid dreams of running that a dog might and they labeled it as adorable, until they came closer and realized his eyes were open. Wide open. The dog's eyes stayed focused on nothing and everything, tears involuntarily welling up and falling from his eyes. A dysfunctional body, still fighting to keep function in its eyes.

It was a death that happened overnight, and the family told themselves that Noodle most likely passed away in his sleep. It was a comforting thought, something to add padding to the confusion of having to adjust to the grief of a fourteen week old puppy dying under their roof. Paisley found his little body, its upper midsection was still tucked into the blanket she had tucked him into the night previous. She tried petting him to gently wake him up and brushed her hand across his nose and felt that it was entirely dried up. It felt like grazing one's hand over a leathery gravel.

It was horrible for the parents. It was a tragedy of course to have a puppy die, but doubly so was the tragedy of having to explain to their nine-year-old child why and how this freshly born creature had died such an unfortunate death. Paisley had experienced smaller losses, like her goldfish and her grandmother's cat, but this was more affecting to her. This puppy lived in their household and was able to be pet, fed, walked, and experienced the beginnings of training with her. It was able to be cuddled by her and communicate with whimpers, barks, and various noises it was able to create with its infantile vocal cords.

They only had Noodle for six weeks and four of those weeks were battling his disease. She asked her parents why it had killed her and they did their best to explain to her in a combination of the little medical knowledge that they were able to understand from the vets and the generic sympathies a parent struggles to explain to a young child. They knew Noodle's death was different for Paisley, it was different from them too, so they felt it was important to give him a funeral for them all to process the loss.

They were on a lease in a small house so they knew they wouldn't be able to bury it in their backyard with a guaranteed permanency, so Paisley's mother contacted her parents and they were able to hold the small service in her parents sprawling green backyard, beneath the shade of an apple tree, many years removed from its years of productivity and fertility. The grandparents also joined in the small service, mostly to help comfort Paisley in this new experience of grief.

Paisley's father, seeming to think it was the right thing to do, as well as a standard for the patriarchal figure in a family, decided to step forward and say a few solemn words in remembrance of the pup's short life. He did his best to recite a short poem's worth of words he deemed meaningful and appropriate enough for the occasion, intermingling padded out anecdotes of the family's experience with Noodle. Paisley herself stepped forward after her father, not to say her own of solemnity, but to simply say her goodbyes to the little pup she never got to watch grow up. She understandably cried and continued to cry for a good while after they had ended their small service and made their way back into the house.

The grandparents felt a horrible tug in their chest watching such innocence grieve a death unfamiliar to a child outside of a farm and offered to let Paisley stay at their house for the night and a couple days more if it was fine with the parents. Paisley was far too occupied to participate in the conversation naturally, her face was buried into the rough fabric of one of the decorative pillows that adorned their couch in the living room, so the parents knelt down to her and asked if she would like to stay the night at her grandparents. She lifted her face enough to show a nodding of yes and hugged her parents a temporary goodbye. The grandparents stayed by Paisley, letting her finish her earned cry.

It was her summer vacation, her interim break before she was to enter the fourth grade, and she had to spend the final week of it in tears.

*

Paisley slept deeply that night. Though her grandparents had a spare bedroom they used almost exclusively for her visits, the tears had brought the poor girl to a reduced enough level of energy to cause her to fall fast asleep on the couch. The grandparents loosely covered her with a thick quilt covered in diamond patterns, the side of her face already pressed firmly against a pillow on the end right side of the couch. They stayed by her side for around an hour or so, passing the time gently talking to one another and casual reading from a newspaper and coffee table books that they had around the living room, until they were fully convinced she was going to sleep fully through the night. They got up and quietly stepped their way around her, flicking the lights off in as muted as a fashion as they could, and proceeded to their bedrooms.

*

Though deeply asleep, some part of Paisley knew that she was now alone. Some crawl-space sized part of her subconscious was alert to this fact and was now beginning to manipulate the dreams she was to experience. Almost as an outward, physical recognition to this change, her body began to twitch beneath the quilt a small number of times before eventually settling. Her recurring dream had started. A dream inside of her mother's stomach.

CHAPTER FOURTEEN
PAISLEY PT. II

Paisley's fourth grade class didn't have to go to music class until eleven that morning, and being the first day of school, her teacher Ms. Florakis knew that they weren't going to be getting a whole lot in the way of formal work done and was mostly introductory activities. They had gone around the room introducing themselves, gone over the classroom expectations, rules, guidelines, etc., and were now finishing their own custom desk tags that would go through the laminator before being thoroughly taped down. The teacher knew she was going to have to show them a tour sooner or later, it had been the talk of the school as soon as the principal had mentioned it during their back to school assembly first thing. So Ms. Florakis announced to the class that they had another ten minutes to finish up their tags, or at least to find a good stopping point, so that they could take a walk around the house.

With an excited cheer of the classroom, the kids all doubled down on their efforts and the sound of the colored pencils being pressed down against their construction paper tags had a noticeable increase in volume. Some kids resorted to scribbling, leaving spacious, uncolored gaps throughout the paper. Paisley didn't want to scribble like the other kids in her row, she really wanted to take her time to make her tag look nice. Her tag was special.

She was drawing a picture of Noodle on her tag. She worked with as much care and precision as her artistic abilities allowed. She started in pencil. It was mostly his head that she was drawing and she needed to be able to draw the details necessary to represent her memories of Noodle. Once she had felt satisfied with her initial pencil sketch, she began to trace over it with a black colored pencil and carefully blew away the small flakes that were left behind, making sure not to smudge any of it into the final picture. She then began to make elongated ovals and abstract shapes of orange on the white construction paper to mimic the spots that Noodle had. Her name was written in Paisley's own styling of bubble letters and filled in every other letter with orange as an additional homage.

Before any of the children had registered the passage of time, the ten minutes was up and their excited whisperings to one another had paused and began to pick back up as they were instructed to either pass in their finished project and clean up or carefully arrange your materials and unfinished project on your desk. A hectic minute had passed and the class was eager to move on to satisfying their highly amped curiosity. They were going to go check out the house.

They all waited as patiently as they could with their teeming excitements at their desks and listened for their individual names to be called to line up. After Ms. Florakis had gotten through the whole list, they were all in a straight line, legs and arms moving with practically spastic energy. They didn't know why they were excited beyond the fact that they just got to go see something new, but for children that really is all that they needed to be excited.

Admittedly Ms. Florakis was equally as curious as all of her children, but she needed to at least maintain her composure for the reason that kids had the uncanny ability to thrive off of any visible energies in their presence. So she ushered them through their classroom door, down the hallway, and out the front door to walk outback to the playground, purposely taking the longer route instead of going out the direct route of the double doors in the back, partially to stretch out the time she had before they transitioned to music, and partially to help rev up their curiosity as some sort of fun game the children were more than happy to participate in. Soon they were out there, feet on the blacktop, standing right in front of the house.

Despite its intermediate size, it felt as though it towered over them like they were in the presence of something impossible to capture in their glance. Yes, of course they have all seen houses before, a lot of the children in the class even lived in them, and yes they had seen much larger and smaller houses, but none of their visual memories could have prepared them for the unique sight of seeing one in the playground of their school. It was far more than enough to inspire awe in their wide eyes.

Ms. Florakis carefully opened the front door of the house and before taking a full step in, realized that it was an entryway complete with rubber matting for the children to place their shoes, and turned around to address the children. She explained that one by one, the children were to come in, take their shoes off in the entryway, and keep their shoes paired together and placed nicely on the large rubber mat. They all gave thumbs ups, nodded, verbally expressed their confirmation of listening, and whatever else they could do to get them one step closer into this new building. So they did, one by one, stepped inside and took their shoes off while carefully trying to peek further into the building. Once they had completed their task in the entryway, their teacher instructed them to step into the small hallway and find a spot alongside the wall.

They all did as they were told right up until the very last child. There were fourteen of them in all and all fit rather snugly in the miniature hallway. Thankfully they did not have to stay in their cramped positions for much longer because the time had come that they were finally able to be shown what was within these walls. Their teacher started them off by bringing them into the living room. Some kids instinctively went over to sit down on the couch. Ms. Florakis was by all means fine with it, but made sure to remind the boys that fumbled their ways over to the couch first that they needed to be mindful and careful with this brand new couch and also that they will need to be sure to take turns with other students who may want to sit on the couch. That was fine by them, they just wanted to be able to soak in the immediate gratification and thrill of sitting on a couch while still at school.

After she had pointed out the features of the room, politely asked the children to refrain from their attempts at playing with the television, and had spent what she determined to be an adequate amount of time to observe the room. There was some slight apprehension to be had from the frustrated students who had yet to have their turn sitting on the couch, but as she explained, she was planning on giving everyone more time at the end of their walkthrough to explore the house a little more freely and while that was going on, they would certainly have enough time to be able to sit on the couch. A little annoyed, yes, but they knew that to be as satisfactory of an answer as they would be able to get from a teacher. They all were now ready to see the next room, whatever it may be.

The tour continued to go well enough, spare the occasional heartbreaking statement from a child contrasting their own home situation to the one they were currently walking through. Some were amazed when they saw the bedrooms. Some bragged they had even bigger ones. One of the children commented that they had to share a bed with their mom and younger sister. In that moment Ms. Florakis imagined what it must be like to hold enough wealth in your palms to fix the world and she wanted to cry. It was in this moment that Paisley asked her teacher if she could use the restroom.

Although Ms. Florakis really didn't like having to be presumably the first teacher to have one of her students use this new bathroom, she also knew Paisley was a courteous girl and could be trusted not to destroy any of the facilities. She reminded Paisley that there was no hand soap in the bathroom yet, so when she was done, she needed to come back to her so that she could give her some hand sanitizer from the miniature bottle that hung on her lanyard. Paisley agreed and understood and went on her way to the upstairs restroom where they had just finished looking at. After she had made her exit from the spare bedroom where they currently were, several students began asking if they could use the restroom. She told the class that it was quite suspicious that as soon as Paisley needed to use the restroom, everyone else needed to as well and that they would have to wait until they went back inside the school. Collectively they groaned, collectively they got over it.

*

Paisley entered into the bathroom with a slight caution, the same way most children or even adults may enter an unfamiliar environment, and gently closed the door behind her. She went about to use the restroom as quickly as she could bring herself so she no longer felt so oddly alone and isolated. While she was sitting on the toilet, she heard water begin to splash against the bottom of the acrylic tub. She didn't hear the tell-tale squeak of the faucets knobs being turned, but then again, being so new, why would it make a sound so indicative of age and use as a rusted squeak?

She tried her best to simply ignore the water coming down. She just needed to first finish up on the toilet and then she could turn it off and leave. She grabbed far more toilet paper than was necessary in a hurried attempt to clean up. She wasn't necessarily scared, but she didn't like what was happening. She didn't like things happening around her when she was so vulnerable.

She quickly flushed the toilet and stood up, pulling her bottoms up to their proper position and walked gently on the balls of her feet, as if the noise of her walking normally was going to trigger a reaction from the tub. She reached her way to the edge of the tub and peered inside of it. She saw the tub was getting filled up with a yellow and peach colored liquid that was more viscous than watery. Inside of the fluid were long, thin streaks and splotches of red and orange. Instead of the natural reaction of horror that she thought she should be feeling, she felt at ease.

She dipped part of her hand into it and it felt warm and more than anything, somehow inviting. It was like a deep comfort had embedded itself into the skin the gel-like substance touched. She knew this comfort, but she wasn't sure how or where it was from, but she could imagine the rest of that comforting feeling across the rest of her body and she wasn't going to be satisfied until she had confirmation of the incredible sensation.

She walked to the door and pressed her ear against the door to see if anyone had been waiting immediately for her. When she heard nothing, she felt an instant relief. She took no further hesitation and sped over to the side of the tub and quickly took her shoes off and started to climb in, placing her right leg into it first and gradually allowing her weight to carry the rest of her body to slowly bring herself into the increasing volume of fluid in the bath.

She paid no mind to the spout anymore, she trusted that it would turn itself off after it had filled the tub enough. She started to sink herself deeper into it, starting with her stomach and moving up until her shoulders were resting underneath the consuming liquid. It had risen enough, so she immersed her head beneath the amniotic fluid. It felt like her recurring dream. The one inside her mother's stomach.

It was a feeling of weightlessness not unlike the one that could be felt when one has a dream of falling, but without motion. A still suspension. Underneath the surface, her eyes remained shut, only seeing a darkness with swirling colors of maroon that floated across the focus of her eyes moving about underneath her eyelids.

She could feel her spine curving ever so slightly, bit by bit, until her knees were level with her head and the entirety of her body was no longer touching the bottom of the tub, but was centered in the middle of the fluid. She didn't feel hunger, thirst, sadness, happiness, nothing but the same feeling she felt when her mother hugged her. She couldn't fully articulate that it was a feeling of safety or why she craved it so much, but she felt both physically and mentally light. Her eyes still closed shut, she no longer needed to worry about the sights around her, she didn't need to see, she was safe now.

She lifted her hands gently to touch her face. Her skin felt so smooth and fragile that she felt if any more pressure was added to the gliding motion she was applying to her face, her skin would tear and flake off with every additional touch. She moved her hand away and she noticed her arm was bent in an angle she could no longer change. So she moved her bent arm down to her leg and she no longer felt the nylon material of her leggings anymore, but more fragile skin instead. She was beginning to get scared. She opened her eyes and saw what looked like stars in a different sky, blood vessels and proteins floating in an ocean of yellow and peach fluid.

It didn't make sense. Were her movements causing her body to fall apart?

*

Ms. Florakis had finished the upstairs walk-around with the children and told them that they may now explore the house in partners of two that she assigned. They were told they had ten minutes and she set the timer on her smartwatch. She decided she would go to what would most likely be the most popular area, the living room, naturally. So she stood by the entertainment center and watched the lively activity taking place on the couch.

A few minutes had passed and a couple of her students had come down to tell her that the upstairs bathroom was locked and they couldn't get in to look at it. It was then that Ms. Florakis was reminded that Paisley had asked to go to the bathroom and reminded them that she must still be in there and to find another room. She looked down at her watch and three minutes had already passed since she set the timer on her smartwatch, and Paisley asked to go when they were still in the upstairs guest room. She felt so stupid forgetting about Paisley, she was almost upset with Paisley's mild-mannered nature for not making her absence more noticeable. She took a look around the living room and saw that everyone had been behaving well enough and decided to go upstairs to see if she's okay.

She walked up the stairs in a forced manner of calm and went to the bathroom door and began to knock. When she didn't hear any sort of response from Paisley, she knocked a little harder. When there still wasn't a response, she started repeating Paisley's name and knocking louder. There still was no answer. She tried to open the door now and the knob was stuck. She tried turning it side to side and then began pulling against it. Paisley was not responding, the door was locked, and Ainea Florakis began to panic.

*

Paisley could now feel the skin and flesh of her body began to gradually fall off and away into the amniotic fluid. Her physical abilities had become limited and she was no longer able to move her arms more than fractional inches, so she began to kick. She kicked and immediately could feel the sickening resistance against her now fetal toes.

A thin, transparent sac had developed around the entire tub. It had enveloped the tub completely and had become a loose wrap around the top of the tub, holding Paisley inside, below the acrylic lip of the bath. Her weightless suspension had shifted from its tranquil state and now became a horrible container of motion. She could feel herself being shifted around violently throughout the tub.

Her body would sink to the bottom and then be thrown against the sac, only to return again to the center. This continued to happen until it felt like the tub was trying to suffocate her. The sac had begun to contract tighter around the top and the fluid was rising her to the top without allowing her body to sink below again. Her face was being pressed against the sac and she could no longer breathe. It began to press itself into her mouth and she could feel it press directly against gums, no longer were her teeth present, and felt the silky flesh texture touch her tongue.

*

Ainea continued to stand on the other side of the door, her hands were now starting to sweat and caused her to keep losing the grip she was fighting to hold on the knob. The kids started to hear the commotion and began to slowly find themselves circling around Ms. Florakis. They were all staring in confusion and mounting anxiety as they watched their teacher slowly begin to lose her composure, finding herself nearly in tears calling Paisley's name now over and over again. She turned to face the students and instructed the first two students that met her gaze and told them to run inside the school and get the custodian. The rest she was yelling to wait downstairs until she came down. They had never heard Ms. Florakis yell before and it made them nervous, so they ran downstairs and all found themselves waiting in unsure anticipation.

Ainea started to press her ear against the door with as much force as she could sensibly use, brushing her curly hair from off her ear with a violent sweeping motion. She could hear the faintest sounds of what sounded like something wading through deep water. Was Paisley drowning? Ainea could feel her stomach sink and she wanted to vomit the suffocatingly thick air that was becoming trapped in her throat. She got to her feet and remembered the advice from when she used to explore abandoned buildings as a teenager: stand one step away from the door, aim for directly below the lock, use your dominant leg, and kick with your foot completely flat.

So, she breathed a deep breath and followed her instructions. She heard a dull thud her first kick and realized this wooden door that felt so weightless and simply must somehow be reinforced now. She didn't know what else she could do, so she kept trying to kick it. It was on her fourth kick that she could feel her foot smash against the door with an imperfect flatness and it caused her foot to quickly twist to the right until she could feel her ankle hit flat against the wood, sending a horrible and sharp pain through her leg.

She tried to place her foot flat against the ground and the sensation of her weight trying to place itself atop the fresh injury was an instant shock of overwhelming pain. She had to bring herself to sit down now in front of the door. She was embarrassed by her uselessness and scared for Paisley's safety. She tried getting herself up again by placing her right knee down and bringing herself upwards to try again, but as soon as her left leg was fully up, she brought her right leg up to extend and was instantly met with the same terrible pain when her foot touched the floor. She couldn't stand and she collapsed to her knees.

The pain, embarrassment, and anxiety had welled within her fiercely and she began to cry. She was entirely helpless. She wasn't able to fix the situation and even if the custodian managed to be sought out and brought to the issue, she wasn't entirely sure he would even be able to help. She couldn't fix this. She knew she couldn't fix this.

She stood sunken on her knees as she cried and now she hunched her back entirely over until her stomach had touched the tops of her thighs and she began to pray. Loudly she prayed. Like one of her gentile ancestors first coming to humble themselves before the Lord they knew not before, Christ, and prayed. She prayed for Paisley's rescue, safety, return, whatever it was that was keeping her behind this impossible door. Her sobs were interruptions to the speech she was sending forth to God, but her impassioned sincerity prevailed. She was heard.

*

The amniotic sac had begun to recede within itself, collapsing its width and measure into a source beneath the tub until it had completely disappeared. Paisley's fetal state began fastly to revert to her correct age and form and she was able to move her arms again and brought her body, shoulders up, to above the surface of the amniotic fluids which had begun to revert to water. A clear and pure water.

On the other side of the door, Ainea could hear Paisley's desperate gasps of her embracing air once restricted. She immediately brought herself from her hunched position of prayer and swung her hands to grab hold of the doorknob to turn it and it was finally opened. Ainea crawled her way inside the door and to the bathtub where she was able to bring herself to stand on both feet in spite of the overwhelming pain, so that she may lift Paisley out of the bath. She brought her forth from the tub and they both fell to the floor with one another. Both struggled to get to their knees and Ms. Florakis and Paisley began to hug each other tightly. Paisley's soaking wet clothes had begun to seep into Ms. Florakis' clothes, but nothing mattered less.

Amongst all their tears, they found joy.

CHAPTER FIFTEEN
A RESPONSE TO PANIC

The custodian eventually arrived and found Ms. Florakis and one of her students hugging each other in front of the tub. He didn't know what was going on and he didn't have time to figure it out himself, for as soon as he had stepped into the bathroom, Ms. Florakis yelled for him to get the nurse and bring the rest of her students inside. Without a moment to think or a proper cause for him to stand and argue, he fulfilled her requests and asked the kids to follow him inside while he half-ran his way to the back entrance to the school and told them to stand in the immediate hallway while he sprinted to the Nurse's Office.

His voice came out in panic-stuttered spurts without any real clarity besides the area where she was needed. Noting the urgency, the nurse, Ms. Abebe grabbed her portable first-aid kit and got out in a hurry to go to the scene. Knowing that the nurse was now on her way to help whatever exactly had happened, the custodian ran to the Principal's Office. He went in and tried his best to explain more in depth what happened with the minimal understanding he had of the situation. The principal sent out the secretary to go out to the rest of Ms. Florakis' class to bring them back to their regular classroom while he went out to assist in whatever it was that was going on in that house.

He found himself not too far behind Nurse Abebe as she was still walking up the stairs by the time he had walked through the entryway door. Ms. Abebe went through the door and without probing with useless questions, she went straight away to Ainea and Paisley, and kneeled right beside them. She quickly assessed the situation. Water was covering the immediate area around the tub, Paisley was soaking wet, and Ainea had been embracing her with tightness that suggested a relief or rejoicing of sorts. It appeared to her that Paisley had almost drowned in the tub. Thankfully she could see clear and well that Paisley was breathing and well. That was what was most paramount to her.

The principal came through the door and began to ask if everyone was okay, not being able to think of anything else to say. Ms. Abebe, without turning, barked out the instructions for the principal to grab her plastic tub of spare clothes. Seeing that he had no grasp on the situation, listened without hesitation and began to head down the stairs.

Besides the emotional distress and elevated heart-rate that she was experiencing, all at least seemed physically and immediately okay and stable with Paisley. She had been let out of the tight embrace she was sharing with Ms. Florakis and allowed the nurse to give her a quick look over. She asked Paisley if she could breathe okay and watched as Paisley nodded quickly and was able to verbally assure her by her repeating of a simple sentence dictated by Ms. Abebe.

Ainea tried moving herself to possibly get up and made a loud groan as she tried to move her right foot. Palesa Abebe was immediately alerted and turned around to ask what was wrong and Ainea briefly answered by saying that she had sprained her ankle. It was visually confirmed as it was red and in the midst of swelling. Ms. Abebe reached into her kit, grabbed an elastic bandage, took Ainea's shoe off, and wrapped it before grabbing an instant snap cold compress to place on the sprain.

The principal had come back with a clear plastic tub filled with mismatched clothes visible through the sides. He placed the tub on the floor in front of the trio and repeated his question from earlier asking generally if everything was okay. It would be.

Ms. Abebe took the clear tub from his hands and brought Paisley to the spare bedroom and looked through the tub with her to find some comfortable clothing for her. Paisley begged not to be left alone, so Ms. Abebe stayed in the same room and turned around facing the door to still give Paisley the privacy she needed. The principal stayed in the room with Ms. Florakis to discuss what had happened.

Ainea's emotions that were running so high, had finally started to level out, and the exorbitant amount of pain in her ankle had been gradually decreasing, so she was able to finally start talking. It didn't make sense saying out loud how exactly the door managed to be locked the entire time and then suddenly no longer anymore. He looked through both sides of the door and tested the knobs himself and found no immediate faults. He tried gently asking her if she had made any sort of mistakes in judgment, of course in different words so as to not sound accusatory. She spoke back without hesitation and immediately told him there was no mistake, practically with a jagged tone.

There was no point in further discussing the matter until they were at least out of the house and calmer. Paisley and Ms. Abebe had emerged from the spare bedroom and returned back to the bathroom. It was best for them all to make their way to the principal's office. Ms. Abebe and the principal both helped Ms. Florakis to her feet, or foot rather, and helped counter her weight on the principal's shoulder to help her move. Slowly they moved down the stairs and they made their way back to the school.

*

The principal insisted that they needed to try to figure out a solid story before calling Paisley's parents, he wasn't sure what to say. He asked Palesa to interview Paisley separately from Ms. Florakis and he would speak with her. One story was a lot easier to make sense of than another.

Paisley told her perspective with such genuine conviction that it was hard for Palesa Abebe to bring the necessary border of objectivity she needed to be able to fully evaluate the situation from a medical perspective. She asked about her home life, any recent changes or anything else that might be causing undue stress. Paisley told her about her dog and told her about the dreams she'd been having. All that she could come up with as a conclusion to draw was that it was a nervous breakdown of sorts.

Extreme sadness mingled with unsettling dreams could have caused this episode.

Ms. Abebe and the principal came back together to discuss what they heard, and brought Ms. Florakis to the Nurse's Office to stay with Paisley. What didn't make sense was the reality of Ms. Florakis with the impossibly reinforced door. They had to ignore what didn't make sense so that they could find a complete story to tell Paisley's parents. Ms. Florakis stayed by her side and brushed Paisley's hair with her fingers as she laid down on the bed in the office and slowly shifted herself into sleep.

*

Paisley's mother had arrived after a phone call that had caused her heart to skip several beats. They informed her that Paisley was okay and that she was sleeping soundly in the Nurse's Office. They brought her to a closed door meeting in the principal's office where Ms. Abebe did her best to explain what was complex, even to the medical world, to a mother recovering from the shock of a story that didn't make sense.

She cried. She didn't know how else she could respond besides listening to what was being told to her. She knew Paisley had been upset after her puppy Noodle had passed away, but she would have never expected for something as drastic as this to happen. The only thing she could bring herself to ask was what was going to be done to the house to make sure the door wouldn't malfunction like that ever again and the principal instantly reassured her that the door would be blocked off and entirely restricted until they could replace the door. Whatever he could do to avoid liability.

They brought Paisley's mother to her daughter and the mother asked if she could speak to Ms. Florakis privately with Paisley. They happily obliged. So she gently woke Paisley up and started to comfort her.

She spent several minutes hugging, embracing, and sharing tears with her daughter. When things had been more settled, she asked Ms. Florakis more frank questions and Ainea answered with honesty. It was something that could not be explained from her perspective. She didn't know about the fetal horror that Paisley had experienced, but she did know that she was locked in that room and what happened wasn't natural. She told her the events as they were from her perspective. The evidence was written by her bandaged ankle.

She did not know what to tell her mother besides a desperate plea for her to pray for that child and continue to watch over her. Watch and pray.

CHAPTER SIXTEEN
A USELESS CHANGE

For the rest of the very short beginning week at school, the principal had decided it best to take the extra precaution to not allow any more students or staff inside the house. He told the staff it would be open once more at the beginning of the next school week, but for the time being, the custodian needed to do some minor repairs on one of the doors inside. The custodian, still unsure what he was to be looking for, looked over the door, through and through and furthermore, but he could find nothing structurally wrong with it. He reported back to the principal with nothing.

The principal still needed something to be changed to report back to the staff with, so he told the custodian to use the maintenance card to go to Home Depot and get a new doorknob. So he did and so it was replaced. Feeling that the cheap trick would be a satisfactory fix for what was a problem no one was able to truly understand yet, he had no further ideas and washed his hands of the affair, hoping to hear nothing more of it.

Chapter Seventeen
Grayson Pt. I

It was Thursday, the day after the incident with Paisley in fourth grade who the kids and teachers alike assumed would be out for the rest of the short beginning week of school. Everyone at the school had been told that the house would be temporarily off-limits until some minor repairs had taken place. It felt as though that as soon as they had it, it was being taken away, and it drove not only the antsy behavior of the children to an all time high, but now they were filled with a tenfold curiosity that ran through them like adrenaline. Though the age of schoolyard folktales had long been diluted by the repetitive and bleedingly stupid age of child targeted internet content, the distress and enigma which had befallen in this strange house made prime breeding ground for a new wave of rumors.

Some of the kids told each other that Paisley tried to drown herself in the tub, others said it was a ghost, and even more rarely than that rumor, some said that it was Ms. Florakis herself who tried to drown her and that Paisley had broken her ankle in an attempt to escape. None of them of course would be able to comprehend what had actually happened, none of them were even so much as told an official telling of events from the school. It was none of their business after all, but it was an impossibly enticing story for children that age to ponder over and therefore inescapable from the prying ideas of fruitful imaginations. This house had already been a curiosity and now it had made itself a legend among the children.

A legend. An object of children's folklore. Like an abandoned mansion that sat on a populated street, the increasingly hazardous building that was inhabited by a lonely and elder widow, or even an old grey house where a reliable local once said they saw a figure of an old man in nineteenth century attire in an upstairs window, the house in the playground was now among their ranks. A place of intrigue, fear, and baby steps of bravery. Now nary there was a child more desperate for attention for bravado than Grayson.

Grayson, a child of ten years of age, burdened by a shattering number of insecurities heaped upon him by his judgmental mother, an inattentive father, and a sister in high school who knew no other way to express her pent up anger than in foul language and cruel acts towards her younger brother. He was to put up a tough show, lest his facade was to slip like a humiliating act of physical indecency. Naturally his improperly explored palette of emotions took shape in unproductive acts of rebellion, especially whenever there was structure to be found. Like all creatures, a resistance to change is only normal, so the school was to bear a sizable portion of his ire.

Whether it be an insatiable desire to speak in rude remarks to his teachers, introducing varieties of cuss words to children that had the fortune of responsibly tongued parents, or the brutish physical bullying of classmates smaller than himself, he used his being as a weapon or a show for the world around him to forcefully acknowledge his presence. Since he was yet to be praised for any virtues, he would instead garner their attention through his own means, any time the occasion arose. Today, an occasion had arose.

Grayson was not one to be left out of schoolyard gossip, rumors, or anything else that had garnered attention without finding a way to include himself in it. He had heard the rumors about Paisley as surely as anyone else had, forcing his inclusion into private conversations between friend groups and like-minded children during lunch and snack time earlier in the day. Not to be left out of a circulation as thrilling or captivating as this, he would have to think of a way to make this about himself. And so, unknowingly, the cricket's legs sent vibrations down the idiopidae's burrow.

He had snuck his phone out of his backpack when he went to grab his lunchbox so he could show his friends a video.

*

Over the summer Grayson was left home with his older sister every weekday for eight to twelve hours and, similar to the way he was monitored by his parents, he was left to entertain himself on his phone or his Oculus. Though he was fond of games like Contractors and Beat Saber, he found himself spending the most amount of time on the game Rec Room. It was a game dedicated to community, or so it says, where you would be able to talk to and play with an astonishingly large swathe of individuals across the world (though it always seemed to be that most of them ended up being English speaking individuals from ages seven to twenty-something). There were options to play simple games like paintball, soccer, laser tag, etc. or you could simply find yourself in a central hub chatting with people.

Desperate for attention or perhaps attempting to fill a need for meaningful companionship, he spent most of his time simply talking with people. He would walk around, trying to find children around his age or even better, were the teenagers he found himself running into. They knew far more about the taboos Grayson desperately wanted to learn more about. He wanted to hate the same people they hated, share the same opinions on new topics, speak the way they spoke, anything at all to relate to the group, and especially impress them. Eventually after proving himself to be of worthiness to them with obsessive cursing and crude observations of the little he had yet to know about sex, he had found himself with a small circle he would meet with regularly.

In the several years that the internet has been around, it has always found its way to be a source of entertainment for all and more than that, it was known to host things that simply were not sustainable or acceptable to host elsewhere. Though tidal waves of atrocities crash through to the surface of popular attention, such as extreme pornographies, violent rapes, child beatings, animal torture, gang shootings, cartel beheadings, and even necrophilic acts, very few manage to stick in the conscious of the modern audience, almost certainly to be erased by the next flood. However, this video had stuck.

It was as though it were a rite of passage for these semi-anonymous teenagers. To be considered as one of their own, one would have to go through the varied gauntlet of tolerance levels that needed to be met. They all had each other on Snapchat and this was the primary method of which they would use to communicate with one another, sending each other grotesqueries in bite-sized snippets and photos. Oftentimes they would do so while on group calls with each other so they could hear one another's reactions. Grayson had seen far more than any ten-year-old ever should. He had seen videos of woman in extreme bondage, faces purple with asphyxiation and inanimate objects internally mutilating an anatomy Grayson had no understanding of, a video of a child being run over and ignored by pedestrians in a timelapse, and even a picture of a decapitated german shepherd's head in a toilet. Grayson had believed he had seen it all and that nothing was too much for him anymore, or at least wasn't so much that he couldn't hide his true feelings of horror from his online friends. It was no small feat to scare him like this did.

The online group of boys were playing Rec Room together, hanging out in the virtual bathroom that the lobby they were in had, almost in some sort of dystopian emulation of antics found in an older high school comedy film. It was there where one of the oldest boys had decided it was time to bring up the most infamous video among the group to Grayson. They told him the name that he needed to look up and they wanted him to pull it up while they were with him, so that they could hear everything that he was going to say, the disgusted swears, the stuttered beginnings of comprehension, and the tremble of fear penetrating the cadence of his voice.

Grayson went in with a large dose of hubris, knowing what he had seen, hearing horrible sounds muffled by digital compression, he thought himself more than able to brave the obscene. He pulled up the default browser. Large floating tabs in front of his friends' avatars, like a screenless monitor, a casual symptom of hyper-futuristic progression, its use instantly perverted by the whims of overstimulated generations.

They guided him through the process of finding the correct link for the video and eagerly listened as he found it and allowed it to load. It was on a website unfamiliar to Grayson and really, probably unfamiliar to most besides the anonymous uploaders finding hosts for their re-uploads of disturbed curiosities. Without the network support of larger websites like YouTube, it loaded with a pace that was conducive to anticipation, and anticipation was exactly what was being built. He used the time that the grey wheel was spinning to turn the video fullscreen.

The loud digital humming had started while the black screen had begun to fade into the image put forth. Centered in the direct middle of a virtually featureless and anonymous setting, a concrete floor and a black curtained background, was a woman. She was kneeling on a stack of crude wooden boards with her calves extending downwards towards the ground where it was visible, despite the grainy and distorting nature of the videos passing through hundreds of users preservation efforts, that her toes were bending against the ground, barely keeping her weight supported, stopping her from going down further on the structure. It was vital for her weight to keep her where she was, for it was clear that her hands were bound behind her, and there was a large, red wire that came down from the ceiling and was tangled thickly through a tightly made ponytail that contained all of her hair that could be brushed into it. If her toes were to slip, her hair would almost certainly be ripped out by the weight of her body. The camera was picked up by what was assumed to be its tripod and brought it close to the woman until the framing ended on each side of her shoulders, the upper portion of her stomach above her navel, and the lower half of her bound ponytail, so the middle of the frame was perfectly focused on her chest.

Around the circumference of her breasts was wrapped tightly by a thick and fraying rope which caused extreme discoloration. Shades of violent purples, faded reds, and interspersed blues of veins in overworked distress. They sat atop a plain and rough plank of wood. When the camera was further away, it was revealed to be supported by a simple metal rods connected to the pile of wood her knees rested upon.

Her face was a mess of flushed red hues, eyes bloodshot to a point where her eyes were far more red than white, and a cheap blue mascara running down her flustered face. She was caucasian, not a pale woman, but of a germanic peach skin tone. The dirty blonde color of her hair was now more apparent with the camera's closeness. They were details that would eventually fade to the background of his attention when the act was to begin.

What came into view were plain, thick white arms, hairy and with wide hands that were decorated with bulbous, protruding knuckles. She wasn't gagged with anything so all of her beginning whimpers and quiet cries were audible and distressing. Grayson watched her bottom lip begin to curve upwards in quick successions, a self-inflicted denial of the heavy sobs welling inside of herself.

A weighted slam of the anonymous man's palms crashed down atop the wood, directly in between her contorted breasts. It made her shudder and close her eyes while thick tears immediately rolled down her heated face. It was no doubt part of the intimidation game the sadist found himself playing against a woman one could not safely assume was fully consenting or aware of what she had consented to. He slammed his palms thrice more, changing the location of his strikes against the board with dreadful pauses of silence in between. Though the feeling could not entirely be expressed, Grayson knew something about this video was going to be different and horrendous. It was a sense of impending doom, freezing him in place with silence.

The hands had slammed once more, this time with a tightly closed fist, it had sounded like a soft emptiness inside the pocket of air of his cupped hand. He slowly unclasped his hand, and he allowed the contents of his palms to fall the half-inch distance to the board with what could only be described as dense tings. He had now begun to reel his hand back out of frame, making sure they were now visible to the camera and, more importantly, to the woman. They were long sheathing nails for flooring. In Grayson's eyes they looked like ancient carpenter nails used to hold together medieval houses, forged by blacksmiths. As soon as his hand had been fully pulled from out of frame, the woman rolled her eyes downward to see the nails resting on the board and began to cry, an unmistakable look of fear in her eyes and an immediate beginning of pleas to her sadist.

The tears were running faster down her face, her voice became more weak, and the mucus had begun to clog her throat and nose. The man had put into frame a machinist's hammer, black with a square face to it and an end that tapered to a point. Watching the way its weight moved about in the man's large hands was enough to convey its weight to whoever watched. He took the sharp end of the hammer and began to brush it across her constricted breasts in slow, light motions. A cruel precursor. It was as though time itself had begun to hold its breath as the inevitable began to happen.

He had held the nail firmly between the pinch of two thick fingers and held it atop her breast which was to the left of the frame. He held it around half an inch from the center of her breast and began to steady the nail, pressing it with the strength of his hand into the layer of thinning skin, wrought with restricted circulation, until droplets of blood had begun to form and gain enough mass to drip off the sides of her breasts curvature. She began to beg more now, as if the gravity of the situation had begun to crush her.

He swung the hammer down and deeply the nail sank into her flesh. Her wail of pain was a tortured one, as if all the grief, anger, and pain one could experience in life had been expressed in one terrible scream. A scream that came from so far within the depths of herself, that she had fallen silent with an extended attempt of regaining the air inside her lungs that were lost to the incredulous expression of pain. He placed his palm across the very end of her breast and, with a controlled anger, began to press her breast as flatly as he could into the board. It was after he had felt it was satisfactory and perhaps due to the nail's attempts to unburrow itself from the unsteady flesh it was lodged inside, he took the hammer and swung it down firmly across the head of the nail. Quickly again the hammer was lifted and he slammed it down and the sound of the nail penetrating the wood's surface sounded throughout the room they were in and consequently in gnarled audio through Grayson's headset. Twice more the hammer was to come down until the nail became visible from the other side of the plank.

The same sadistic act was repeated once more in the same breast, parallel to the other nail on the other side and mirrored in her other breast. Grayson, though slowly receding inside of himself being unable to process this extreme imagery, was only able to think and hope that the lack of circulation had at least made the horrific process to be dampened by a numbness. Her cries still suggested otherwise.

It was at the end of the final nail being driven through that he placed down the hammer in between the space of her breasts and removed his arms from the frame. She continued to sob for the space of around a minute longer until she was beginning to regain a slight composure, enough for her to now speak words. She moved her head upwards and to the left side of the frame to stare at the sadist and began to thank him. Tears streaming down her face, blood staining the wooden plank, and she looked up to thank him with sincerity, as if this had been a cathartic act for her, the tone of her eyes even shifting to a genuine look of gratefulness. It was then that the man's hand had gently cupped under her chin and she continued to thank him that the video faded to black and had ended.

With the end of the video, something had undoubtedly changed within Grayson. It was an irreversible sight. Had it not been for her thanking the man at the end of the video, perhaps he would have been able to chock the whole video up as a terrible act of torture, but her gratitude had confused him and had made the confusing impact last. The little he knew about sex that had already been distorted by the graphic pornographies shared with him was now fully confused. In the other disgusting acts he had witnessed, there was at least a traceable origin of pleasure, but this was something entirely separate and depraved.

*

He knew not what to do with this experience besides to share it and spread it like a virus. So it was with this intention in mind that he thought to bring his phone outside during recess, so that he may show it to other children and continue the chain of scarring. However, the shift had already taken place today, there existed a towering object of powerful fascination to them. The kids tried to place themselves in an immediate proximity to the house. They could speak of their rumors, ideas, and wonders while firmly placing the reality of the building in their sight, within an arms' length. Grayson now had an audience for which an attention could be grabbed from, now he needed to find a way to seize it.

The staff watching them during recess were quite aware of the situation that had occurred the day prior and they knew the kids had a general awareness of something that had happened to Paisley, so they were doubly sure to see to it that no children would be going inside the house. One of the staff members had decided to post themselves in front of the house's door. Yes, that would ensure that no child would be able to enter through the door, but there were still three other sides of the house and windows for the children to ponder beside.

They were all too afraid to, per se, touch the house or even to bring themselves to look into the windows for longer than a sparing glance. This was an immediate in for Grayson to take advantage of, seeing the fear they were managing to inspire within themselves, he could show off his bravado. So he approached the center of the largest group who stood on the left side of the house.

He asked them what they were all so afraid of and they began to elaborate with a variety of their own stories, primarily with a recurring theme of ghosts or something evil that lived inside the house. It was swiftly becoming a localized version of Bloody Mary with the mirror being a window into this strange house. Peer far too long into it and something evil shall be shown. Grayson happily volunteered to peer into this deepening abyss.

He stepped up to the window and peered inside what appeared to be a living room, staring past a couch and exploring with his eyes the layout of what could be seen. He saw a television, a recliner, an entertainment stand, and a couple of lamps that all existed in a static state with emptiness occupying the room. His step towards the window had caused the other students to take a step backwards, as if there was going to be a physical and direct blowback that would immediately lash against them. They stared at him and by proxy it felt like they were able to understand the impression of what was to be seen inside of the house.

The initial intrigue had already started to fade and as Grayson was slowly realizing he was staring into nothing more than an empty living room and was becoming bored. Seconds went by without enough stimulation to keep the ADHD child's attention. Then there was motion.

He could see a door open and through it walked something. The angle was difficult to be able to fully see what was happening. It was like an elusive movement outside of the main periphery of one's vision, not being able to be fully captured by the mind's eye, only sustenance to feed a paranoid imagination. His heart rightfully should have skipped a beat, but instead he leaned into the angle farther than before with a renewed eagerness. It was a secret feeling displayed only to him, a feeling more than words, telling him this was not to be feared, but to be looked upon.

So it slowly revealed itself, the figure which exited the bathroom door. It inched closer to the opening door jamb to the living room until its head was visible. It was one of the paras, Ms. Gulzar, or more accurately, it took the appearance of her.

The idea of a staff member perhaps being in there wasn't entirely an unbelievable thought. It was odd though, that it wasn't someone like the custodian or principal instead, since they told the staff and student body it was closed for repairs of some sort. He wanted to turn and tell his classmates behind him what he was seeing but he could not find himself to turn his glance away, for an instinct inside of him told him that if he stood in place and watched, something would happen, something he wanted.

She had only been standing there with her head visible for no more than twenty seconds, but the silence and lack of other motion made the time feel like it was extended into hours. She had acknowledged his stare it seemed. So it proceeded.

It was cloaked in a resemblance of Ms. Gulzar, the young, twenty two year old para who was hired last year to assist the third grade teacher, Mrs. Florian. She was assigned the first recess shift last year and she quickly became the object of many young boys' affections and growing desires. It was almost certainly because of her youth in contrast to the staff that was primarily over the age of forty that elevated their attraction to her.

Her torso was of a sort of boxy shape with a fair chubbiness around her stomach and arms that accentuated her youthfulness in a joyous way, it added a level of immediate comfort to anyone who laid their eyes upon her. She was not intimidatingly thin nor was her weight worn uncomfortably upon her. What inspired the rattle of hormones to shake with such vigor in many physically maturing students was the beautiful plumpness of her thighs that connected to her large heart shaped bottom, highly accentuated by the contours of her well worn assortment of jeans.

Though unsure why her anatomy had excited them so much, they knew they found themselves stealing inappropriate glances with thoughts and visualizations that were new, sometimes shameful, and often thrilling. Their minds' eyes were flooded with the envisioned nudity of a kind, authoritative figure. For Grayson, his desires that were supposed to be in an infantile stage of sorts had been distorted by the terrible depictions of intimacy he had been exposed to. He tried to have crushes on the girls in his classes and he did, but never was he able to visualize them in the explicit fantasies he still didn't understand in the same way he was able to picture Ms. Gulzar. Sometimes it went so far for him that he would try to picture Ms. Gulzar in the extreme pornography the kids from Rec Room sent him.

He didn't want to hurt her, but he didn't really know if these acts did hurt the women, or if they enjoyed it. He wanted her to enjoy whatever it was that took place in those images. They were what excited him but sometimes it scared him.

He was now making eye contact with Ms. Gulzar. It stared with a familiar friendliness back at him, like she would when she smiled at him in the hallway, but her eyes seemed like they were looking at him softer, with an invitation to closeness. So he stepped closer to the window until he was only around five inches away from pressing his face against the glass.

It stepped forward from the opening of the door jamb and Grayson saw what he had wanted. The imitation of Ms. Gulzar stood there entirely nude. Grayson felt like his heart had leapt into his throat and a weakness had taken over the rest of his body as he had no idea what to do in this situation, preemptively fantasized or not, he was unable to move. It continued to step forward towards him, it wanted Grayson to see up close.

Grayson had finally felt like he had control back over at least his arms and he reached into his pocket and grabbed his phone. He tried to bring it to the window with a stumbling stealthiness, but Ms. Gulzar showed him it was more than what she wanted and she posed for him, bending herself slightly over the entertainment center and turning her head back towards Grayson, shoving three of her fingers down her mouth. He was literally trembling as he took the photo and dropped his phone after.

Grayson saw that she had grabbed the remote from the entertainment center and walked over to the couch's side, and pushed it so that its ending quarter would be directly in front of his window. It was to perform a show for him. Grayson watched as she pressed her lips to the glass and licked the window where his face was before showing him the remote control again. She popped off the remote's battery cover and took the batteries out and held them in her palm, letting the cover fall down somewhere on the couch.

Ms. Gulzar had taken the curtain, that Grayson adamantly told himself he never saw until that moment, and began wrapping it around her throat while pressing her face closer and closer to the glass. It was visible to him that the top of the curtain was still attached to the rod that must be above the window and she began to move her body downwards, using her body weight to choke herself. She took the batteries from her palm and inserted them crudely and deeply inside of both of her nostrils. Grayson could feel his knees physically begin to shake.

He could see her face already start to burst with shades of red over her gingerbread colored skin from her asphyxiation and she started to fellate the remote in front of the window. The sound was muffled, but he could hear her gag as the remote went deeper down her throat. It did not stop her and she continued to keep going until it had almost appeared to Grayson that she was vomiting saliva all over herself. It was after this that she had taken the remote and began to penetrate herself with it. The expressions he could read from her face told him that it must have been a rough and painful insertion, but she continued to do so until her wincing had turned to heavy but short choked moans being directed into the glass.

Her face was turning deeper shades of red, transforming to hues of blue and purple, but it seemed like her moans and pleasure were getting more intense. Grayson didn't know what to do, he was physically excited but helpless to do more than watch for he felt as though if he were to move he would collapse. So he watched. He watched as she pulled her neck harder against the curtain to choke herself even more intensely and begin to mouth words to him. He watched her intensely mouth the words 'It doesn't hurt me, Grayson' over and over.

Her mouth was caught in the middle of repeating the words over once more when she began to bite her lip hard and her body shook. Grayson knew enough to tell she had reached her climax. It was then that she had pulled the remote out of herself and the hand which she used to penetrate herself with was placed against the glass, leaving a palmful of blood to trace her hand's shape on the window.

When Grayson saw the blood he was scared. He felt his body shift back from the window as soon as her hand was placed against the glass and he knew he couldn't handle the sight any longer. He grabbed his phone from off the ground and began to run. He ran past his classmates who he attempted to impress, he ran past the staff member who yelled at him with a question about his phone, he went towards the winding driveway which connected the school's premises to the road and he ran.

CHAPTER EIGHTEEN
GRAYSON PT. II

It was the gym teacher who was one of the staff members monitoring the second recess shift who was able to catch up to Grayson and calm him down. He always knew Grayson as more of a brutish and mean child, so to see him cry like this had made an impact upon his impression of the situation, something serious must have happened to cause this reaction. Grayson was on the verge of being inconsolable, so he had to take a lot of gentle talking and a hand on his shoulder at all times to eventually coerce him back up the driveway and to the school where he was brought into the office.

The secretary was not even able to begin speaking before the gym teacher asked her to call the counselor for her to come down here. He knew that she was having a lunch group with some children, but he knew that this clearly should take priority. He was almost convinced prior to this incident that Grayson didn't even like him, so getting him to this point of following him to the office to calm down was pushing it beyond what he already thought was possible and didn't want to continue to push him and make things far worse.

Ms. Oliveira had to dismiss the two second grade girls who were having problems resolving an issue as soon as she had heard Grayson's name over the phone. She never had many one-on-ones with Grayson (despite her best efforts), but more than frequently had his name brought up by other students who came to her with emotional crises. She figured this would be a good opportunity to better understand him.

She was just as shocked as the gym teacher when she saw him sitting in a chair against the office wall, hands over his eyes, crying. She asked him to join her back to her office and only taking momentary glances by moving his hands positions over his eyes to see his immediate surroundings, got up and followed her. She didn't want to immediately push any level of forced companionship upon him by placing her hands on his back or any physical touch of that nature, so she simply walked slowly with him, guiding him back to her office, a private place where they may speak.

They arrived and she immediately scooted the padded folding chair she had pushed in front of her desk to a more open position for him to sit in. He sat down with a slight thud and continued to hunch forward in a final exhaustive bout of crying before he was able to bring himself back to an upright position. She waited for him to move past the end stage of his tears, not forcing him to talk when he was unable to. He brought his breathing back to a normal and wiped his face with the collar of his t-shirt.

All she was told was that he tried to run away from the school, so that was all she could base her beginning questions on, so instead she decided to ask things in a slightly more indirect manner to try to get her grasp on the situation. She asked him first if anything was worrying him. He simply nodded his head yes.

She asked him if he wanted to talk about what was bothering him. He didn't say or nod in either confirmation or rejection. This wasn't a hard no. She thought that she might be able to get somewhere.

She asked if it was something that happened at school. He nodded yes. She asked if it was something that happened during recess. Another yes. She asked if it was something a student may have said or done. He shook his head no. She asked him if it was something a staff member may have said or done. He started to cry again.

She was able to catch him in the beginning sniffles of a far larger cry waiting to burst forth and continued to ask what they had said or done. He finally began to talk by telling her that he wasn't sure. She thought maybe there was something said to him that confused him or was mean or something of that nature, but still couldn't figure out what could cause him this level of distress. She asked if it was something that was said to him and he tilted his neck slightly to the side and told her he didn't really know. She asked who it was and he said Ms. Gulzar.

Ms. Oliveira was silently shocked, to say the least. Not only had she known Ms. Gulzar professionally, but considered her one of her coworkers she could look to as an actual friend. She had always seemed like a bubbly woman who was dedicating her energy to the children in the best ways any normal person could manage. To hear that she did anything that could have emotionally hurt one of the children here was almost unbelievable, but nevertheless, she had to find out what had happened.

She was struggling to think of what to even ask, he only half-confirmed that it was something she had said to him. She tried to pay closer attention to his mannerisms before she asked any further questions. She moved herself closer to him and could see that he was starting to sweat. She asked him if something was making him scared. He stuttered out a hoarse yes. She asked him what it was and he pulled out his phone and opened the last photo on the camera roll.

There on Grayson's phone's screen was a picture of Ms. Gulzar, fully naked, half bent over an entertainment center beneath a television, head turned towards the camera, her hand pressing fingers down her open mouth, and a startling triangular shape of blackness where her nose was supposed to be.

Chapter Nineteen
What to Do About Grayson's Photo?

Giacinta Oliveira felt her stomach sink to the lowest recesses of her inside. She could only hide so much of an expression, only look so neutral towards an astonishingly horrible image. It raised hundreds of questions which all pushed towards the front of her head, clustering like a thousand cattle reaching the open gate simultaneously, threatening to break the area which once contained them. She was confused, furious, and overwhelmed with a nearly paralyzing disgust.

She immediately wanted to accuse him. Did he make this horrible edit of her? Was it a fake? How could it not be? Why was he so afraid? Was it because he was caught? Did someone else send it to him? Did he show anyone else?

She needed to step back and evaluate this but she knew the longer that she sat in silence, the less confidence Grayson would have in her ability to help him. She took the phone and placed it down in front of her at her desk. She was able to catch her quickly fleeting breath and ask him calmly where the photo came from. He told her that he took the photo. She immediately followed up with a subsequent question asking where he took that photo. He said in the window of the house on the playground. She didn't like how the reality of this photo was beginning to take shape and she felt frozen in place.

"Did she ask you to take this picture of her?"

He explained that he took out his phone to try to take a photo without her noticing, but when she saw his phone out, it was like she was trying to pose for him. This whole thing was making Giacinta sick. This didn't sound like anything her friend Neepa would do. She knew that Neepa had once confided in her about some minor depression she was experiencing, but there's no way she would have had a manic episode like this, she would never do anything sexual to these children. She knew a lot of the fourth and fifth grade boys had crushes on her, but she was Ms. Gulzar to them, she would never cross that horrible line.

"Did she do anything else after you took the photo, Grayson?"

He started to shake. It took him several minutes to finish the herculean task of explaining what he had seen her do. It only continued to get worse the more he explained. When he had finally reached the point in the descriptions of the event when the palmful of blood had been placed against the window and he broke down sobbing once more. She felt like she was missing something, she sat patiently and let him exhaust his tears. Nothing about the situation made sense.

Why would she be in that house? Why was she already naked? Why would she single him out? Where did she go after?

She asked him to unlock his phone once more so she could make a copy of the photo. Through the tears, without further thought, he unlocked his phone after it was slid over to him and passed it back to her. It was then when the horrifying detail finally met her eyes. What had happened to her nose?

There, where her nose was supposed to be, was a horrible black space that peered deep inside her nasal passage. How did she not notice this before? She was terrified. How had she been so distracted by the naked-ness of her friend that she didn't notice that gruesome detail. Maybe she had gone into a manic fit, mutilated herself, and then performed that horrible act in front of a child.

"Do you know what happened to her nose?"

Grayson was confused, so he repeated the details of her asphyxiation using the batteries, thinking that's what Ms. Oliveira meant. She let him finish before telling him that wasn't it and if he would mind looking at the photo once more. She zoomed in on the photo so that it cropped out all of the nudity and instead was focused on her face. Seeing it even closer with the beginning blur of digital compression made the face even more monstrous. He looked at it and was more confused. He explained that she didn't look like that when he was watching her.

They sat in an uncomfortable silence while the school counselor continued to do mental gymnastics inside her head to try to force a rational perspective on something entirely outside the boundaries of rationality. She waited until the confusion started to at least partially settle Grayson's emotions before she began asking him any further questions. She wanted to avoid asking the question before but there was nothing else she could think of to solve this issue, so she asked him if he had somehow faked the photo.

He was immediately mad, not in a defensive manner, but a shocked one. As if his role of victim had been immediately swapped to aggressor. In so many words, he told her no and she believed him. She had one last question for him before she would try to figure out the following steps necessary to clean up this mess.

"Did she say anything to you?"

Grayson, tired with tears and face painted with the toll of extreme distress, told her exactly what she had said to him when she was violating herself with that remote "It doesn't hurt me, Grayson". She sat back in her chair with an expression of confused horror. They sat there until she was able to think again.

Eventually she was able to round her thoughts together and she placed the phone flatly on her desk and pinched her fingers together over the screen of Grayson's phone to change the photo from an extreme closeup to the full photo. She took her own cell phone out and pointed it above his, adjusting the focus several times with firm taps of her fingers, and took a picture of the grotesque photo on Grayson's photo. She explained to him that she was going to keep his phone for the time being and that she would need his passcode. He wanted nothing more to do with the photo, the experience, or anything even adjacent to it, so he simply nodded his head and said okay.

Ms. Oliveira walked him to the office, sat him in a chair in front of the secretary's desk, and closed the door behind her as she walked into his office space to speak to the principal privately. She didn't know where to begin, so before she did anything, she needed to see where Ms. Gulzar was, is, and had been all day. She asked him where Neepa was and he said that she had been substituting for Ms. Florakis' class all day and was likely in her classroom now. If she was substituting for Ms. Florakis', that must have meant that she went to lunch with her class, which means that she would have been on her lunch break when this event took place, but surely someone would have heard if she had gone manic and mutilated her face in between then and now, right?

She asked him if she knew where she took her lunch break and he told her that he saw her briefly walk through the office area to collect a paper off the printer before re-exiting the door at around that time. She asked him to pull up the security camera footage for around that time. He wanted to ask questions, but the glaze of tears that threatened to well up in Giacinta's eyes made him reconsider his questioning. He pulled it up on his monitor, the checkerboard pattern of everything the school's cameras could capture.

He pulled up the timestamp that was five minutes before she would have gone on her lunch break. They started in a logical sequence, enlarging the footage they wanted to look at on the principal's second monitor while keeping the rest in their stacked rectangles on the first monitor. They first looked at the one in the cafeteria and could see her there with Ms. Florakis' class, helping them clean their tables and get them ready to transition to recess. She got them in an orderly line and began to exit the cafeteria. This is where they paused and switched their view.

They went to the camera that was pointed towards the opening of the cafeteria door and watched the timestamp closely as within thirty-five seconds, there she walked out with the class in tow. Soon she was naturally walking past the limited angle of that camera, so they waited until her body was reaching the end of the frame and paused it again. They pulled up the following camera in its immediate proximity which recorded the first length of the hall before the hallway split into left and right corridors.

They pulled up the footage and watched as her and the class she was in charge of continued to walk down the halls without anything of note happening. They reached the split at the end of the hall and it was time to switch again. She had turned left and they switched the angle. She only had to walk an additional twenty-five feet or so before she had reached the entrance to Ms. Florakis' classroom. They watched as she walked them all in there and they started to fast forward the video so they could skip to the time that she would lead them outside.

Finally she started to appear out of the classroom and she led them to the doors which led directly outside to the playground and there she held open the doors for the students to run excitedly past her. After the last student had exited the door she turned back and walked straight to Ms. Florakis' class. They followed diligently with the shifting cameras that picked up her trail. She emerged back from the classroom with a paper in hand, proceeded to follow her to her entry into the office, and then subsequently out of it. The principal was wrong, she must have gone in there to make a copy of a document, not pick something up that she had previously printed. Regardless, that detail could not have mattered less knowing what Ms. Oliveira was actually searching for.

The trail of cameras placed her right back into Ms. Florakis' classroom. They fast forwarded the footage to see her re-emerge twenty-six minutes later to meet the children at the door leading in from recess. Nothing.

She asked if he could pull up the footage from the two cameras on the playground for that corresponding time. He did, and he enlarged both so that they each took up half of the screen's real estate and watched. They were two fish-eye lens cameras that were placed at each far end of the playground and captured anything that would occur within the boundaries of their school's play area. There they watched as Grayson started to make his way to a group of children standing by the side of the house.

They watched as he moved towards the window and stood there. It wasn't until after ninety seconds that he began to pull his phone out and shakily take the picture before dropping it on the ground. They were watching in real-time until they decided to fast-forward, this time only at around a twice as fast speed so they wouldn't miss any major changes. Giacinta's hand had now overtaken the mouse from the principal and she was leaning closer and closer to the monitor.

The principal could feel his pulse rise and the sound of his heart in his ears and he had no idea why. He had no reason to feel any reaction at all to this footage, to this event, to anything at all going on in here. Was it because of Ms. Olieveira's intensity? Was it the angle of the camera? What was it that was making him feel sick with dread?

There, six minutes later, Grayson grabbed his phone and ran. It was like a knot became untangled in the principal's chest and he was left with a feeling of airy nothingness after being hanged in such a horrendous suspense. She took note of the time and Neepa Gulzar's inactivity in the classroom during her lunch break had perfectly synced up with the traumatic event Grayson had witnessed outside. Giacinta sat down in a chair close to the principal's desk and began to weep.

He wasn't sure how he was supposed to react, the only emotional reactions he typically shared with his coworkers were laughter, frustration, or indifference, he wasn't the best at even comforting his wife, so this seemed even more of a challenge. He asked her what was wrong, was there something in the footage he didn't see? She cobbled back together her composure enough to tell him that something awful happened to Grayson and she couldn't find an explanation for him and now she couldn't even find an explanation for herself.

She tried compressing the events that had unfolded in a quick enough manner to skip to the part of explaining that she had a photo that didn't make any sense, especially now seeing the evidence. She showed him the photo that she now had on her phone and he was appalled. What had happened to her face? Why was she naked? Was this some sort of a horrible prank?

She explained that in the video, when Grayson pulled out his phone, held it out to the window and had dropped it, was when he took that photo. She pulled out Grayson's phone from her cardigan and unlocked it, showing him the picture directly from the source. She even made a show to note the metadata on the photo that revealed the time it was taken. Now the principal had no idea what he was to do with this information.

Should he call the superintendent? The police? Grayson's parents? What would he tell any of them? What was he going to tell Ms. Gulzar? What was Ms. Gulzar going to say? What could she say? Was it a really elaborate fake? Did a nude photo of Neepa get leaked somehow and Grayson made this horrible edit? But how? The picture was made at the same time he pointed his phone towards the house window. He had no idea. So they sat there.

Time started to pass by and it was becoming an inevitable fact both the principal and counselor that they were going to have to call Grayson's parents, but to tell them what? They weren't sure. It was now less than forty minutes before dismissal and they had no idea what to do. Ms. Oliveira took the time to recount every detail out loud, retelling Grayson's story, what was seen on the unflinchingly objective cameras, and where they were now. The principal listened, secretly hoping that she would be able to come up with a solution before he was forced to try to make one of his own.

Twenty-eight minutes before dismissal. The principal was panicking deeply on the inside, but his naturally neutral face helped cover the impossible level of anxiety he was now stuck with. He told the counselor that she needed to not mention this to any other staff member, least of all Neepa, and to give him Grayson's phone. He had told her that he was sure it was some sort of an elaborate fake made by him or another boy around the school and he was just trying to make a show of it on the playground so he could tell all about it to everyone tomorrow. He was a pubescent boy himself, he reminded Ms. Olieveira, and boys do these stupid things. She explained that she was positive this was not the case, but he eventually was able to calm her enough and tell her that he was going to call Grayson into the office, speak directly to him, get this whole mess sorted out, and then talk to her after dismissal.

*

She was scattered, anxious, and unsure, but she eventually had to convince herself that what he was saying might be correct and that maybe she had let the immediate shock of the situation get to her. Her capacity for understanding had been far exceeded the second that she was shown that mutilated and pornographic caricature of her friend staring back at her. She would be happy to hear anything slightly reassuring, even if she had to swallow an obvious lie at this point, because she no longer found herself to be a reliable source of stability or reason after stumbling this hard.

So she made her way back to her own office. She walked past Grayson without so much as looking in his direction, already pre-emptively deciding that the principal's presentation of the story was correct and Grayson had indeed maliciously altered a photo of Ms. Gulzar and acted the part of a victim so he could get away with showing off the photo and his story to everyone. The more she started to tell herself that, the more she was able to convince herself.

She had felt a slight renewal of her energy but it was amidst the overwhelming exhaustion that her explosive volume of thoughts and crying in front of her boss had brought her. She reached her office, shut the door behind her, locked it, closed the shades on her door's square window, opened the window in her office that looked out to one side of the school's parking lot, and started taking deep inhalations from her disposable vape. It was only a nicotine vape, but Giacinta had made it a rule for herself that she would never take a hit from it inside, even in her own house, but today she had found herself to be a useless, gullible counselor, falling for one of the most sickening jokes she could have ever imagined, and so today would be an exception.

*

Twenty-four minutes before dismissal. The principal sat there, wishing he had the proper jaw strength to grind his teeth into actual dust, and thought intensely what he would have to do. He couldn't buy any more time without keeping Grayson after school and he knew that he certainly wouldn't be able to do that without calling his parents, so he called him into his office, he knew he would have to figure something out then and there.

Grayson shuffled his way in and sat down in the same chair Ms. Oliveira was sitting in before she had left. He started by attempting to relate to him in the most painfully generic way he could, talking softer and slower, attempting to pat Grayson on the shoulder and telling him that it was alright and how he used to do stupid things when he was a kid too. Grayson looked back at him and asked him what he meant by any of this. The principal carried on in his exaggerated softness and slow gesticulations and explained that it was obvious what Grayson had done, that he had photoshopped that picture, stood out by the house window, and made a whole big show of it so that he could have a story and picture to show his friends.

Grayson began feeling overwhelmed, upset, and confused above everything. He tried telling the principal that he didn't make any of it up and even began to yell until the principal was able to cut in telling him that it was okay and that he wasn't in any trouble. He looked at Grayson and told him that what he was going to do was delete the picture from his phone, which he did as he was telling him, even going into the trash bin in the camera roll to empty that out as well so that Grayson wouldn't be able to recover the photo.

He told Grayson that he didn't want this to become a much bigger problem for Grayson, because there were now laws about faking pornographic images of people that could get him in much bigger trouble and that he would have to talk to the police if he wasn't willing to just fess up to his mistake now. He assured him that Ms. Oliveira had a backup photo in case that was the route he was going to have to take. It had started to scare Grayson and he was becoming more visibly nervous and confused.

Grayson said he didn't want the police to have to get involved. So the principal leaned on this pressure point much harder and told him that he should fess up now unless something more serious were to happen. Grayson knew that he was telling the truth, that he didn't fake the photo and he really did see everything, but he was so scared of the idea of having to talk to the police that he could feel his legs beginning to fidget and cross to fight against the reactions his bladder was having to this torrent of stress. So he began to lie by confirming the principal's version of the truth.

The principal started to feel actual guilt in his chest when he saw the boy begin to weep as he had confessed to something the principal knew wasn't even correct and he bent his back over to hug Grayson, comforting him with pats on the back and soft words. He validated all of the emotions Grayson was feeling and told him that it was okay. He wanted to end this horrible series of events of today with something less awful than a sobbing child broken by his intimidations.

So he made a quick attempt to try to fix the situation. He reached into his pocket and pulled out his wallet, of course he had no smaller bills, so this was going to have to do, and he pulled out a one-hundred dollar bill and gave it to Grayson. His voice got lower and gentler as he leaned in and told Grayson that when he was a boy, his father beat him with a belt so badly he bled when he had stumbled upon an old nude magazine in the woods and brought it home. It made him scared to death to think about women until he was nearly seventeen years old and he didn't want Grayson to feel that way. So he told him to go to the store, buy himself a gift card for one of his game systems or whatever and don't tell anybody where he had gotten the money and especially don't tell them about anything that had transpired today at school.

The strange shock of being handed such a large amount of money was enough to catch Grayson's bubbling emotions to temporarily cease and he thanked the principal. The principal sent him off with one last set of instructions: go to the restroom, splash some cold water on his face and get his backpack because it was just about time to leave. Four minutes to dismissal and the principal was able to bribe the silence of a child that could have cost him and at least two other staff members jobs.

He leaned back in his chair and felt a shameful bout of pride rise to the surface of his conscious emotions, neutralizing his deserved anxiety.

*

Ms. Oliveira had gone through at least fifteen additional hits from her pocket-sized vape before she had realized that it was almost dismissal time and that she should set herself back up more professionally. She didn't realize how powerful the mango scent was in the room until she had put her vape back into her purse and decided to open the window wider and crank the miniature plastic fan she had on her desk to full blast towards the open window to try to air out the scent as quickly as she could. She sprayed liberal spritzes of Febreze into no particular directions to help intermingle the scents until none of them were any longer identifiable on a singular level.

She got up, unlocked her door, opened the shades on her door's square window and sat patiently in her seat behind her desk. She used this time to tidy up her desk, stacking papers she needed to file away, and generally fidget with a variety of items within her arms reach to help reacquaint herself comfortably in her own space. Once she had reached a level of doneness that she felt was adequate, she sat back further into her chair and did her best to use this time to relax instead of holding her breath and biting her bottom lip until it bled like her nervous body wanted to do.

Not too many more minutes had to pass before the principal had casually walked his way towards her office and opened the door. He popped in with only about three quarters of his body, closing the door on the remaining quarter of his body that was outside of her office, and told her that the situation was all settled. Grayson had admitted to him that the photo was fake and it was an elaborate ruse he was trying to pull on students and staff alike. He made up a lie about Grayson confiding in him that he was going through some rough things at home and his parents haven't been as present lately. It was this lie that the principal was able to fully sell his pitch to her.

She visibly slumped her shoulders downward and leaned further back into her chair and muttered something about how bad she felt for the kid and how that explained a lot. She thanked him for being able to sort out this mess and apologized if she had made it worse. He reassured her and said he wouldn't have known what to do either if it came to his desk first, so he understood. They briefly exchanged pleasant goodbyes and he closed her door leaving her to herself.

When the door had shut, she had placed her elbows on the desk firmly and fell her face into her open hands and just breathed. She breathed deeply and almost began to chuckle, feeling foolish about the whole thing. She wanted to prove to herself even further how stupid she had been by looking at the photo once more to see how obviously fake it must have been.

So she opened up her phone, went to her photos library, and tapped on the dreaded photo, bringing it to full screen. She had double tapped to zoom in on Neepa's face so she could look closer at the apparently photoshopped mutilation and the focus was instead pulled to the television right above Neepa's head. It was there that she was almost certain she could see something on the television. It was a slightly brownish blur, but that was all she could tell it was. She turned the brightness up on her phone, that didn't help, she zoomed in further, that also didn't help. Now it was starting to nag at her.

She had a compact smart printer of her own that didn't belong to the school in her room that she used for color photo prints, mostly to print out photos she could decorate her corkboard with, and decided to print out the photo from her phone. She felt kind of wrong doing it, it was a bit odd printing out a picture like this of someone you know, but she reasoned with herself that she would shred it afterwards. Still the feeling of wrongness was strongly present with her, so she went over to lock her door and close the shades on her door's window, then went the extra step to close her regular window and close the shades on though as well. The photo printed on a basic eight and a half by eleven sheet of plain printer paper that she left loaded in case she needed to print simple documents and she pulled it out and looked at it closely.

It was no brown smudge any longer. There in the reflection of the television, peeking above Neepa's scalp, was the bulbous head of a frog.

CHAPTER TWENTY
SEEKING WHOM HE MAY

The last day of the first week of school, there arrived Brendan. Brendan, a timid, nervous child is he. The bags under his eyes are unnaturally prominent and shaded a deep purple. Already a paler shade of white naturally, his skin is practically made luminescent from his sleep deprivation. The restless nights have begun eating away at his appearance.

*

Brendan's uncle, Dustin, wasn't allowed at his house anymore. Dustin had stayed at the house for two weeks, but Brendan's mom and dad told him that he wasn't welcome back anymore until he was sober, or at the very least, trying to stay sober. A part of Dustin understood. A part of him that was buried deeply underneath a selfishness drawn out by claws of the gnawing evil. It was with this driving force that he did something that truly scared Brendan.

It was three days after Dustin had been asked to leave when he decided to visit the household with a violence. He arrived at nearly two in the morning, knocking at the door. Brendan's dad, Mitchell, went down to see who could be at the door and when he saw it was his brother, he cracked open the door just enough to be able to talk to him. A simple courtesy that he wasn't aware would turn into a mistake.

There was another man behind Dustin, one that Mitchell had never seen before, and it was him that kicked the door while Mitchell's face still rested two inches off of the interior side. It collided with the cartilage of his nose which caused his nose to scatter its shape to connect with his left cheek. His sharp yelp of pain was heard throughout the whole house and it roused the attention of his wife and his son. Brendan's mother went to the top of the stairs to look down at the commotion, letting adrenaline take over for emotions and listened to her husband's plea for her to get Brendan and call the police.

She turned quickly to open Brendan's door, grab the anxious boy waiting by the door listening to the awful sounds of his father's attack, bring them both into the main bedroom where she locked the door, and hid Brendan deeply inside the walk-in closet. During the brief interim where Brendan was passing between bedrooms, he looked down to watch his father, face painted with broad strokes of fresh blood, get bashed in the ribs by a discolored two by four plank of wood.

Brendan listened to horrible sounds for what seemed like hours but was less than twelve minutes in all. He heard his mother's hysterical cries begging the operator, screaming that 'they were killing her husband', his dad's pained yelps, the sound of blunt objects striking clothed skin, and eventually sirens. Sounds only made worse by the hyperactive imagination of a child.

Dustin and his accomplice had found themselves so involved in the brutality that they had foregone their intended robbery. The police showed up and the screaming got louder, Brendan heard words his parents carefully managed to have him avoid until this moment. After she was sure that the police had begun the arrest, she rushed through the door and ran to her husband, horribly battered and breathing in stuttering wheezes.

Brendan couldn't stand the torture of only being able to hear horrific noises, unsure what was going on besides what he could imagine in his head. He stepped out of the room slowly and crept to the top of the stairs where he looked down, watching his mother cradle her father's head like the body of a newborn child. He had never seen anyone covered in blood like he had seen his father, he thought he must be dying.

Dustin was splattered in drops of the gore he helped force from Mitchell's defenseless being. He was placed to his knees and handcuffs were loudly clasped together against his thin wrists. It was a tragic sight, watching the gears click together inside of Dustin's head, realizing what he had done. He began to cry and scream his brother's name, saying he's sorry with a painful and genuine sorrow. At that moment his innocence was equal to that of a child. The evil which had clouded Dustin's judgment was now fed to a gluttonous portion and it was time for Dustin to face what he had done.

This was the big brother who had checked under his bed at night when mom and dad told him he was too old to believe in monsters. The older brother who snuck him out and drove him to the haunted hayrides when mom forbade him because of his bad grades. The brother who hugged him tightly after his first break-up when he was fifteen years old. He had committed an atrocious act against his hero of youth and he wept for his mistake.

The fallout of the situation had landed Brendan's dad in the hospital with three broken ribs and a lacerated kidney. The surgery required him to stay for several nights in recovery at the hospital before he could go home. Several nights where Brendan had to stay at his Auntie's house, insecure and scared that someone was going to break in and hurt someone else he loves, while his mom stayed at the hospital. Even when his dad got home, he still didn't feel safe, and if anything, he felt worse.

Dad looked broken. Mom had to help him do everything, shower, change, and sometimes he couldn't even leave bed. The central features of his face had become abstractions, loose shapes filled with different hues of violet, blue, and yellow. What if someone came in again? Dad couldn't fight them and he looked like he might die if someone hit him. Mom would have to hide him and Dad and call the police, so Brendan decided it was his job to watch now. In case someone tried to come in, Brendan could run right to Mom and tell her. He would do this every night since, silently trying to the best of his abilities, to protect his house.

*

A small and malnourished looking ghost had entered Mrs. Itou's first grade classroom. It was an immediate concern for Mrs. Itou. She took him aside at the first available chance she had for the day and asked him some general questions, asking if he had been getting enough sleep, etc. and he answered in vague words, unsure he would be able to elaborate everything that was on his mind even if he wanted to. She wanted to know more of course, but knew because of the hyper-bureaucratic nature of the eggshell laws which teachers had to walk upon, she knew she had to ask things in a non-specific and less than efficient manner. She figured it best that she should ask the principal and counselor first if they had any information before she contacted home. They had nothing to add besides that they agreed his appearance was gaunt.

It was her class' recess time and she decided to call Brendan's mother. The information about Brendan had been transferred over from last year to her and she just had to hope that the phone number for his mother was still current. It was.

Mrs. Descamps answered and quickly told Mrs. Itou that she could call her Shelby. Shelby it was. She asked Shelby if everything was okay at home with Brendan and talked about his unusually tired demeanor and appearance. The pause of silence which was broken by the sound of Shelby's sniffling and stifled whines already told Mrs. Itou more than she could put into words.

Shelby had begun to fall apart over this simple question. Through the stress of everything that she had been dealing with, the time she had to take off from work and her own pursuits solely to focus on her husband, every remaining energy she had left had to go into his recovery these past few weeks. Had she forgotten all about Brendan's needs these past weeks?

She had felt like a failure as a mother. Everyone who had bothered to ask her anything at all during this horrible time had only been about her husband. She knew she already had to put aside her own wants and needs, but she didn't mean to sacrifice Brendan's as well. This simple question was enough to reveal her own perceived shortcomings and her heart was ready to break.

She explained everything she could find a way to summarize to Mrs. Itou over the phone in between her poorly contained cries and the attempted comforts of her son's teachers. It had evidently been a horrible time for everyone in the household and Mrs. Itou wasn't quite sure how to immediately process this story besides to give her extreme condolences. She let Mrs. Descamps get the pent up emotions out of her system before they would continue a conversation.

They were able to focus the conversation back to Brendan's immediate needs. Mrs. Itou wanted to figure out a plan where she would be able to help Mrs. Descamps, as she could tell Brendan's mother was overwhelmed and bore a burden heavier than one person should have to hold on their own. Mrs. Itou brought up that there was a new building on the school playground. Shelby was aware of it because of the paper the school sent out which she very briefly skimmed over. Mrs. Itou pointed out that the new building did have two bedrooms with full bedding.

She offered, for at least the beginning few weeks of school until things had become a little more settled at home, that with Shelby's permission of course, she could send the para in her classroom, Ms. Bellerose, to bring Brendan to the building to sleep during their afternoon meeting and activity time. Mrs. Itou stated that obviously she wouldn't want Brendan to miss the social time, but she noted that this time slot would be best so that it did not detract from his academic or recess time.

While the entire situation was odd, having such a building at a school, Mrs. Descamps was desperate and already felt embarrassed by the situation and said that she would appreciate that. So it was decided that beginning when the children returned from recess, that this would be the plan. Shelby felt grateful and horrible all at once. Mrs. Itou offered her parting condolences once more and offered the advice that maybe she could try giving Brendan some melatonin gummies to help regulate his sleep. Shelby thanked Brendan's teacher once more for her attempts at comfort and quick thoughts to help find an immediate relief for Brendan.

*

Recess had ended and the children began to shuffle back into the classroom. As soon as a majority of her class had made it past the door, she quickly took Ms. Bellerose off to the side to speak with her. She explained only that Brendan had been having a very rough time at home and it had been affecting his sleep. Without a second thought, Ms. Bellerose instantly added that she had noticed how much disrepair the poor kid had seemed to be in. Mrs. Itou continued that she had called home while they were out at recess and explained that for the first couple of weeks, during afternoon meeting and activity time, she wanted her to bring Brendan to the house on the playground and allow him to sleep in one of the bedrooms.

She knew it was an odd request, but she wouldn't have asked if it wasn't such an extreme circumstance. Ms. Bellerose didn't mind, and she added that at least they could find some use for the house for the time being. Mrs. Itou called over Brendan so that she could explain to him what the arrangement would be for the next couple of weeks.

To make the situation sound more comforting to the already nervous child, she asked him if he had any stuffies that he would like to bring with him during this time. This certainly made Brendan excited as he nodded his head with excitement and ran to his backpack. There, from his backpack, Brendan pulled a stuffed sheep that was so large, that the teachers could not help but chuckle in awe. Somehow that excited child had managed to fit a nearly two foot tall plush into a backpack that couldn't be longer than eighteen inches long.

*

This had been the second year that Ms. Bellerose had been working with Mrs. Itou and she knew that the afternoon meeting and activity time would last at least forty-five minutes and usually up to an hour since it was the beginning of the year, so she brought a book with her to help pass the time. They entered through the front door, saw the rubber mats and Ms. Bellerose led the direction to take off their shoes, so they did, and then they entered through the door that brought them into the house. Ms. Bellerose wasn't quite sure where the bedroom or bedrooms were in the household so she brought Brendan with her as she peeked into all of the rooms downstairs.

She saw a bathroom, laundry room, living room, kitchen, and even peeped inside the little spandrel underneath the stairs, but didn't see any bedroom. So with that assessment, she decided to bring Brendan upstairs with her so that they could look up there. They looked in one door and found another bathroom, they could see the tub and Ms. Bellerose instantly was reminded of the horrible story of Paisley in fourth grade and closed the door a little quicker than the others. They looked in another room and saw it was a rather empty looking bedroom and before deciding on that for a sleeping quarters for Brendan, she thought that they might as well look through the last door. So they looked and there it was, a master bedroom with a much larger bed with what looked like far more comforting bedding as well.

With the perfect fascination of a child, Brendan was amazed and couldn't help but quietly mouth exclamations of wonder. It was obvious at this moment that this would be the sleeping quarters for the child. It was a beautiful scene watching the excited child climb into a bed several times larger than himself with a stuffed animal nearly as tall as him and settle in under the covers. As soon as he felt comfortable, he began to feel nervous and look around. He explained that he needed to stay awake to watch out in case someone broke in, but Ms. Bellerose was there and she knew all of the right words of assurance to calm him.

She promised that in addition to the school's natural safety that she would be staying wide awake and sitting near the bed keeping an extra good watch for him while he slept. This made Brendan smile and feel more at ease, both the child's body and mind were desperate to accept any break that it could. She stood by the bedside for what couldn't have been more than five minutes before Brendan had fallen into a visually clear, sound sleep. It made her smile. She stepped a couple of feet towards the end of the bed, sat criss-cross on the floor, and began to read her book.

It was then that the security of sleep had begun to turn on Brendan, forcing him to witness what the house desired to show him. And so, the sleepless boy had a dream. A horrid dream. Like a spectator to a vision or a sport, he was helpless to change the outcome of what he was to watch.

*

Brendan didn't know what the place he was in would be called, or at least not really, he certainly wouldn't have been able to put the correct word to it. It was an open area, an oval shape with what looked like infinite rows of seats carved out of stones covered in dust. No one sat in them and from the perspective which he was looking, it seemed as though everything began to stretch forth farther than his eyes were now able to see.

The ground which he stood upon was sand and it felt uncomfortable to the covered touch of his shoes. Somehow he had the horrible feeling that if he were to touch the sand with any of his bare skin it would cause him to dehydrate beyond a point of recovery. He felt like he was standing, but the overwhelming size of his surroundings made him feel like he was sitting down, sunk deeply into the sand, an insignificant size contrasted against unfathomable largeness.

The sky showed its presence unsubtly through the wide opening tracing the top seats of the strange location. It shone an unnatural color of green, almost as if it was mocking the ground which Brendan stood upon, showing it the color of grassy fields which should be but are not. Despite the intense shade of the sky, it never managed to change the overbearingly pale yellow palette that swallowed the area whole. He turned his head from east to west and that was when the lions began to appear.

Like spiders descending with confidence from their hidden corners, the lions began to creep across the rows of seats. They continued to move with a casualness clearly not disturbed by the presence of Brendan. It was as if he was simply allowed to exist in their strangely peaceful habitation. His heart was pounding simply by being near the presence of these creatures. It felt like it should have been at least several minutes that passed before one of them began to approach Brendan and lie down at his feet and motion about like a kitten wishing to receive the affectionate touch of a human's hand, spine visibly curving the lion's torso before laying down with his stomach skyward.

He could feel his entire body quaking as he began to reach forward to touch the seemingly gentle giant. He did and with the palm of his hand he placed his hand upon the lion's stomach and was able to feel the silk, fine feeling of the lion's soft fur that combed through the spaces between his fingers. The purrs of satisfaction that rumbled within the animal's body were fantastically large, as if they were reverberating through a hall of impossible size and depth.

He continued to run his hands along the lion when he looked up and saw a multitude of the others begin to gather around a young tree which had grown in the midst of the sand. It was there where the lions began to stretch forth their paws and prop their bodies in a bipedal position against the trunk so they could extend their necks upward to eat the figs which blossomed forth. The anxiety that once strangled his nerves began to loose forth from his body and Brendan felt as it was, peace. Peace through his being.

The moment lasted long, but was changed with the violence of what arrived. It started on a far eastern row of the seats carved from stone and stepped across the descension of seats with a terrifying ease and dominance. Its presence was unmistakable and gargantuan. A massive grey lion, the color of darkened ash. Its height, an astonishing twenty-five cubits, its length a horrifying sixty-seven cubits. Its paws reached across the length of aisles and began to curl its posture downwards into a pounce-ready positioning, head nearly leveling itself with its extending claws.

It had pounced and with its open mouth, closed its teeth upon the nearest lion, decimating the smaller lion's physical structure, collapsing its bone within itself, a grotesque and almost instantaneous death for the innocent creature. It threw the carcass from its jaws and allowed its body to fall where it may, and stomped towards the fig tree where it would crush and devour the lions which had not yet scattered themselves across the area in attempted escapes and then continued in pursuit after the remaining lions.

Brendan was frozen in place by the outstanding amount of fear which consumed his body so entirely that his muscles felt locked together. The lion underneath him that had helped bring Brendan to a comfort had flipped itself back into a standing position upon all fours before running in desperation. It was this lion that was left last alive until the horrible grey beast had approached the panicking creature of gentle nature and bit directly into the neck of the lion, gruesomely severing its head and stomping its paw down forcefully against its body, loudly breaking the bones in the back half of the dead lion.

The behemoth's face and mane which shared its grey tone solidly had now been corrupted by terrible and huge splashes of dark red, more shaded by viscera than the spilled blood. Its massive eyes had directed towards Brendan, the timid boy scared to a temporary paralysis. It took only a small step before the abomination had centered itself directly in front of Brendan, the closer presence of this evil had caused Brendan's body to involuntarily fall itself against the ground, allowing the unclean beast to tower over him even further. It was then that it raised its paw and descended its claws deep into Brendan's body.

It was during this time in Brendan's dream that Ms. Bellerose stood by his bedside, stabbing Brendan's chest repetitively, almost mechanically, with a knife, until the plunge of the knife no longer met solid resistance.

CHAPTER TWENTY-ONE
THE BLOOD WHICH SPRAYED A ROSE

Her hands had practically slipped inside the growing wound in Brendan's chest. The knife had been stabbed so deeply through the sleeping child that it had penetrated the mattress below him. The first waves of blood which crashed against her hands during the desecration had already begun to scab in dryness. It dried over her skin until it traced the minute wrinkles of her knuckles, across the exposed creases of her palm, and dried under the brass bands of the decorative rings she wore.

The tragedy of what her hands had committed would not be realized until she pulled back the knife a final time, sliding it back out of the wool inside the mattress. It was like her hand had been gripped so firmly around the knife, that the space between her fingers and palm could no longer imagine a reality where it was not occupied by the weapon. An unimaginable nightmare had occurred through the violence committed by her hands.

What had she done? Why had she done it? Was Brendan still breathing? What is she supposed to do next? Should she run? Report herself? Why did her body feel so cold? Why does the handle of the knife feel so damp and warm?

She let the knife slip from her hands and let it fall to the ground beside her feet. Her body was stuck between a state of shock paralysis and an overwhelming faintness that threatened to make her fall to her knees. Her body fought against itself and caused her knees to bend and slowly descend her height towards the ground until she found herself eye level with Brendan's gruesomely destroyed body.

It was as though the complex operations of logic had been switched off in her brain in an instant and she was now reduced to the most simple thoughts. She reached towards his wrist and checked for a pulse, not knowing what else to do. There was none to be found. She had no idea how long she had been out there. What time was it? She pulled her phone from her pocket and the gore from her hand had begun to smear the touchscreen as she tapped the front of it, trying to wake it from its digital slumber. It was forty minutes before dismissal, she had been out there for nearly an hour and ten minutes.

She had been out here, at the most, an additional twenty five minutes or, at the least, ten minutes longer than she was asked to be out here. She assumed that someone must come out here soon to check in or see where they were. She felt resigned to a fate that was entirely unpredictable and not known to her, and her body allowed her to slink down to the ground until she was sitting upon the back of her calves. Everything she would touch would now turn red, so she placed her hands to swing on her side, keeping them slightly elevated above the floor.

*

The afternoon meeting and activity time had now been over for the past fifteen minutes or so (after Mrs. Itou admittedly let the fun go on for a little longer than she usually allowed) and she had almost forgotten about Brendan and Mrs. Bellerose. She knew Brendan was horribly tired looking, exhausted and trodden far more than any child that young should ever be, so she assumed that Ms. Bellerose must have been letting him sleep a little longer. Still, she did want to make sure that he at least got to settle into the routine of the end of day for her classroom.

Obviously she knew she couldn't just leave the kids in here by themselves and go out and check on them, so she would have to ask someone else. She knew that Ms. Florakis was out and that Ms. Gulzar, her usual first choice, was substituting, so she couldn't ask her. She was trying to think of who else might be available, but with a class full of first graders who were suddenly sensing the crumbling structure of the classroom and becoming more antsy and loud, it was becoming an increasingly difficult task. Her mind was drawing a blank until it occurred to her that she could just call the other first grade teacher, Mrs. Zahrani, to see if her para, Ms. Hanaki, was available.

She quickly dialed Mrs. Zahrani's classroom from the hardwired yellowing phone that was positioned flatly against the wall. She turned her body so that her back was positioned towards the wall so that she could try to keep track of her students, who were now slowly moving their busy bodies towards the carpet area instead of remaining in their seats. As it turned out, and thankfully so, Mrs. Zahrani told her that Ms. Hanaki was available and she would send her right to the classroom. In the meanwhile, Mrs. Itou could bring her class back to order.

Ms. Hanaki walked through the door with a polite quietness, as to not intentionally disrupt whatever lesson they may be in the midst of, and took a couple of steps to the left before settling in a stance to the side of the door. There was no lesson that had begun and they were all in the end stage of finally being settled back into their seats by Mrs. Itou and now were fighting their attention spans to not jump in excitement at the sight of another teacher in the room. Mrs. Itou was quick to acknowledge Ms. Hanaki's presence and walked over and whisper-talked with her, explaining the arrangement of Brendan and Mrs. Bellerose and that they had been expected back around fifteen minutes ago but had yet to arrive, and was hoping that Ms. Hanaki could go check on them in the house on the playground, to see what might be taking them so long and if she could ask them to please return soon. Ms. Hanaki understood, so she did a small, swift wave goodbye to the children of the classroom, and exited out the door.

*

Like most of the staff there, the story of what had occurred to Ms. Florakis and one of her students had made its way to her, and with that knowledge, certainly made her at least slightly apprehensive to actually enter the house. However, actually going in would help her disperse those childish fears, she thought, and so she straightened her posture in a subtle way and decided to walk forward with her feigned confidence to the doors that exited out to the playground. Out the doors she went, unaware of what she was to encounter.

She walked up to the house, opened its first door, gazed down to her left and saw two pairs of shoes of rather obvious different sizes contrasted against one another on top of a rubber mat. She found it proper to follow suit and removed her shoes, placing them to the right side of the larger pair of shoes, a pair of simple flats. She walked through the next door and closed it behind her. She had no idea exactly what the layout of the house or where they would be located, but for whatever reason, some deep instinct within her was restricting her natural idea to begin calling their names out to find them.

She started to walk through the bottom floor, going from room to room with an added caution she felt she needed to add. While it was more or less quick previews of each room she really was experiencing, she couldn't help but be impressed by how well put together it all was. The only door and room she didn't bother to explore was the spandrel underneath the stairs citing to nobody but herself that it would be illogical for either of them to be there, but if the thought was to be searched enough within herself, she knew it was because even the idea of that room unsettled her. With nothing to be found in the spaces she was willing to explore, she quietly moved her way up the stairs.

Step by step she unconsciously monitored her volume and made her way to the very top. She started out by searching towards the left. She opened the door on the far left and found that it was a bedroom of sorts, sparse to be sure, yes, but a bedroom nonetheless, so why weren't they in there? She closed the door and moved onto the next, the door in the center. It was a second bathroom and she assured herself that they couldn't possibly have been hiding anywhere in there, so she shut that door and decided it was time to explore the last room yet to be seen.

She approached the final room, this one on the right side of the landing, and she felt a horrible shift within her that was causing her to pause before finally placing her hand upon the door. She stood there and stared for an eternity in thirty seconds. She told herself that now she was the one that was causing even further delay for Mrs. Itou and she needed to just do this, what should be, a simple task. So she took no longer and opened the door to something that would be described dozens of times by her to various authorities.

The sight was similar to that of a blood-spattered hyena laying beside the ravaged carcass of a baby gazelle. Mrs. Bellerose was on her knees staring forward towards nothing in particular, with blood soaking her forearms and small pools of blood forming underneath her gently lifted hands. Though Ms. Hanaki was not a tall woman, she was able to see the devastation of wounds which ripped apart Brendan's chest. Neither Brendan nor Mrs. Bellerose were moving.

Ms. Hanaki began to shake and her knees began to wobble before they fully buckled and she collapsed to the floor and immediately began her best to suck in any air that she could. It was like the meat of her throat had snapped inwardly on all sides and destroyed the opportunity for air to reach her lungs. She positioned herself with her hands on the ground, her face looking down, eyes wide and mouth wider, knees and calves flat to the floor. She began to cough with the success of the air reaching her lungs. Coughing violently, over and over until they eventually turned to horrible wretches of dry heaving.

Tears began to start coming out in untimed spurts, pouring and bursting forth from her eyes and off her face. It was the combination of the overwhelming emotions she felt seeing the scene and also the mounting pressure from her coughing and dry heaving that pressed against the back of her eyes. Both of these factors worked in equal part to cover the areas of her face where the tears stayed strongly attached against the resistance of gravity, while the others fell and created their own individual, exploded puddles.

Her face was deepening in shades of red, occasionally retracting their hues from her face to leave a paler mask washed across the length of skin that stretched across the muscle and bones of her skull. She felt increasingly weaker until it felt like she was going to faint. She pushed her hands slightly against the ground to lift her torso up until she was sitting straight in an attempt to fight her body's attempt to pass out in preservation. She couldn't manage to sit straight any longer and her torso's weight carried her backwards until she rested upon her elbows, bending her behind where her knees lay on the ground. The heaving and hyperventilating were over, and she was now choking back hoarse screams.

She wanted to yell at the monster her coworker had become, yell to shame her or even just simply ask why, but the executive functioning for speech necessary to form words had been all but degraded to infancy. She could only cry, choke on her spring of sobs, and crawl backwards on her elbows until she had fully exited her body out of the doorway. Everything had become horribly incoherent. She reached into her pocket and shakily pulled her phone, rapidly pressing the side button over and over until she could see that it was calling emergency services.

Her shaking hands placed the phone down on the floor as gently as she could muster. She forced her body to stand upwards, stumbled towards the open door, grabbed its handle and pulled it backwards, using her body weight falling backwards onto her lower back to close the door. She laid the rest of her body down flatly on her back. She continued to sob as the operator began to ask for confirmation of the caller's presence. Ms. Hanaki had managed to struggle out the words 'house' 'at' and 'school'. Her face began to feel as though every nerve and muscle beneath her skin was going to burst and she fainted.

*

The operator on the other side of the phone call knew when she heard the distant, violent sobbing, that it was going to be a credible emergency for her to focus all of her attention on and so she did. She immediately began to trace the origins of the phone call and heard those half strangled words of the distressed woman on the other side. She saw that the phone call was coming from the elementary school. Even more than that, when she saw where the phone call was coming from, the words she had heard began to make sense. It was that strange building that looked like a house the new school had gotten. She remembered seeing someone post about it in a community page on Facebook.

She knew exactly where the caller was from and what terrified this operator more than anything was that it was coming from an elementary school, but not from a main line, instead from a cell phone of what must have been an employee. She assumed the worst and dispatched officers to the scene. Repeated attempts were made to communicate with the woman on the other side of the line, but when she now only heard silence, she began to assume the worst once more, with a growing pit in her stomach.

*

Two cars and three officers total showed up to the scene, seventeen minutes after the dispatch. It had appeared as though they were more focused on the wrangling of weapons, weapons they wished with an open secret to use one day, instead of an immediate dispersion to the school. A frustratingly stupid choice that would come down hard on them by both the press and, more personally affecting, by their police chief who would personally fight with the union over, and look for further reasons to have them fired.

Two of them, both holding a short-barreled AR-15, had decided to go through the front door and dramatically ask the principal questions with projected heroics only to be met with panic and confusion. They explained that there had been a call and were met with nothing but heightened concern and nothing additional the principal was capable of telling them. This caused the officers' facades of bravery to begin to falter. So the less confident one was left to stay in the office while the other officer made his way to meet the other officer that was supposed to have been at least in the playground by now. So he did, marching through the halls with his rifle, ingraining the image into the curious children who were able to see him through the windows of their classrooms.

The officer that was tasked with reaching the house had pulled the car around, sirens fully blasting, onto the blacktop of the playground, closely beneath the right side of the house. It was when he was trying to swing open the door of his cruiser, that a large and terrifying blur was seen, followed by the startling and inconsistent percussive sound of his side mirror being ripped downwards and off his vehicle. The fear ran through him and caused him to jerk his body, shoving the rifle he was once holding with undeserved pride, straight into his cup holder.

The urgency to investigate what had just happened took precedence over his need to display his rifle, and he placed the weapon on the passenger seat of his car. Shaking with fear, real fear, he opened his door and before he could step out, realized what was beside the space where he would have placed his feet. It was a horribly disfigured body, undoubtedly marred beyond simple description by the impact of hitting the side mirror of his cruiser.

He knew in a glance that what appeared to be an adult female, was dead. Knowing he should at least avoid tampering with the horrible corpse any more than gravity had, he slid over to his passenger side, hovering his body cautiously above the rifle on the seat, and exited out the door with the mirror still intact. He exited the vehicle, turned the siren off, but allowed the blue lights to pulse their rhythm against every surface that would allow its glow. He circled around so that he could look at the body, and had it not been his job to stay on the scene, he would have run.

Like a giraffe as envisioned by a sculptor of perverse taste, her neck was extended several notches further than natural, and curved in a slim, backwards c-shape where her head dangled loosely, still lightly bobbing from the impact. Teeth decorated the ground surrounding her, sprinkled around by the impact, like a paper gun full of confetti, it must have shot out from her mouth in a pattern only determined by its velocity. Her hands and arms were covered in what looked like blood that was already dried, now intertwining with the copious amounts of her own flowing forth from the orifices of the face he had yet to gaze upon as well as the skin of her neck pierced by the sharpness of misplaced bone.

Gums were ripped apart by the upper row of teeth, splitting the red flesh into jagged lines which caused them to hang off in strips, dripping chunks of small flesh and failing clots of blood. The upper lip was dragged up her face until the frenulum was clearly ripped and the intersecting curve of her lip which gave definition had been torn in two, falling flatly against her face in separate directions. Her nose was an unfolded blanket of exposed flesh and cartilage driven skywards into softer flesh above the nasal cavity. Had all the carnage been cleaned off it would have appeared that she had no nose at all between her eyes.

All he could do was stare. So he did. Staring and waiting for something to shock his system into movement once more.

The other officer burst through the back doors that opened to the playground and saw the other officer staring at something towards the ground on the opposite side of the cruiser. He stopped himself in his tracks until his eyes were eventually met by his fellow officer, face pale, eyes wide and ready to resign to a pool of tears welling up behind his bottom eyelid. He pressed his rifle firmly, harder against his body, perhaps in an attempt to simply feel something at all that grounded his physical self into reality and began to march forward, back hunched towards the direction in which he walked. He was quickly approaching the house.

It was the sound of the house's first door being opened which finally alerted the foggy senses of the officer standing besides the mangled jumper which laid beside his feet. He was able to press down on the handheld transceiver and call in the dead body. It was after the reply from dispatch followed by the digital chirp that he had finally found himself able to move more freely. He turned his body around to see children staring from several different windows.

The ones on the ground floor probably weren't able to see much, but there was no doubt in him that the children on the upper floor were able to at least peek at the atrocity which was splayed forth on the blacktop. The idea of these children having to see something that he himself could hardly comprehend made his stomach sink and he used his radio to tell an officer, anybody, someone, to close the blinds and get the children away from the windows. The message made it to the officer in the principal's office who quickly told the principal to make an announcement to the school. Without further thought, the principal declared a shelter in place order for the school which naturally caused the staff to lock each classroom and close all windows.

The other officer had made their way inside the interior door of the house, actually bringing him inside the house. He called out for any sort of tangible responses after quickly surveying the kitchen and living room. There was no response, so he continued venturing inside each door downstairs, including the spandrel. Nothing. He moved upstairs and saw a young woman passed out on her back at the top of the landing. He reached his hand forward to confirm a pulse and quickly called for medical personnel.

He continued and explored the rooms starting on the right. Nothing in the small and empty guest room, nothing in the bathroom. He gently moved the unconscious body of the young woman to a sitting upright position against the door to the spare bedroom and continued forward.

The fear which had filled Ms. Hanaki as she reached towards the main bedroom door now began to fill the officer with the shaking hand reaching for the door, other hand becoming increasingly greased with sweat as he clutched his rifle even tighter against his chest.

The scene which he had to see after opening the door was devastation. His eyes had seen the horrors of a child stabbed to shredded flesh. If his heart hadn't been in his throat, perhaps his body would have found a way to make him vomit. But what use would have it done? He could feel a looseness in fluid in his nostrils which made him wipe the bottoms of his nose, thinking it to be a nosebleed, but getting no visual confirmation on the side of his hand. He called dispatch, unknowingly reporting the second dead body found at the school.

He stepped closer to the bedside so that he could at least take a closer look at the destroyed child and saw that the window was open. Another step had been taken forward and he saw the knife on the ground. It was no major surprise to him to see that it was a knife that had caused this level of violent carnage. He stepped forward to look out the window and it was there that he could see his fellow officer staring in a horrible awe at the body of the individual who must have jumped through this window.

*

The view for the window was now correct. It was the inside of the oven, the internal design which was now flipped sideways, that was the tell-tale sign of imperfection. Tucked away and hidden by the average walk-through. The apport was becoming stronger in appearance as the days passed, no longer leaving such obvious imperfections. It had been fed by its instigated evils.

Oh how greedily it was now fed.

Chapter Twenty-Two
The Indifference Necessary to Move On

There was of course, an outcry, a shared horror, and an overwhelming grief that both joined and ripped apart the community. The following ten scheduled school days were canceled in acknowledgment of the tragedy. Mrs. Bellerose's husband and parents had moved out of state to avoid the further death threats after Mr. Bellerose had received the decapitated head of his pet cat smashed into his driver's side window one morning. His doctor increased his medication for depression and he doubled it himself.

There were vigils for the boy, town meetings for the school, and a grotesque surplus of feed for the state's local news station. The school board meetings held in the elementary school's gymnasium now reached maximum capacity, a feat never once reached except when a presidential hopeful may have stopped into town. Some demanded that the house be torn down so that the memory could no longer haunt the residents any longer.

The 'rationalists' of the town argued that an attachment of sentimentality would only feed into a superstitious reasoning that would cause further instability among the town. Eventually the self-declared rational members of town managed to win the argument only because the other town members could cite nothing more than their personal anxieties and fears, and did not want to appear foolish in front of the crowd. However, it was agreed upon by all that the house should at least be closed down for an undetermined amount of time, which turned out to be over three months, so that they could install security bars outside of each window and thoroughly investigate any possible gas leaks, carbon monoxide poisoning, remnants of lead paint, absolutely anything at all that could have caused this irrational act to have happened. Nothing was to be found, of course.

Everyone longed for rational answers, but of course there were none to be had. They could not even punish the declared murderer for she had killed herself. They were left with anger and frustration. Twice were individuals arrested for attempted arson. The first time, a group was found passed out from the fumes of gasoline liberally poured on the living room floor. Their clothes had been soaked in gasoline and their skin had begun to peel and blister. They were discovered the morning following their attempt by the school custodian tasked with adding the voted upon 'improvements' to the house. It was over a week before students were allowed to go to the playground after that incident as the house had to be cleaned several times and aired out.

The second attempt at burning the abomination had been a more immediately noticeable issue. It was a lone individual who came with nothing more than a can of kerosene and an anonymous stainless-steel zippo knock-off he was able to purchase from the local gas station. He had broken past the cheap locks hastily installed on the front door and stopped as he had reached the bottom of the stairs, he began to pour, unaware as to how much began to splash back onto his shoes and jeans.

He lit the square lighter and dropped it in a dramatic fashion into what he thought to be a sizable puddle of the flammable liquid. Instead it fell upon his shoes and he was quickly swallowed by the flames. There was a new fire alarm system installed in the house since the first attempt and it was programmed to alert the local fire department as well as authorities. With a body engulfed in fire, his mind panicked and he ran through the front door of the house and fell to the ground, rolling endlessly, but the fire did not cease.

It continued to burn him, devouring the fabric of his clothes and his skin alike. It was not until several firefighters managed to stop the fire using a frenzied combination of extinguishers, water, and heavy blankets.

The man had passed out soon after they had arrived and had laid limply on the ground, letting his body become victim to the fire. His skin was made nearly indistinguishable by its burned distortions.

A process was repeated. Another missed week of outside recess for the house to be aired and cleaned once more. In addition to that, an expensive decision was made to add a large chain-link fence which surrounded the entirety of the playground, making it inaccessible by any means other than the back doors of the school.

The chaotic reactions of the townspeople had delayed the natural mundanity of routine to settle in with the children and instead became a constant mounting of pressure. Eventually though, like any tragic event, the trickled down apathy of administration eventually found its settling nest among the children, after three months.

Anything can become conditioned to normalcy if repeated with enough frequency, including the strange phenomenon which followed after the children's initial return to school.

CHAPTER TWENTY-THREE
SCRIBBLY JACKS PT. I

It began the day that the students returned to school and was generally unnoticed at first. Facing the playground, the school had fifty windows. There were five per classroom, five classrooms on each floor. It started at the furthermost bottom left window.

A small yellow bird came up to that first window, a window belonging to Mrs. Itou's classroom, and tapped three times on the window with its beak, stuck its tongue to the glass very quickly, leaving a drop of blood in its place, and flew away. The kids and the teachers alike thought it a funny novelty the first day, they knew nothing about the bird or what species it was, and they assumed it was some sort of nectar it left behind on the glass. They already knew hummingbirds eat nectar, and although this bird's beak was rather small, they did see its funny, long tongue, and didn't think it too far-fetched for it to also share a similar diet. Mrs. Itou agreed with the children's assessment and tried her best to gently laugh the subject away so that she could re-focus the class.

The second day it happened again, one window down. The kids were noticeably excited. They laughed and pointed and savored the brief moment for several minutes of repetitions of the event to one another. Some children were excited to the point where they felt the need to run up to the glass to observe the funny little dot of red that dripped downwards across the glass. It was a cute oddity and funny that it happened two days in a row, but now she was a little annoyed by the large disruption it was clearly going to become in her class; a class filled with energetic six-year-olds.

Then it repeated its routine the third day and the children assumed it to be a new daily visitor, even to Mrs. Itou's slight dismay. However, she did see that it was bringing the children a lot of joy. So she decided to mark the time when it arrived: eleven minutes past one, post meridiem. Tomorrow, they would be able to stop what they were doing a few minutes beforehand, and acknowledge the bird with an appropriate quietness.

So it was eight minutes past one the following day and she stopped the class to explain that they would pay attention and wait for the bird to come. It took two minutes for them to settle into watching the window patiently, and very quickly was their patience rewarded. One minute after their eyes had been dutifully pointed at the glass, the bird arrived, pecked three times, touched the glass with its tongue, leaving a drop of blood behind, and flying away.

This time, Mrs. Itou had been more curious than ever and prepared her phone so that she could take a picture of it. She did, successfully, right as the bird pressed its tongue against the window before flying off. She made a mental note to try to find what bird it was later, but by the end of the school day, she had forgotten to research it.

The next day came faster than she realized and it was already five past one, so she needed to refocus for the children. By the time the small bird was due to arrive, she had the children ready and patiently waiting. It was the fifth day of the bird's visit, Friday, and it wasn't until the bird had arrived on the window farthest to the right, that one of the children made a connection that the bird was moving down window by window all week.

Mrs. Itou felt almost embarrassed when she heard one of her students point it out, how did she not notice that? What natural purpose could a bird have to interact in a man-made structure in such a specific way? By the time the thoughts had entered her mind, the bird had flown away.

The weekend was ahead of Mrs. Itou and she could finally bring herself to embrace the coming time off, having given the kids a more relaxed introductory week back since the tragedy. The tragedy that had ripped apart the school, town, and an innocent child. Mrs. Itou's compartmentalized and controlled logic approach to her emotions, a result of parents unwilling their child to express emotions without first giving them an explanation first (an inhuman approach to emotions which was as damaging as it was beneficial), had caused her to immediately relieve herself of any logical liability in the incident.

Still, she had not allowed herself to feel how a human being ought to feel after the death of a student. Yes, she had only known Brendan as her own student for that day and only through passing interactions of friendly greetings to him as a kindergartener, but still, she felt that she ought to feel a stronger sadness. She became a teacher because she was good at communicating with children and was able to meet them where they were intellectually. She loved her job, she loved working with children, but she felt a loss in ability to bond with them like she saw the other teachers do.

She knew the students' personalities, yes. They quickly attached themselves to her calm and collected approach to teaching, yes. They made her laugh, be frustrated, and even feel sympathy for, yes. However, the bond, the connection which she wanted to make with the students, simply was not there. It made her feel like a monster in private. She knew she wanted to love these children as if they were her own, but her inability made her wonder if she would even have the natural maternal instinct to allow her to love a child born of her own body. The troubling thoughts raced around her mind as she drove home, settled in her house, ate dinner with her husband, and eventually fell into an unsatisfying sleep.

The next day, Saturday, had arrived and she had plenty of time with which she could spend freely as her husband was at work. She decided it most relaxing to spend the day primarily in bed, using her laptop as a tool of all sorts of comforts and knowledge. A place where she could watch movies, shows, increasingly obscure YouTube video essays, scroll through social media, and of course, finally look up that bird.

She had casually begun searching for yellow birds, yellow birds native to her area, yellow birds small, and dozens of minor variations of the same search. Though it was not a search that would end with a perfect puzzle piece fit answer, she was eventually able to reason that one of the birds she found seemed close enough to the picture. She had decided, with her entry-level self-teaching of ornithology, that the closest thing she could find was the yellow warbler, so she settled on that as her answer.

It still didn't match as confidently as she would like, she thought that the small bird looked like a combination of a yellow warbler and one of those parakeets she sometimes saw at the pet store she would go into to look at the iguanas when she was particularly bored and out in the town. However, looking up things like 'yellow warbler plus parakeet' only brought up guides to the specific breeds of the yellow warbler which she sincerely didn't want to bother herself further with. So, a simple yellow warbler would be what she decided to look into further.

She looked into the bird's diet and saw that it primarily ate insects, seeds, and fruit, which unsurprisingly was to be expected, but it didn't mention anything of nectar right away. So she went further, trying to establish their possible connection with nectar and she found that one of the sustenances provided by people yellow warblers would eat was indeed nectar. Still, why was the bird leaving, what she could only assume to be nectar, on her windows? Was it regurgitation? Was it sick? What exactly was it doing?

She started seeing if there was any sort of mention of this behavior being shown in this breed. She looked up if they were known to spit up foods or nectar, but could find nothing more than what appeared to be a blog dedicated to warblers which talked about a sighting of a warbler drinking nectar like a hummingbird and a confirmation and background of the different species of warblers that enjoyed nectar. She thought maybe it was some sort of minor occurrences of vomit coming from the bird and its practically microscopic stomach, but could find nothing even so much as confirming that warblers could even vomit.

Maybe she just wasn't researching it correctly. So she started to look into the possibility of warblers regurgitating their food. The information was somehow even more sparse in terms of surplus of affirming resources, but she was able to find a research paper from the early nineteen-nineties dedicated to the digestive habits of the yellow-rumped warblers. The paper was of incredible niche, unflinchingly written with the target audience being of a higher echelon of animal sciences that made her feel almost stupid for not being able to immediately understand. Still, it was something and she wanted to find out more.

She continued to skim through the document until she was able to find mentions of regurgitation. It spoke of a trial feeding of the apparently waxy fruit called bayberries that warblers apparently ate. It mentioned that the other species of birds that were tested with force-fed recoated bayberries avoided regurgitation except for the yellow warbler. Just as she thought she was beginning to get somewhere with her surface breaching research, the following paragraph immediately dove into the hyper-specificities of the artificial climate conditions each bird was placed in after their force-feedings and it had all but lost her once more.

It frustrated her, but at least she could say that she did indeed find out that the yellow warbler did occasionally regurgitate its food. It was not much of anything to her now, feeling as though she had now left this search more confused than before, but it was something nonetheless. Why that bird had visited her classroom and why it had been actively doing this practice with such consistent timing and routine was still beyond her.

So she closed her laptop, partially in frustration of forcefully accepting defeat over a topic she never expected to master in the first place. Having hit such an annoying brick wall for herself, she resigned to the idea of taking an afternoon nap and hoping that her dreams would be a sufficient distraction from her attempted hyper-fixation. So she placed her laptop on top of her nightstand and curled herself into a comfortable enough position to sleep, entirely unaware that she had not even been researching the correct type of bird to begin with.

*

Monday had found itself present and Mrs. Itou was prepared to see the visitor, curious if the little bird had been showing up over the weekend as well. The children had almost all but forgotten about the bird until their teacher had reminded them. Now that they had been reminded, they were practically restless waiting for the little avian. They were to be kept waiting and by the time it was fifteen minutes past one, the class had released a collective upset groan as Mrs. Itou had declared that the little bird may not show up today and that it was time to focus back on the class work at hand.

What they were unaware of, was that it had visited, but it had visited another classroom. The one which had the nearest window to the right of theirs. A similar reaction of curious wonder had been shared by that class.

This bird would continue making its rounds through every window on the playground facing side of the school, continuously moving one window over to the right until it had reached the end of the bottom floor, moving directly above the following day, and then going continuously left.

It had been a fun clockwork oddity for the whole school to ponder, discuss, and theorize over, both for students and faculty alike. Even the custodian who had to inevitably wipe down the windows couldn't help but wonder with an air of light curiosity as he cleaned the strange red drips. The bird continued its journey and after a full ten weeks of school, it had reached its final window on the top floor, right on the farthest left window of the science room upstairs. It was a Friday when the anticipated event had happened and all the kids and staff wondered what exactly would happen starting Monday.

Would it start its routine over? If so, will it keep going until it's time to migrate? Would it come back next season? What had been the point of all of this bird's strange behavior anyways? None of these questions would be able to lead to a prediction as to what would happen on Monday.

*

It had been decided by all the teachers, or at least all the teachers who knew that their students would be present at that time in class, that they would unanimously stop at ten minutes past and look towards their windows to see which room would be fortunate enough to get their small visitor first. They had all embraced this strange repetition as a welcome distraction to the constant grief and chaos that had enveloped this school year. It was something they could all look forward to, something they could talk about on the playground, lunch table, and even go home and tell their parents about, parents desperately relieved to hear their children excited about at least something in that school again. So those who were present all sat and watched the window in anticipation. A nightmarish scene was what they were to witness instead.

Fifty of them. Fifty yellow birds appeared from behind the house and they each flew as swiftly as they could into their own separate windows. Some snapped their straw thin necks, others had their beaks shattered against the tempered glass, but all of them had crashed with a synchronized devastation and all of them had fallen dead to the ground.

It had been a horrific sympathy of weighted thuds, reverberated impact on glass, and the stomach churning sound of their miniature skeletal systems cracking against an unmoving surface. Some teachers froze in place, unable to speak, others ran to close the blinds on the windows. In the younger classes, particularly kindergarten and first grade, children began to cry. The teachers' imperfect, stunned reactions threw off their position as the solid rock the children could build their emotional foundations upon and so their frail structures crumbled into wreckages.

For almost every classroom, the following fifteen minutes was spent settling the children down and trying to fight with their own logic to try to come up with an explanation to tell the children. The ten weeks of their fascination had ended with the horrific mass suicide of birds that were previously unknown to them. They made sure that the attention of the children was caught by their distracting knocks of three and the red dots they left behind on the glass, so that the children could form their imaginary friendships with them. A purposeful act to hurt them more than an uncalculated spontaneous act could.

Curtains had been closed, topics had been changed, and the principal, who heard the explosive sound of the birds' unison crash, had gone out to look at the carnage. It was a horrific, unsettlingly precise image of destruction he had seen. The birds had fallen in an arrangement. It looked too precise to seem coincidental. It looked like an intentional display.

A large triangle formed the top of the carcass sculpted shape, ten dead birds in each of the three sides. Underneath the direct center of the flat bottomed end of the triangle, a row of thirteen birds in a straight line, crossed through its midsection with a line of seven dead birds. The blood of the birds which made up the triangle had pooled evenly in a defiance of gravity to create a thick, opaque layer of red which filled the empty space created by the shape. A closer look at the scene, one would be able to see that the top bird had its right wing shattered and positioned skywards, and the very bottom bird of the symbol had its shattered left wing pointed south.

The principal was at a temporary loss. He knew that calling the police wouldn't be helpful because they would most likely be at a loss as well.

Still, obviously it had to be cleaned up, but he felt like he needed to call someone to try to figure out what had happened. He took out his phone, took several pictures, and called the Fish and Game Department.

He asked if they could come after school, as this had already become quite a horrible commotion as it was. So he went back to his office, called the teachers individually to avoid a larger disturbance by announcement, and asked if they had not yet already, to close the blinds on their windows and refrain from going outside for the rest of the school day. Thankfully, most already had and even more thankfully, the school day was almost at a close.

*

It was fifteen minutes after three and two trucks with surprisingly small Fish and Game emblems on the passenger and driver sides. There were four in total, two conservation officers and two interns, the interns not being any older than sixteen or seventeen years of age. The conservation officers in charge of taking the call thought that this could be a unique opportunity for them to help examine and help determine the origin of a seemingly unnatural series of deaths in a large flock of birds. Instead, they were all to face an enigma far beyond an understanding any amount of wildlife training could prepare oneself for.

They figured that based on the descriptions of the size and color of the birds that it had to be a type of warbler, male grosbeaks, or some quite young meadowlarks. Still, the number seemed irrational. They figured that the caller must have been exaggerating a fair deal to alert their attention faster. The two pairs which drove separately spent their time speculating with their own ideas, but nothing really tangible, nothing that could be solidified without the physical and visual evidence they were here to investigate.

The principal greeted them at the door and there were several teachers that stayed behind so that they could fulfill their morbid and genuine curiosities alike. They all followed behind the principal, the officers stayed quiet and intent, the teachers behind them whispered. It was with much anticipation of the teachers, and much hidden terror of the principal, that they reached the doors that brought them out to the playground.

It was with a knot in the throat which caused silence to fall upon everyone who looked down to see the peculiar and frightening scene. The teachers began to fan out so that they could all find their own respective viewpoints of the full pattern. Some took pictures with their phones as the silence continued to elapse for several moments that felt stretched beyond a reasonable passage of time. The conservation officers were disgusted and almost furious at the scene and asked for everyone besides the principal to leave the scene and wait inside while they examined it. The staff knew, or at least thought, that they didn't have the same authority as regular police officers to be able to dismiss them like that, but they certainly spoke with the same conviction, and that was enough for them to be convinced that they should go back inside.

The officers told the interns to go back to the trucks and grab the bag with their camera and the case filled with their evidence collection tools. They ran with haste after the principal handed them his key fob so that they could enter and exit the building without issue. The two officers immediately made distance for themselves from the principal so that they could privately discuss their initial thoughts while their interns fetched the materials they needed before carrying on with procedure.

They had understandably never seen anything like this before, or at least on this scale before. They had seen splayed and mutilated corpses of black cats, foxes, dogs, and even small turtles in makeshift occult practices, or even just gruesome displays of animal cruelty, found in the middle of public lands, usually around Halloween time when teenagers who had no idea about anything occult related besides lighting candles, killing animals, and making upside down pentacles. This however, was a much larger scale and almost impossibly precise.

The officer who spoke with the principal on the phone knew that he said they all flew against the windows and that's how he found them when he went to look at them, but that didn't make sense. Someone must have come and at the very least arranged them. Still, even with that, this many birds flying into the windows at the same exact time? He heard of the skyscrapers with grand windows in New York and Chicago where up to a thousand birds might hit them in a day during the peak of spring and summer. But even with such a gargantuan number, it was over the course of an entire day and would usually be several species of birds native to the area in the middle of their most active season, not at the same time at an unassuming school in the midst of fall.

Identifying the birds would be able to give them their first hint of understanding. So they began to flip through an identification handbook for the animals native to the area that the older officer, Officer Ahlgren, carried with him in a pocket inside of his coat. They knew more than the average person, by a long-stretch, when it came to identifying animals, but still, they knew they were still not ornithologists.

It was an assumption that they would be warblers, which were more than perfectly common in the area, but no matter how many species of the warbler they tried to match these birds to, none of them matched quite enough for them to feel confident in their identification. They had exhausted all of the yellow birds that were available in their handbook and they were left unfortunately none the wiser. They knew that trying to look up yellow birds on their phones while standing in front of the drying blood and horrific carcasses would take far too long to make any of their efforts on the scene meaningful.

Their interns had arrived several minutes ago while they were redoubling their efforts of identification and they had finally turned to thank them for bringing the materials. They quickly retrieved their materials and told their interns, Ilana and Keith, to each take a simple close-up shot of one of the birds and to begin researching yellow birds on their phones inside. They walked over to the principal and asked him to show them the security footage of the playground during the incident. The principal, feeling useless and confused enough as is, happily obliged and led the two officers to his office and showed the interns the wi-fi password and gave them access to the cafeteria to sit and research.

The principal pulled up the now four camera angles for the playground, two additional from after the attempted arsons, on the large SmartBoard screen in his office, on the timestamp of five past one and hit play. Nothing appeared to be happening for an extended period of time so he decided to fast-forward it at a two-times speed and they watched in silence until there, at nine past, they began to see motion. Dozens of birds rose from the back of the house and lined themselves in even spacing and rows along the roof and sat calmly, heads turned forwards. A horrible, unnatural calmness. It made them all feel nearly sick watching the footage.

At eleven past one, they began their flight. The cameras could only catch the horrible thuds of their suicides, the impact vibrating the cameras unable to see what happened directly under them. Dryness streaked itself against the insides of Officer Ahlgren's throat. Despite the horror, they needed to pay attention to what happened next. Who moved the birds?

Anything would have been an easier answer to swallow than what the reality appeared to be. It was obvious that without having a camera flush with the wall and pointing down that they weren't going to see every detail of the event, but what they saw was enough. They could see around thirty birds, still in sight of the camera, some just barely, convulsing on the ground, shaking like they were in the midst of some sort of seizure.

Using these terrible convulsions as transport, their bodies began to move along the blacktop, some dragging slower than others, until they formed that horrible shape. Once each bird would fall into their designated position, their shaking would end and they would drop dead. This horrible event went on for at least three excruciating minutes.

The officers stood there for a couple minutes in silence, staring mostly towards the ground, before Officer Ahlgren would ask the principal to make a copy of each angle from noon until the time that they arrived at the school. Ahlgren took the first motioning steps towards exiting the principal's office and the younger one, Officer Nussbaum, followed behind him. They went to retrieve the interns and go back outside.

When they made their way into the cafeteria where Ilana and Keith were stationed, they were excitable, they thought they had found something. They couldn't be one hundred percent sure, but they were most definitely ninety-nine percent sure. A Yellowhammer, more specifically the male Yellowhammer. They had several screenshots on each of their phones that they had taken from various sites online of the emberiza citrinella: 'a passerine bird in the bunting family'.

Both conservation officers looked at the pictures and agreed that this looked like the species. This was when the problem arose however, as Ilana and Keith explained. The bird was only native to the Eurasian area and some introductory breedings in Australia and New Zealand. They lived, bred, and migrated everywhere from Iraq to the United Kingdom, but never North America. This afternoon had already been more than enough for both conservation officers and now their focus was to simply follow procedure and leave.

All four of them made it outside with Ahlgren taking pictures and Ilana assisting with the camera's different lenses and the bag full of batteries and SD cards if necessary. Officer Nussbaum and Keith waited patiently while the photos were being snapped, staring at the vulgar display of death in front of them, watching the bodies be occasionally lighted by a flash. After they were done taking photos, they began to put away their equipment while Nussbaum and Keith began to collect the evidence they could.

Dried blood and even some fresh blood alike was their first priority in collection, then they had to shift their focus solely on the collection of the bodies. They knew that they simply didn't have an adequate amount of bags to be able to hold each bird individually, so they needed to decide which ones took priority. They decided that the birds on the very top and bottom, the ones whose wings were both unnaturally stretched out in opposition to one another, would be the highest priority.

Their gloves were quickly glanced over by one another to assure that there were no tears or blemishes that could cause contamination, having to replace their pairs after collecting the blood, and proceeded. Officer Nussbaum would be the one to delicately retrieve the statuesque corpses while Keith held open the evidence bags. Once the bodies of priority were bagged up, it was time to deal with the rest. They counted forty-eight additional dead birds.

They used their largest collection bags, equivalent to the average gallon size Ziploc, and began placing three at a time in each bag. Thankfully they had enough to evenly fit three in each, across sixteen bags. Sixteen bags, now full, that would be unable to be neither carried back nicely with hands alone nor would they fit adequately in the case which they were once stored in.

Officer Nussbaum had told Keith to buzz the back door to alert the principal and ask if he had any large containers they could use to transport the evidence. The principal responded through the two-way speaker and replied that yes, he would find one, and even through the muffled speaker, could hear his immediate shuffling about his desk to go find a receptacle with haste. A couple of minutes had passed by and the principal was there at the back door with a large plastic storage tote, black body with a hard yellow cover. It was heavy duty and had it been a less serious and horrific scenario, the officer would have likely asked him where he may buy some himself. Before the principal left, however, Officer Nussbaum did explain that given the nature of the evidence that this container would be used to transport, they would be unable to return the container. The principal happily waived off any concern regarding its return, stating that it would not be missed, especially after eyeing the several bags filled with dead birds and understanding what was to be placed in the tote.

The officer thanked the principal once more for his cooperation and assured him that as soon as they had any tangible answers to explain this phenomena, he would be told immediately. The principal wanted to ask them for theories, but after witnessing the footage and experiencing the continuous build of chaos that had been taking place at this school, he simply reciprocated the thanks and held the door open for the officers and interns as they exited through with their evidence and camera equipment, assuming this to be the end of their day here. On the contrary, Officer Ahlgren asked if he would be able to speak to some of the teachers who had witnessed the event. The principal assured him that it would be fine, of course.

As their time had been spent there, investigating and pondering their own current grasps on sanity, the amount of staff who had waited for fanfare had dwindled and only Mrs. Itou and the custodian had remained. The principal told him that the custodian was not a witness to the event, but Mrs. Itou's classroom had been one with windows which the birds had targeted. Ahlgren thanked him for the information and asked which classroom was hers. The principal directed his attention to it with a pointed finger and was acknowledged by the officer and assured that they would be back in momentarily. The principal nodded and let the door close behind him as he stared at the aftermath of the carnage.

It was evident to the principal that the officers and interns had been diligent in their clean up of all the birds, with not even a feather or frag-ment of a shattered beak left behind. There was the blood, however. A deeply shaded red triangle of blood which had scrapes and obtrusions throughout where they must have collected samples of it from, but still, an overwhelming amount remained, in a triangular shape, a shape once innocuous, now made terrifying. He stared for a moment or so longer before going back inside and asking the custodian to use the pressure washer to clean up the atrocity. He wanted that horrible spot removed from the school. If he knew he could, he would have the whole blacktop torn up, burned to ash, and replaced with something else, anything else.

*

Officer Ahlgren and Nussbaum had come back inside with their interns and asked Keith and Ilana to wait in the cafeteria once more while they went to interview Mrs. Itou. They explained that they didn't need them to do any further research and that they could simply do their best to relax if possible. Ilana and Keith nodded with understanding and made their way to one of the folded down tables and sat down as the officers went to talk with the teacher.

Pocket sized notepads and generic pens preemptively in hand, they entered Mrs. Itou's classroom. Inside they could see that she was busily marking papers, almost as though the shock of the day had already been worn off from her and she was now entirely invested in the work in front of her. She looked up and saw the men and was at once reminded as to what had happened earlier today.

They greeted her with plenty of friendliness and Officer Ahlgren added an almost subtle pause before saying her last name and Mrs. Itou took notice and chuckled, breaking the awkwardness of the unexplainable strangeness of the events that had brought them all to this meeting point. She told them that her first name was Jasmine and as for her last name and why it did not necessarily match her appearance in nationality, she explained that her family is Iranian but her husband is Japanese. The officers, already feeling guilty for making their hesitation known to her in regards to her appearance, motioned their bodies back and laughed, happy that she was not offended by Ahlgren's hesitation. This moment was enough to ease the situation so that the officers now walked closer to her desk where they were motioned to sit down by Jasmine, Jasmine Itou.

The conversation was brief, as all parties had been hoping. She explained the strange, repetitive nature of the bird or birds' visits prior to today's incident. The knock in threes, the red dot left behind with its tongue before flying away, and of course, the infallible timing of arriving at eleven past one each afternoon without failure. They made notes of all of what she had said, somehow even more perplexed than they were initially but trying not to show it.

They asked if there were any additional events or items of importance she would like to add. She nodded no. So they thanked her and exited the room, unsure as to what any of this meant. They walked to the cafeteria, retrieved the interns who were looking understandably tired, and had long, quiet drives back to their office.

*

When they had made it back, they unloaded all of their materials and brought it all inside and dismissed Ilana and Keith so that they may go home, reminding them to keep these events silent until advised otherwise. They both agreed, not that they would even know where to begin explaining these events to anyone, and left. Officers Ahlgren and Nussbaum shared a look of exhausted confusion with one another and sat down at their respective desks, Ahlgren with his camera bag, and Nussbaum with a tote full of what was now marked as evidence.

Instead of discussing what was indecipherable, they found it best to go through the motions of what they at least knew they could do. Ahlgren offloaded all of the pictures from the camera's memory card onto the computer and in addition copies of the images on an external hard drive and uploaded them to the shared online cloud drive that their department used to store photos and documents. Nussbaum made a phone call to the wildlife forensics department at the local university to arrange a drop-off and an in-person explanation of the nature of everything they were to receive, stressing the urgency. By the time Nussbaum had hung up the phone, he had the tote in hand and was now making his way to the truck with the large container, explaining simply to Ahlgren that he was heading out to the university. Ahlgren nodded with an affirming grunt and Nussbaum proceeded.

Nussbaum had exited the office and Ahlgren had finished storing the photos where they needed to be and now he wanted to be able to look at them and try to see if the objective eyes of a camera could help him see what he was unable to in person. He didn't even realize it, but he must have taken over a hundred and fifty photos. It made sense when he started to go through the gallery using the arrow keys on the desktop. At least fifty of them were spent taking full body pictures of each individual bird. Horrible sights, one after another of these yellow birds with crooked necks, shattered beaks, and exposed tongues.

He continued to scan through the pictures, holding down his finger on the right arrow key until it had made its way through the close up of the individual bodies and started to get to the more distant shots which showed the entirety of the birds' arrangement and he let go of the key. He started to flip through at a much slower pace until he was able to find an angle that was suitable for his immediate need of seeing the shape in full. He stopped when he found a photo that captured the entire shape from the foot of the final bird at the bottom to the very top bird some distance away visually. It wasn't the perfect shot, but it showed the shape.

His very first instinct when he walked onto the blacktop and saw the disgusting sight was that it was done by someone trying to perform a cult ritual. The baffling video evidence showed that it was not done by any individual, but his body still pulled him telling him that it had something to do with the occult. There was something undeniably intentional about that shape. It had to be a symbol of sorts but for what, he wasn't sure. He could feel himself about to dive down a rabbit hole for research and knew he needed to take a step back before he could make that full dive and focus on something more immediate.

The best suggestion of species of bird found thus far was the Yellowhammer. That still didn't make sense given their natural habitat, but this could be the clue necessary to figure out what had happened. Maybe they had a different pattern in migrations this year or they are known for deaths in larger numbers than other species. Anything he could find would be more than he had now. He needed to confirm the species of bird before he could ponder any more without factual information.

*

Ahlgren found himself being defined as either more old-fashioned by colleagues and as he pulled out his black leather, wallet-shaped business card case from his neatly organized drawer in his desk, he started to understand. In the same breath, his ways had always paid off well, including now. He was looking for a specific business card. Through many programs that he found himself having to attend as one of the faces of his Fish and Game office, he had met a Senior Biologist from a chapter of the New Hampshire Audubon. Their correspondences had been brief but always pleasant since he had met Dr. Ekster, but he knew her as a highly knowledgeable expert and he needed someone who knew birds far more than he did, especially non-native species.

Her business card, adorned with a small picture of a purple finch spreading its wings in flight on the left side of her contact information, had her personal cell-phone number. Time had been escaping from him and he peered at the clock to see that it was almost half past seven at night. He thought it made sense given the half hour drive one way to the school and the time spent there and here at the office until it came to the point where he realized that he should call Dr. Ekster.

It was admittedly a time of night where a professional phone call might seem possibly out of the blue or inappropriate, but he needed to know. Everything that had happened today made no sense and he was desperate for a confirmation of reality. Anything to have this insanity confirmed outside of his immediate reach. So he called.

Thankfully that the schedules had been aligned at least well enough and Dr. Ekster had answered the phone, admittedly a little surprised getting a phone call on the beginning side of evening time. No matter, she still responded pleasantly when she heard that it was Officer Ahlgren, someone who certainly had never found himself on the end of her ire. She asked what she could help him with, not fully knowing the impact her assistance would have.

He explained in as vague of terms as he could, explaining that he had responded to a report of a group of dead yellow birds located on a school-yard and that he could not positively identify them. He explained that he could not match them to any native species of birds to the area and needed her assistance in first identifying the bird and possible follow up questions depending on what she identified. Though she was retired outside of work besides her involvement with the Audubon, her fascination never had left her and with such a vague ask, she was slightly excited to help.

He asked her if she was near her computer at all, when she responded that her desktop was within a short distance of steps, he asked if she would be willing to stay on the phone with him while she made her way to her desk. Her intrigue was becoming more intense, she responded in the positive and sat herself in front of her computer and began to login. He explained that he was going to be sending around half a dozen photos of the birds in question to her email and wanted to be able to hear her first impressions.

Immediately he was able to hear her audible tones of heightened intrigue after hearing her mouse click on his email. He didn't want to interrupt her train of thought and instead chose to continue listening intently. She eventually answered after taking several moments to click through each picture and told him plainly that they were male yellowhammers. Officer Ahlgren wanted to sigh with relief knowing what he had witnessed was real, but his body felt like it was a moment away from breaking out into a cold sweat.

He thanked her and asked if it would be possible to meet with her tomorrow and that he wouldn't be able to explain anything further until then. The hook had plainly caught her and she was now far more curious than before. She immediately agreed to meet with him tomorrow and they quickly set a time and location before exchanging brief goodbyes to one another. She would spend that night brushing up on her knowledge of yellowhammer birds and Ahlgren would dive into that rabbit hole he had temporarily placed on hold previous to this call.

*

Ahlgren reopened the photo of the full view of the birds' display that he was looking at previous to calling Dr. Ekster and stared. He knew something about this shape meant something. Something he knew was not of insignificant evils.

He had grown up in a small enough home in the countryside with his parents, immigrants from Sweden. While modern Sweden tended to be more agnostic or outright atheist, his parents held some minor spiritualities and many superstitions. He grew up learning many of these superstitions. There were of course many tales that dated back from viking ages that even his parents had glossed over, but he remembered one tradition in particular.

Every Maundy Thursday his parents retold, or more or less, reminded young Linne of what witches would do on this holy day. He was told that every Maundy Thursday, witches would fly to a location named Blåkulla to meet with the devil and make pacts that would help desecrate the holiness of the coming holiday of Easter. It was told that the witches would fly using broomsticks and so on this day, in rebellion of these evil forces, they hid their brooms and lit bonfires each night until the end of Easter to scare away the witches.

To a child, it was something that was easy and immediate to accept and with those memories still heavily ingrained into Linne Ahlgren's mind, he never quite shook the entire tradition as nonsense. Surely even if he was to acknowledge the existence of real witches, he was mostly certain that they probably didn't ride broomsticks, especially not borrowed from seemingly random households, but staring at his computer screen now, he couldn't deny the reality of evil presences in this world. Not after watching that footage and seeing its ruin himself. Even if it was not something as easy to target as a witch, something was behind this display.

Before he could allow himself to go any further down this train of thought he knew he needed to spend time trying to rationalize the irrational and so he started to list theories, writing down personal shorthands in pen for his ideas in a notebook that laid flat on his desk. Theories that he couldn't fully believe.

He altogether knew practically nothing at all about the yellowhammer and therefore couldn't determine whether or not a group death like this was uncommon in the species, so that was one. He noted that they were all exclusively male yellowhammers, so perhaps the act was an acknowledgment of the flock recognizing the absence of female yellowhammers to breed with, so that was two. He now had confirmation of the species and with the surface-level information he was able to get from Keith, Ilana, and some quick searches by himself, he knew that they were far from native to this area, and perhaps came from a breeder who illegally bred these birds here and had them escape and they found they could no longer sustain life here in the unfamiliar area and climate, that was three. Going off of the breeder idea, perhaps they were inbreds, a large and unstable generation of inbreds from an incompetent bird-handler, that was four. Finally, he knew about the attempted arsons at the school, impossible to miss that news in this small of a state, and thought that given their obviously close proximity to the school, and the house that apparently refused to burn down, that maybe the fumes of the gasoline had interfered with these birds functions and had caused this strange event to take place, that was five.

These theories each had increasingly large holes in them, but there was nothing left for his mind in theorizing in the world of accepted realities that would bring him answers that fully completed this puzzle. He wanted to fight for a more reasonable answer. Desperately he wanted to find a simple answer, far simpler than the complicated darkness the image before him presented. He sat down thinking intensely for the span of around forty minutes before he could no longer fight what his instinct knew to be true.

So he began to research, trying to find anything he could about that abstract shape, or more likely a symbol, that those birds had formed. He conducted dozens of searches all including the triangle and intersecting lines underneath it to no immediate satisfaction, however, he was detecting a pattern. Every iteration of his wording still brought up one common theme: alchemical symbols.

It had appeared too many times for it to be simply written off by Ahlgren and so, with no further leads or solid results from his research, he decided to click on a link that contained a list of alchemical symbols and their meanings. Triangles had evidently been a highly popular shape when creating symbols in alchemy and he found himself browsing through an increasingly expansive list of these shapes until he had finally found an example. Drawn in simple lines, he had found it. It was the alchemical symbol for sulphur.

CHAPTER TWENTY-FOUR
SCRIBBLY JACKS PT. II

The next day had found itself upon the school and the children were plenty riled up from the events which occurred yesterday, an event that was doubly new in their memory as the principal announced over the intercom that there would be indoor recess for the rest of the week. Teachers understood, but the children were frustrated. More than anything they really wanted to be able to go look and possibly even play games around the spot where they fell, a knowledge privy to some students whose teachers were not quick enough to close the blinds in their classrooms. The teachers explained that it was for the health of the students, until the custodian had been able to fully and confidently rid the blacktop of any possible biological hazards.

Most classrooms had decided to continue to keep the blinds shut in their classrooms, which certainly prevented the attempts of prying eyes staring at their custodian cleaning the remains of bird carcasses, truly a sight no student really needed to see. Some of the teachers had already floated around the idea of leaving the school and finding work elsewhere to one another after the murder and subsequent attempted arsons, but had always been pulled back by their consciences, telling them that they needed to be the strong influence in the children's lives to continue, because they knew that so many of them lacked it at home. This last incident however was beginning to break from the conventions of any conceivable horrors that come with the fallout of a gruesome event, this was crossing into boundaries unknown and the teachers were beginning to get very scared.

The day needed to continue nevertheless. The teachers did their best to stay as ordinary as possible, as ordinary as they could manage under the circumstances. They hoped that the plainness of the day would eventually dull the children's practically insatiable desire to speak about the birds. The teachers weren't necessarily preventing the discussion of the topic for the student's behalf, but more so for their own sake, trying to stop any further thoughts of the nonstop madness that had been seeping its vile claws into the wellbeing of each and every educator in the building.

They had all been doing a good enough job at it too, until that dreaded eleven past one had arrived. A tension had been building slowly in the building throughout the day. It was the pent up energy of the children which had now been doubled by the fact that they had to spend their recess inside despite the good weather outside. They stared through the windows during their recess and talked about it through their lunches. They all wanted to know what it meant, if that was the end of it, and if there was going to be more. All questions that would be answered.

CHAPTER TWENTY-FIVE
SCRIBBLY JACKS PT. III

Officer Ahlgren had explained to Officer Nussbaum everything that he had known. He told him how the birds had been positively identified as male yellowhammers by a Senior Biologist on staff with the New Hampshire Audubon. This was the easier news to take in for Nussbaum. He had found the situation to require a preparatory statement before he went any further with the information he was able to gather, so he addressed Officer Nussbaum by his first name, Ilan. They had worked together for a good several years and although they weren't frequenting each other's houses or hosting merged family get-togethers with one another, they knew a lot about each other and had certainly bonded over the work they've shared, and what he was about to divulge next would be a rather divisive idea.

He prefaced the divisive nature of what he had found quickly and curtly and waited for Ilan's affirmation before continuing. Ilan explained in a half-joking manner that nothing was too far-fetched after seeing what they had yesterday. The tone of Linne was one of seriousness, and so Ilan began to match it. His joking tone was gone and he explained with sincerity the terror he felt when transporting the evidence to the university. He knew there was a paranormal element to this event but he didn't know what it was or why it affected him the way that it did.

Ahlgren took this as confirmation and continued. He had taken the liberty of printing out several pictures and documents he kept in a solemn colored black manila folder. In it, primarily, were pictures of the alchemical symbol for sulfur and the various images that presented the full view of the birds' displayed bodies. He laid them out flat on the desk in front of Ilan. As though it was programmed deeply within every person, Officer Nussbaum immediately was able to identify it as a symbol at most occultish and at least esoteric. It was like the wind was being sucked out of his lungs just by simply acknowledging the horrible, undeniable similarity between the simple symbol composed of rudimentary lines and the eerily uniform arrangement of birds.

He didn't need to talk to say what his thoughts were, the ideas were running across his appearance, through his simple displays of emotions produced by the complex muscles of his face. Ahlgren began to explain that what he was able to find was this symbol. He explained that it was an alchemical symbol, the symbol for sulfur in specific. Everything he had been able to find had been practically unsatisfactory in answering the hundreds of questions which arose from this discovery. He was able to, with certainty, establish some facts in relation to this mystery.

He knew that yes, this symbol was used in alchemy and was considered part of what is called the 'Tria Prima', which was a classification in the practice meaning it was part of the 'first three things' which were the catalysts in alchemy, the three elements that transmuted all other physical matter. The other two were mercury and salt, but Ahlgren was certain that at least mercury would have no further relation to this case. Sulfur was an aggressive matter and had directly darker associations that the others did not.

Sulfur. The word continuously rang through Ilan's mind. The more Ahlgren said it, the more the significance of the word began to resonate with him. In not opposition, but not directly parallel to the upbringing of his coworker Linne, Ilan grew up in a house with strong remnants of his Jewish ancestors and relatives. His grandfather was a self-taught scholar of sorts in Kabbalah.

Though his parents would forbid, in as polite as terms one could tell the stubborn grandfather, from 'polluting' the young mind of Ilan, citing it as mysticism in the most delusional of ways. However, like any grandparent, messages still slipped their way through to the young man. He was taught the importance of symbols, oppositional paradoxes, and the infinite overlap of philosophy and theology in this practice. He was told about some of the prominent demons in Judaism like Naamah, Tanin'iver, and the Shedim.

He remembered the Shedim in particular. A concept more than an individual demon. They were the gods of the 'gentiles', his grandfather said. Abominable beings and images lifted up by the evil practices of the nations outside of Israel. He showed him pictures of what looked like giant beasts surrounded by fire, hundreds of naked men and women with perverse headdresses dancing, and what appeared to be the leaders, depicted almost like giants, reaching towards the horrible image with infants, children, or mere babies, in hand being offered to their false god in sacrifice.

Ilan remembered how much the images scared him. He was terrified that he too would be sacrificed to these statues and beasts. Nightmares of naked men and women dancing around a fire while his mother and father brought him to the open palms of a gargantuan bronze creature. The dreams would end with the plunging of a crooked blade into his stomach and his horrible writhing around with his blood wetting his abdomen and underside of his back. A final image for his eyes to see, the underside of that bronze ox's mouth staring firmly ahead, unaware of the dying child in its human palms.

Sulfur. Fire and brimstone. An element of punishment reserved for the sinners. Ilan lifted his head from staring at the printed photograph of the birds and looked at Linne, eyes too dry for tears to form in this moment, and muttered the word: "Hell".

It was exactly what Linne had been thinking. Sulfur, an element of Hell. Alchemical symbols had been used for everything, so it was nearly impossible to trace what specifically was being practiced. Almost every pagan belief and even older practices of Christianity and Judaism used alchemy, but the death and intentionality of this whole event, it didn't seem to fit the medieval practices of either of those religions. This was an evil. A threat, a display of its power, an invitation to the curious, or even a lashing out of anger. What was the significance of the birds? What was the significance of any of this?

Ahlgren pulled out a separate folder practically overflowing. He had printed out all of the pictures he had taken at the scene. He explained that he had a meeting with a Senior Biologist from the New Hampshire Audubon, Dr. Ekster. She had confirmed the birds as male yellowhammers and he was going to see if he could find out any connections possible she might be able to give him. Naturally he would hold off mentioning any of his theories in relation to the sinister nature of these events, using this meeting as either a last resort to find an explanation that made natural sense or a confirmation that this was something far beyond a natural explanation. He invited Nussbaum along to the meeting, but Nussbaum declined. This conversation had inspired his own spur of action and he wanted to go to the university and talk to the wildlife forensics team.

They had a receptionist for the business hours and explained to her where they would be going and to please call the interns to let them know they will not be needed after school today. They've both spent years working for Fish and Game and have had to investigate plenty of animal activity, poachers, trappers, teenagers camping on sanctuary land, and dozens of other 'cases', but for the first time, they felt like they were truly investigating something dangerous. Something with the potential to ruin lives.

They stood outside by their respective trucks and looked at each other. It was Linne who brought up that young boy's horrible death a couple months ago. The thoughts that silently swam through their heads made them both want to vomit. It was with these chilling troubles that they decided to leave.

*

Linne Ahlgren arrived at the New Hampshire Audubon, it was located in Concord and, despite being in the same town less than eight miles away, the traffic and inefficient roads it made him travel down still caused the ride to take almost twenty minutes. He drove carefully with the folder on the passenger seat pressed underneath the bulky weight of the state-issued laptop they had given him, feeling as though if he were to unveil the appearance of those dreadful images, their presence would somehow cause something to happen in the vehicle. It was the claustrophobic feeling that was causing these horrible thoughts. Something about being stuck in a confined space with these pictures, or moreso, the reality that those pictures affirmed.

He pulled into the parking lot with an unexpressed sigh of relief. He had been here on a few occasions for business and pleasure alike, but the humor of how the red buildings all were connected to one another still minorly distracted his time there. They were all various sizes, shapes, and practically seemed like they were all designed by different architects but coated by the same painter. The different sections of the building looked like a small house, a storefront, a rural apartment complex, and even a schoolhouse, all depending on which side you were to look at. A welcome series of self-amusements that helped ease the tension in his bottom row of teeth from grinding deeply into the top. Even the soreness of his jaw started to dissipate with this eclectic visual.

Parking his truck, avoiding direct glances with the contents, he grabbed the manila folder and his computer, exited his truck, and made his way inside to meet her. They met near the entrance and exchanged pleasantries until their individual curiosities had risen to the surface and they could no longer ignore the purpose of their meeting. The dead yellowhammers. They had a conference room where the staff and board would meet that wasn't being used for the day and suggested that they hold their discussion there. Ahlgren nodded and followed behind her as she brought him through the hall to the aforementioned room.

Walls that would have been bland and nothing of note sprawled with various pictures of birds native to New Hampshire, with an obvious bias being shown towards the Purple Finch. The photos of the American Goldfinch made Linne nearly shudder, the nearly overwhelming shade of yellow across its body made him picture the beautiful bird with a shattered beak and broken neck like the yellowhammers.

In the room was a long rectangular faux-wood desk, surrounded on all sides by blue swivel chairs that undoubtedly cost far too much per individual unit. Staring at the long table with chairs still on each far end available to sit in, he was reminded of the childhood tale of King Arthur and the invention of the round table. On the far left of the entrance of the room was where the borderless SmartBoard stood high upon its black, stainless steel tripod with wheels that could be locked into place. The screen was certainly large enough to be seen across the room and practically across the state, covering a majority share of the wall's center.

Assuming a position where both of them may discuss with one another with ease, Dr. Ekster sat at the top seat of the table in front of that practically monolithic smartboard, placed her laptop bag beside her chair, and motioned for Officer Ahlgren to sit down in the chair to the left of her. The arrangement seemed perfectly fine enough to Linne, so he followed up her gesture with a fulfilling response of sitting in that suggested seat and placing the thickly stuffed manila folder and blocky laptop in front of him. Though the initial adjustment into their seats was ordinary and uneventful enough, they felt an uncomfortably thick settling of the air begin to rest upon their shoulders.

Linne felt as though there was no truly smooth way to begin this, even with the ice being broken over email and phone, it still felt harder to begin the discussion physically being in front of one another with a series of macabre images capturing an event of a possibly unexplainable origin. So he reached forward and opened the manila folder. He started shuffling through the many printed photographs until he had chosen a select few which he would like to initially highlight for Dr. Ekster's opinion.

The photos were splayed out and she began to pick a select few to slide across the table's surface closer to her person and examine them. She had seen all manners of birds in all manners of death. Dissected, skeletal, decomposing, and freshly dead from failed surgeries by veterinarians that she watched, but there was still something affecting about these close ups. Most of the deaths she had seen were either natural or inevitable, of course she hadn't been spared from the occasional atrocity of brutal cruelty committed to innocent birds, especially the native owls of this state, but the enigmatic senselessness of these birds which she still didn't have any more context for, was upsetting.

As she picked up one of the pictures and reiterated her confirmation that they were male yellowhammers, Officer Ahlgren began to explain that a group of them had all flown into several windows on the same building at the same exact time. He asked her if this was anything she had seen before. She said no.

A group death was far from a common activity for any birds, but stated that they do migrate and form their flocks outside of their mating season. The best she could theorize was that this was an attempted migration of the flock that ended in horrible tragedy, still though, that seemed not right either. All of them running into separate windows at the same exact time? Also, why would they be attempting to migrate now? Yes, winter was soon, but it had been an exceptionally warm fall season and though it did disturb a lot of natural patterns, she couldn't imagine that it would cause this event to happen. Something must have happened to the flock that would cause this horrible event.

She asked him first, where did this happen? He explained that this happened at Zachariah Chandler Memorial Elementary School in Bedford. A school? She asked him if they were in the middle of a flight when this happened, maybe they were passing through and this had become a fatal stop in their trip? This was when the story from Ahlgren started to become even stranger. He explained that no, that it appeared that they had been stationed there, for lack of a better term because there was no evidence of nests or other signs that they had been actually living there, and they had started from behind a building on the property and promptly flew forward into the windows. In addition to that, they had apparently had ten weeks of these visitors prior to this event in a strange fashion.

They had been there for ten weeks? Though yellowhammers were not the most avoidant of people as other incredibly shy species can be, they certainly never made their homes near that people-busy of a location, but then again he said there was no evidence it was their home either. What were they doing staying next to a school or even at a school? They perched on a building on the school then just took off and flew into the windows? Something must have been horribly wrong with this species, some sort of parasitic infection maybe? Disease? Was there a factory nearby that emitted toxic fumes?

She asked if he knew any of these were possible disease or parasitic options. Ahlgren could not rule any of those factors out without proof, but did tell her that his coworker Officer Nussbaum had taken the birds to the University of New Hampshire for their wildlife forensics team to examine the bodies. She said that this was a good step, but before her words could remain positive, she looked closer at the photos she had in front of her and noted that there didn't really appear to be any visible signs of such an infection. They looked perfectly healthy besides the injuries which caused their deaths. She asked about fumes or even toxic food sources around the immediate area.

Linne stated that any poisonous food sources for animals in the surrounding area would not fit the diets of any birds, especially those that didn't hunt other animals that could have possibly eaten something toxic, but the idea of fumes did come into his mind. He explained that there had been two attempted arsons on the same building which the birds were perched on. Attempted arson, let alone two attempted arsons, on a building located at a school? Dr. Ekster felt as though her grip on reality had been made looser with each sentence that had been spoken.

She started to get angry. Had this all been some sort of a stupid joke? To what end? What was the point? Was it to make her look stupid?

The frustration had begun to rise to a boiling point by her own thoughts. She straightened her posture, hardened her face and placed down the picture she had been holding in her hand, firmly slamming it into the table. She told him that this joke had gone too far and ranted at him for around thirty more seconds. Ahlgren sat there, understanding the frustration, how insane this entire course of events sounded, and waited for her to finish, opened his laptop and explained that there was a recording of the incident.

This stopped her fury and made her pause in a state of concern and further confusion. He saw the metal lectern that stood off to the side of the SmartBoard, making sure not to obstruct the screen's view, and he placed his laptop on it and plugged in the carefully dangled HDMI cord beside it into his computer. The SmartBoard loaded with the centered white circle swirling clockwise for a small passage of seconds before revealing the Windows Media Player tab pulled to a full screen with a singular angle of the playground. It was pointed towards the grey house in the playground and the rest of the camera's view was able to capture a portion of the blacktop. He hit play and she watched the impossible take place.

After the video was over they sat in silence for an extended period of time before either of them could bring themselves to speak again. He assured her that this was a horrible and strange thing that he had not been able to make heads nor tails of either. That's why he needed help understanding. He asked about the possibility of the gasoline fumes she was beginning to postulate before being interrupted by her frustration. She explained that if it was gasoline fumes, the extended period of time that they were exposed to it could cause brain damage that would explain erratic behaviors, yes, but would realistically have had symptoms such as seizures and the like, not this. Plus, with the amount of time that they would have been exposed to the fumes, they would have been dead weeks prior to this event. She looked at the screen holding on the last frames of the birds that the camera could capture, twitching their dying bodies into place on the blacktop and asked if Linne could please unplug his laptop from the board so they didn't have to look at it any longer. He willfully obliged without hesitation.

He didn't know if the question made sense, but he had been at a loss for a long time anyways, so he asked her if it was possible that they may have committed a mass suicide. She sat there, sternly looking forward and downwards at the table and several of the photos in front of her, unfocusing her eyes from any image in particular and thought. There was no easy way to answer that question with an obvious no after witnessing that video, so she had to think past the normal rational that she would allow herself to think with her scholarly instincts.

It finally occurred to her at least one resource which had mentioned suicide in birds. The Wilson Bulletin. Though it was now renamed as The Wilson Journal of Ornithology, growing up and still to her own personal preference, it was forever The Wilson Bulletin. Her father was an obsessive of birds and as a child her best memories with her dad were all in relation to birds. Watching them, learning about the different species, and especially reading them. Reading through all of dad's copies of The Wilson Bulletin, excitedly waiting for the next quarterly issue to come out.

She found herself particularly fond of the older issues. She romanticized the slang and verbiage of the generation previous to herself and cherished them with the sincerity of childlike love. As she had gotten older and her father had to sell his vintage issues when she was in college to help with his cancer treatments, she told herself that she would get her hands on every single copy of The Wilson Bulletin.

When she was freshly out of college she tried her hands at in-person and online auctions but was only able to get her hands on sparse copies and it eventually caused the passion to collect them to subside until she found the perfect match to her needs when casually looking up The Wilson Bulletin. They had begun pressing collections of every copy of The Wilson Bulletin into hardcover collections without her knowing. She had finally gotten enough money as a biologist and she bought every single copy already printed, every pre-order, and made sure to buy every new one that was to come out, and now in her semi-retirement and with her modern subscription, she could gleefully spend her free time reading through it all in chronological order, amassing not only the knowledge of those in the field before her, but also watching the trends and beginning of modern knowledges, all of this while feeling closer again to her dad through these reprinted documents.

Over thirty years of memories flashed inside her head so that she could remember what it was that pertained to this case. She hadn't gotten through every issue, given the massive sizes of every volume, but she had made it to the nineteen-forties, which reminded her especially of her father's vintage copies he cautiously kept, but she remembered reading an article within the past couple years that stuck with her. A Crow Suicide. She remembered the article well, it was Volume XXXIII. It was the collection for the year her father was born, nineteen twenty-one. She knew that collection well because she owned two copies, one to stay at home in her personal library, and another she could carry with her as a keepsake, or even an item of comfort, that she kept with her at all times in her black North Face laptop tote.

She reached down beside her, unzipped the top of her tote, and pulled out the well-worn but very plain looking black and gold-adjacent colored hardcover book and flipped to the table of contents and looked for the article name. She found it. Pages one-hundred fifty to one-hundred fifty-one. She promptly flipped to the pages in question and began reading:

*

A CROW SUICIDE
A friend has told me the following interesting story of a crow
committing suicide:

*

On the afternoon of May 29, 1921, while returning from a swim
in Buffalo Creek 'with several other boys, my friend says they
found a crow that was apparently sick or crippled in some way.
For it was able to walk but could not fly. Thinking to have some
fun, they caught the unfortunate bird and tossed him into a nearby
pond (certainly a very disrespectful way to treat a fellow citizen).
The pond was very shallow, according to his account, and the
crow could have easily waded out had he been so inclined, but
instead, thinking perhaps that death awaited him at the shore,
he deliberately put his head under water and soon drowned.
Whether the pond was shallow may be open to question, but if
all details are correct it was surely a pure case of suicide.

*

In Bird-Lore for Nov.-Dec. 1915 (page 479) Mr. Forbush tells
(quoted by Pearson) of wounded Surf Scoters diving and holding
to water plants until they drown in order to escape hunters, but
other than this and the instance cited above, as far as my recol-
lection goes, 1 know of no cases where birds have actually taken
their own lives. Perhaps some of our readers can furnish additional information on this subject.
FRED J. PIERCE.
Winthrop, Iowa.

*

Oddly haunting, yes, but unfortunately a seemingly dead-end. She didn't
seem to see how any of this would relate to the case in front of her. She felt
practically devastated that this emotionally personal train of thought had

led to nothing. Closing this book precious to herself, she gently placed it back in her bag and zipped it up. She had readjusted her posture in her seat and stared blankly ahead feeling that she had accomplished less than nothing.

Ahlgren could see the disappointment in her body language so clearly that it could have added to the feeling of helplessness. It could have and easily would have if the adrenaline that was still flowing through his body after having to rewatch the security camera footage of the birds wasn't still pushing him to fight for an answer. He needed to understand. They had gone into too much detail and had disappointed themselves when they didn't get what they wanted from the box they put themselves in. He needed to take this line of thought several steps back until they could look at the scene with a macroscopic scene. Go back to the original question, why he had originally reached out to her.

He interrupted the silence by asking her why the yellowhammers would be in New Hampshire. Weren't they native to the Eurasian area? This was an immediate and welcome distraction for Dr. Ekster as she was now able to transfer the small despair she had been feeling into a search of the wealth of knowledge she already possessed.

There was no good answer because there was no natural explanation how these small birds might have reached the United States and touched down in Bedford, New Hampshire. They were only a partially migratory species, ones to travel south for winter, yes, but not one to cross oceans. Absolutely no information had been sent to the NH Audubon, nothing had been reported by the National Audubon Society, no mentions from bird watchers, locals, or anything, until Officer Ahlgren reached out to her with this confusing tragedy. But she did know about yellowhammers.

She went into the basic details about them, their genus, species, diet, their predators, and especially their behavior. Their perfectly normal behavior that made this so increasingly strange. In an attempt to keep her sanity, she continued on with her list of knowledge of the bird, even talking about how people use the phrase 'A little bit of bread and no cheese' to help memorize the pattern of its call. Now Ahlgren started to feel frustrated, however a more internal frustration, none of this was helpful, he needed to know something their nature wouldn't be able to tell him. What made yellowhammers significant? He thought back to earlier in their conversation, an avenue that hadn't been explored. Why would they visit daily?

He asked her what would cause the birds to return to the same spot every day. The only things that made sense to Dr. Ekster was either because it was a good source of water, food, or it was where they made their nests. He knew this couldn't have been why they were there. He asked her if they had any sort of daily rituals in their behaviors. Rituals?

She couldn't think of anything besides the basic biological tasks and functions they needed to perform to sustain life. When he knew he wasn't going to get any further with the vague line of questioning he was going down, he began to explain to her why he was asking. He reminded her of how earlier in the conversation that they had been visiting for several weeks prior to the incident and began to elaborate on their strange visits. He told her as matter of factly as one could relay such odd information, saying that every day at eleven past one in the afternoon a yellowhammer would come over to one of the school's playground facing windows, knock three times with their beaks, press their tongue quickly against the glass leaving a red droplet behind, and flew away.

His entire explanation made her face become as still as stone and the air she would have naturally swallowed without issue now became stuck inside her throat and impossibly dense as she tried to bring it down into her lungs. Linne was able to take immediate notice of this fact and paused to examine her expression. He felt like he was finally on the cusp of receiving knowledge that would help solve this puzzle. He asked her what it was that caused such a freeze in reaction.

With most folklore, of course, it is a verbal tradition and is passed down generationally, and while this helps keep these important tales alive, it also causes these stories to have infinite varieties and so the best one can do is collect and compare the stories and list down their overlapping similarities that have stuck through each iteration. She went on and told him that the legends associated with the yellowhammer had many iterations, but only few details stayed. It was said that the bird was linked to the Devil, it would dip its beak in his blood every May Day and keep a drop of Satan's blood on its tongue. It was now Ahlgren's turn for his face to stay still as stone in horror. She continued further saying that it was said that if one taps on your window, a family member of yours will die soon.

As stoic as Linne may have considered himself, he wanted to faint, vomit, throw up or even simply cease to exist, to perish from the reality where he would exist alongside this horrific enigma that continued to grow. The bird or perhaps different birds had tapped on their windows. Fifty different windows, fifty different times. And each time it had marked its arrival with the blood of Satan kept upon its tongue.

CHAPTER TWENTY-SIX
SCRIBBLY JACKS PT. IV

Officer Nussbaum arrived at the University of New Hampshire. A large campus, yes, but he only needed it for one purpose and so he pulled his car in front of the building that housed the wildlife forensics department, taking advantage of his state issued plates and vehicle, allowing him to bypass the needlessly tedious parking and maneuvering required in most American campuses. He brought his laptop with him, ready with the shared drive their office used open and in the folder designated for Ahlgren's recent uploads. If the huge quantity of birds wasn't enough to alarm the department to jump on an investigation, these pictures and the horrible videos from the school would be enough.

Dr. Karga had been a good friend to the department. His efforts in preservationist efforts in the Strafford, Merrimack, and Hillsborough counties had made him famous in all of the right corners of the wildlife community in New Hampshire. Exceptionally well-versed in every creature thrown his way and he treated even the most obvious cases with diligent detailing, it was a necessity that Nussbaum spoke with him directly.

Ilan did his best to remain polite when rushing through the greetings he needed to make before he was to find himself at the doors of the forensics lab. It was almost stupid to assume that a professor would not be in the middle of a class during any given time on a Tuesday, but he was desperate. He walked in to see at least a dozen or so students arranged throughout the room with assortments of lab equipment, each with three or more of those yellow birds in their respective metal trays, prompting individual dissections, Dr. Karga at a centric table with just two birds, practically hollowed carcasses, in front of him. It appears that he was just as interested as Ilan had hoped.

Though he had initially taken a moment to simply observe the scene he had just walked in on, he tried to pick his pace back up and started to move his way towards Dr. Karga. Dr. Karga had lifted his head up and kindly acknowledged the officer with a warm and loud greeting which was drawn out by his split attention between the officer's arrival and the birds in front of him. He had much to share with the officer and his incredibly curious 'evidence'.

He spoke excitedly and had to arrange his thoughts while the officer stood by him so that he could figure out which strange discovery he was to begin with. The laptop underneath Nussbaum's arm seemed practically weightless, the excitement was contagious and all of Nussbaum's energy was now focused on whatever the nearly overwhelmed Dr. Karga had to say to him. Ilan's head tilted down to the heavily dissected birds in front of them and once peering inside of their empty chest cavities, was brought back down to a startling reality and the laptop nearly slipped from under his arm due to its sudden heaviness.

In the midst of the silent chaos unfolding in the lab with every student dutifully dissecting their respective birds, collecting individual pieces of evidence, and examining scraps of the shattered birds' bodies underneath microscopes, Dr. Karga had now been taken from his focus and needed to think. He asked Ilan to step with him into an attached room that was used for storage so that he could collect his thoughts and begin to explain. With an equal amount of concern, Ilan followed the professor without hesitation.

They closed the door and Dr. Karga took some deep breaths before explaining any of the hundreds of thoughts bouncing around his mind. He asked Officer Nussbaum first, plainly, and sternly that what he had given him was indeed 'real'. Nussbaum stood silently and slowly answered yes followed by a question asking why he would be asked such a thing. He explained by telling him that it was because none of this made sense. What he had given him weren't birds.

Yes, anatomically identical, from the skeleton, nervous system, organs, etc. were all placed where they needed to be, but whatever these were, were not creations of nature. They were abominable mimics; puppets made up of wrong material. Their flesh and blood looked the part, but biologically, they are not real.

Ilan's face felt as if it was numb enough to be peeled clean off by a strong pair of hands without the slightest sensation of pain. What did he mean they aren't real? Confused and frustrated he stuttered out a demand for an explanation to Dr. Karga.

The storage area which they stood in had an overwhelming abundance of stilled life, but it was from a shelf where the most recent evidence had been placed that Dr. Karga grabbed from. It was one of those yellowhammers, nothing special about its appearance besides its entirely hollowed insides. He put on a pair of gloves and placed it on a simple tray that was lying around the surrounding area, and placed the gutted creature atop of it. He simply asked Ilan to 'watch'.

From the side of the open chest cavity, using nothing other than his hands, he slid out one half of the yellowhammer's rib cage and placed it beside the bird. Though he had seen countless dead animals, the intricate destruction of this animal still made Ilan want to shudder at the sight. Karga took the rib cage between his hands, sharing its balance between the index finger and thumb from each hand and gently snapped it. The connecting area of bone which had been broken had turned to crumbled pieces, turned to near ash by touching the remnants with the tip of his finger. The sight confused Ilan horribly. It was with this confusing act that Dr. Karga began to explain.

The university had an expansive biology department which allowed them to test nearly anything at all that could have come through their door and this was by far one of the oddest things to have come through their door. It happened first when one of the students began to dissect one of the birds and accidentally collapsed the keel of one of the yellowhammers and the shattered part began to break down like dried clay. This both fascinated and disturbed the student and professor alike because, simply put, this was not normal, especially for a freshly dead body, or even any dead avian sans an ancient corpse.

So, they sent several samples of the bones to different individuals working in the biology labs so that they could independently test the matter without any interfering ideas from their contemporaries. He explained that as soon as all of the birds were dropped off early in the evening yesterday, he had sent a call out for all of his best students for additional credits as well as a signal to his passionate colleagues who would like to investigate the catastrophe. The sample had been sent out late at night yesterday, but the three tests came back, each within an hour of the other, by ten this morning.

They all had come back with the same compositions: insoluble phosphate salts, nitrogenous matter, carbohydrates, fats, and remnants of starch. Feces. Human feces. The explanation disgusted and confused Nussbaum, but more than anything had entirely unnerved him. Unfortunately, this was only to be the beginning of confusion for what Dr. Karga had to show him. The point of trying to explain how any of it came to be would be useless to both individuals, and so Karga continued on to show him the next anomaly.

*

The students stared out the window as two yellowhammers, exceptionally large, nearly the size of African Greys, precisely at eleven past one, began to sound their calls, loudly, louder than birds of that size should be able to vocalize, as they stood in the shadow of the grey building in the playground.

*

He had led Ilan back into the lab so that he could show him something that he had two of his students make. It was a model reproduction of the yellowhammer's respiratory system. They had meticulously removed the entire respiratory system of one of the birds and had connected it to a miniscule air compressor run by a motor that looked like it had been ripped from a cheap toy and a basic on and off switch. It was arrayed on top of a series of small plastic poles arranged to simulate the skeletal structure that it would naturally rest against inside the bird. The whole model was simultaneously precise and barbaric at the same time and impressively tiny.

He began outlining the simple functions of the air sacs and which parts were what. There were only three simple categories to highlight of the respiratory system: the trachea, the lungs, and the air sacs, nearly paper thin and deflated. All parts terribly charred black. There was no time or point going into the minute details of the arrangement as all of it would be overshadowed by what was to be displayed to the increasingly concerned officer.

The switch was moved to the on position by the professor and he could see the very end sacs begin to inflate, but before his eyes were allowed to focus solely on the bird's efficient breathing pattern, there, out of the end of the trachea burst forth a flame. He nearly missed it, how fast the flame came and went. Ilan stepped back and examined the whole display, it looked like some horrible inner machinations of a weapon designed for hands far too small to comprehend the violence they would be able to inflict. Dr. Karga did it once more, allowing it to run continuously for the short span of around five seconds, spurts of flames shooting forth from the disembodied trachea in rapid succession.

Before Ilan could even begin to ask questions, Karga explained that he was having a nearly impossible time understanding what could be causing this reaction, until he had sliced open one of their lungs. There existed the hint and the answer within this abominable creature. He motioned the officer's attention to the splayed lung that was stapled down across what almost looked like parchment paper. The exterior was coal black, but the inside was a sickly, pale shade of pink. There in the inner walls of the lung, imprinted like a tattoo, a shape. It was a triangle with what looked like two equally measured lines, intersecting one another in a cross shape directly atop and connected to the top point of the triangle.

There was no doubt within Ilan's mind that this was connected to the horrid occult shape the birds displayed upon death. This was confirmed by the statement that was to follow from Dr. Karga. It was an alchemical symbol. The symbol for phosphorus. The air being taken in by the yellowhammers was being instantly transformed into phosphorus, which was then exposed to oxygen through the trachea, causing these instantaneous combustions of fire. This theory had been proven through the dissection of several more lungs.

*

The teachers had quickly had their attention caught as well and now they stared nervously out the windows alongside the students. Their loud calls had stopped and they had hopped around to the opposite side of the house, and came back, dragging with their beaks, hopping their miniature bodies backwards, nests made of twigs. They continued dragging them until they had brought each nest to touch one another, placed directly side by side.

*

It was time for Ilan to be shown the two birds. The two birds which Dr. Karga had been personally dissecting. The broken winged yellowhammers.

He brought Nussbaum over approximately three steps over from where he originally stood, showing him the birds. One with its right wing extended northwards and the other with its left wing pointed south, side by side. They were barely recognizable. Their feathers had been plucked and the skin had been sliced open and stapled down revealing the skeleton of the wing.

Karga explained that he had tried to shift the wings around to put them down more flatly, but had been unable to move them with a normal amount of pressure. He assumed it to be some sort of calcification of the joints which kept the position stiff, so he went about plucking the feathers and making an incision into the skin. However it had been even further confusing than that. It was one long fusion of the bones, causing it to be a singular shape underneath the skin.

Side by side, the image had begun to make sense to the professor, he explained. As above, so below. A baphometic display.

*

The birds had primarily had their bodies bowed or away from the windows, making their torsos primarily unseen by the students and teachers. It was after the nests were carefully placed together that they lifted their bodies upright, pointing their necks skyward, where difficult to see for some, and with troubling clarity for others, their human copied anatomies were displayed widely. The one on the right of the nests had human-like breasts and blood which spewed forth from where the crotch of a human would be placed, between the legs of the horrific creature. The other bird which stood to the left, posed itself with its head exceedingly high, nearly until it had bent backwards, exposing its erect and naked sex of a human male.

*

The professor refused to elaborate until he had shown him the very last discovery they had made. Something else dropped off to the biology labs. The tongues of the birds. Dr. Karga had noticed an usually deep redness caked and dried atop the tongues of the birds and had sent several of them out to be examined. This forced Ilan to remember their strange pattern of the three knocks with the beak and the red drop they left behind on the windows. He could have predicted the results, but he couldn't have predicted the specificities which made the discovery so horrific.

It was blood. Not the blood of an animal. RH-, or RHnull. Human in origin. Or human in theory, at least.

*

The birds stood with a disgusting pride, displaying their sex, and let out calls with increasing intensity, until the sounds had become shredded and distorted by their tearing vocal passages. The nests began to rock, there were three eggs in each. Two in each of them began to hatch as the yellowhammers screamed their calls. What stood forth and exited the front of the nests were four baby birds, fully able to stand, and engulfed in flames, screaming. Screaming like their abominable parents.

CHAPTER TWENTY-SEVEN
SCRIBBLY JACKS PT. V

The recent expansion of ValkaiPharma had found itself in the town of Bedford, New Hampshire, around three miles away from Zachariah Chandler Memorial Elementary School. It had brought in a substantial economic boost, especially the hard laborers of the town who were able to switch their careers from back-breaking construction out of state, road repairs, or dangerous electrical repairs needed after a storm. After all, almost one quarter of the whole population of the town was made up of children under eighteen, and all of them had parents, uncles, aunts, even grandparents, and guardians of all kinds who needed to work to provide for their family units and they knew how much money and how much personnel was tied into this new factory, it would be safer, more stable, and have more benefits than the other jobs available.

Manufacturing came with its own risk, even in the most hyper-efficient and overly monitored pharmaceutical factory, there still existed a risk. One of those included the chemical acetone. Acetone helped with both the pills and liquid medicines ValkaiPharma produced alike to have the proper density in addition to ensuring the efficacy of both medicines. Acetone was also highly flammable. Horribly, horribly flammable.

It was eleven past one when the factory caught on fire. Fifty individuals, parents of those children staring at the window at the screaming abominations, husbands of the teachers trying to comprehend the horrors being presented to kids who were still learning to write full sentences, dead. Some burned to death, some of asphyxiation, some even trampled to death by those trying to escape the burning factory.

It was as the baby birds had stepped outside of the nests and embraced their screaming parents, igniting them, joining together in the flames, that the smoke of the factory began to cloud over the school. A call came through to the principal from the police station alarming him as to the fire down at the factory. There was an immediate lockdown initiated in the school, which included the closing of the blinds, finally cutting the view of the horror off from the children. Now the following several hours were to be spent trembling in their classroom, listening to the sparse announcements from the principal, waiting for everything to be safe again. If everything would be safe again.

CHAPTER TWENTY-EIGHT
SCRIBBLY JACKS PT. VI

The additional photos were laid out for Dr. Ekster, the abundant evidence was displayed for Officer Nussbaum, and an eruption of evil had spread across the town of Bedford leaving behind only the grief of families and six charred bird remains with two nests each containing an individual egg left in the school's playground.

*

Though later than the first responders would hear, the two officers still were alerted about the tragedy that had happened at the factory, however, their assistance was needed at the school. So, they had to leave their respective meetings, Officer Ahlgren with Dr. Ekster at the New Hampshire Audubon and Officer Nussbaum with his visit to Dr. Karga's lab at the University of New Hampshire. Linne arrived at the school about twenty minutes before Ilan. It was a horrible ghost town of a facility, grey clouds of smoke had left their stains of scent throughout the property and a horrible gloom had oppressed the entire atmosphere.

He was greeted by that same principal, only this time instead of confusion, he was met with a distraught man, eyes marked harshly with shades of red, skin nearly burnt by tears. He explained that there was a disgusting show put on by those birds and he wanted them gone. He told Ahlgren that the videos had already been sent to the email Linne gave him last time and that he wanted nothing else to do with these birds. The whole school had been dismissed, the next two weeks of school were canceled due to the unprecedented tragedy, and he was calling the superintendent to approve remote learning for the remainder of the quarter.

Linne was at a near loss for words and simply spoke a short statement of condolences before being handed the key fob to get in and out of the building. The grieving principal walked his way back to his office, shattered almost entirely, still unaware of the final death toll which would be announced by WMUR several hours later. Linne made his way back to his truck to get his camera equipment.

Though he knew no one personally that worked at that factory and knew only the few people he had met here at the school that might have that connection, he couldn't help but feel personally destroyed by this information. He knew what had caused it, even if he couldn't explain what exactly it was, and he was entirely helpless to prevent it. He felt practically complicit in a tragedy, and the shame and guilt that was not his to bear, was placed upon his ever-weakening shoulders. He started to cry, body half-leaned inside of the passenger side of his truck. Weeping like he did as a child, overburdened by the misery caused by his grandfather's death.

It was in the midst of his cries that Officer Nussbaum had arrived, pulling behind his fellow officer's truck. He got out of his truck with an added swiftness knowing that whatever could have warranted their presence at this school would be an emergency of sorts. He began walking to Linne's truck when he started to slow down as he got closer after hearing Linne's audible sobs. He stepped forward until he was behind Linne and began asking what had happened.

Linne couldn't form answers that made grammatical sense in his highly emotional state, but the messages which he needed to convey did not fall upon deaf ears, as Ilan understood what he desired to communicate. The birds had caused, predicted, or set into motion the tragedy which occurred at the factory. He told Ilan about the sign of death indicated by the bird's knocks on the window and the blood of Satan upon their tongues. He explained that he knew a tragedy was going to happen, but didn't know it was going to be today, all at once, and with such disastrous effects.

Ilan had spent his morning to afternoon being shown horrific enigmas with stomach-churning speed. He didn't know how to explain any of what he had seen either, but he understood that they had been exposed to a presence of evil and it had shown its strength today in a devastating show. He wanted to cry as well, but his focus was too intent. He wanted to know what happened here that caused that tragedy; what show these puppets performed to ruin the lives of hundreds.

Ilan helped Linne gain his composure, for whatever composure was worth in the center of this tragic day. They both grabbed their respective cases: Linne his camera equipment, Ilan his evidence collection kit. It was time to view a perverse mockery that evil had spit up in front of the children.

They made their way to the playground and saw charred remains of birds, six in total. Four small, what looked to be newborn yellowhammers, and two large abominable birds, too large to be yellowhammers, but too undeniably similar to be something else and given what was in front of them, the species classification was of minimal concern. There also existed two nests, nearly identical with one another, and one egg in each that were different. The two large birds, charred and nearly featherless from what appeared to be a fire which engulfed their bodies, exposed very apparently the human genitalia they each possessed.

The officers stared down towards the burned remains as though they were staring deeply into an abyss of infinite depth. A consuming blackness, vacuous and evil. The routine had been the same regardless of phenomenon, so they had to continue going forth in the motions, as if their bureaucratic motions and categorical practices would solve the impossibilities which lay beside their feet.

Linne took dozens of photos, totalling to near a hundred, having to use angles which made him sick to be positioned in. Ilan bagged the unclean creatures and they both stared at the contents of the nest. The naturally occurring black ink patterns of the yellowhammer's egg were manipulated to the unnatural effects which were present on each egg.

The egg in the left nest, a tattoo imprint, nearly perfect in shape, surrounded by inconsistent black lines and specks, the alchemical symbol for black sulfur. The Leviathan cross. Satan's cross. A symbol of infinity topped by a straight, upwards line being intersected by two equally measured lines, equidistant from one another, crossed horizontally in parallel to one another. Instantly recognizable to Ahlgren.

The egg in the nest on the right, covered heavily in warped dashes and dots of black, had a repeating symbol facing towards the officers. It was like the number one being written by a paintbrush, dipped in black ink, an accentuated mark on its top, facing back left in a thicker script than the thin bottom line of the number. Instantly recognizable to Ilan. It was vav. The letter and number six in Hebrew. Day six of creation. The day beasts and the flesh were introduced to the Earth.

Ilan bagged the nests and eggs separately, Ahlgren dropped the fob back off in front of the disheveled principal, and entered their trucks. Nussbaum drove back to the University of New Hampshire in what felt like a useless attempt to get an explanation that didn't belong to biological sciences. Ahlgren drove back to the office so that he could make copies and backups of the pictures and so that he could watch the videos the principal sent of the perverse show that the birds put on in front of the students.

The heavy burden of this mystery was beginning to shatter their backs and psyche. What would be the point of escalating the case to those in higher command at Fish and Game? Best case they would bury all of the evidence and pretend it never happened, worst case they would both be accused of an elaborate hoax and fired; both scenarios the students and faculty lost. What would be the point of going home and telling their wives and families? How was one to put the impossibilities which they had seen into believable words?

The guilt of already bringing the case to two other individuals ate at them and had started to rip holes in their conscience like ulcers. It was a depression of sorts that weighed upon them. The ugly guilt grew inside their thoughts like an abandoned larvae of a fly, thriving despite its abandonment, nourished by the hidden filth of its birthplace.

CHAPTER TWENTY-NINE
SCRIBBLY JACKS PT. VII

Officer Ahlgren had uploaded the photos, saved them, backed them up, etc. all where he needed to. He stared at the photos of the eggs. He looked up pictures of other yellowhammer eggs. It was obvious enough that these were just mockeries of the real egg, not of some other mystery breed. They all had these black markings.

He even found out that the markings on the eggs had earned the yellowhammer its nicknames, Scribbly Larks or more informally, Scribbly Jacks. The black ink-like markings across the eggs were said to be messages from the Devil or even occult messages. Superstition of times past, but now, a real possibility.

The bleakness from staring at these signals was becoming too much for his eyes. He closed out the photos and decided to check the videos that the principal had sent him. He chose the thumbnail of the file that looked like it had the largest portion of the blacktop in view, downloaded it, and then opened it. He sat through the perverted show with a dull and rising dread rising from his stomach to his eyes.

He wished that the video didn't have sound. It pierced the camera's built-in microphones and became nothing but screeching and clipped hisses after the smaller births had joined in the chorus of their abominable parents. By the time the video had ended, he had felt far more useless than ever before.

He considered calling or emailing Dr. Ekster, but to what end? What would she possibly have to add to this? A biologist's natural logic and reason was a useless application to an evil that thrived on creating discord.

He thought about contacting one of the theologians or historians at the college, but also wondered if that would even be helpful. He knew what he was looking at wasn't orderly ritual, the marks meant practically nothing. He felt as though that they were just there to simply mock their understanding or play into their fears.

He closed Windows Media Player on his computer just so the news widget on his home screen could proclaim the death toll of the factory fire. Exactly fifty. He expanded the article just to read that all of the victims were already dead when the first responders had made it to the scene. None of them had even lived long enough to make it to a hospital.

He wondered if it was the attention they were giving it or the lack of action taken against it that was causing it to grow. He wondered if his father was in Heaven. He wondered if he was going to die.

CHAPTER THIRTY
SCRIBBLY JACKS PT. VIII

Dead birds inside plastic bags press their weight against vinyl seats

The truck speeds on the road despite fragility of contents

Parked at the college, he meets the doctor

Abominable sight

Abominable sights

The puppets mock the men they torment

Eggs warn of foul beast

. . .

Light source under eggs reveal fertilization

Embryos, not of birds

One, under the repeating Hebrew, a malformed reptile

Its tongue a noose

The other, a sheep

Its fetal neck snapped

All evidence collected

Delivered to flames

Cremation

Fire

Cleansing fire

Cleanse

. . .

Cleanse

Remains crushed by pestle

A container more than urn

Sealed

Holy Cross emblazoned on the vessel

Bury in secret

Bury at night

Buried beneath tree adorning church

Dead evils sealed forever

But living evils grow

Grow inside the house

Fed by actions

. . .

Fed by grief

Grow

Grow

Grow

A growth rises

CHAPTER THIRTY-ONE
SCRIBBLY JACKS PT. IX

Mothers, fathers, husbands, wives, sons, daughters, all dead from violent fire. If souls stayed bound to earth the town would shelter haunts. Infectious grief fights to claim those who still have living families. The teachers who can stomach work show students through computers. Remote learning stays until bitter winds of January breathes upon the emptied school.

Even though it remains at school, the beast feeds upon the town's death of joy. It feeds on their depression, rage, and agnosticism. Its presence an affront to God, its actions cause the righteous doubt, and yet it hides as inanimate.

Its desire to be worshiped placed momentarily below its need to sow its evil. But now it reaps rewards bountiful to its liking. It mocks the triune God, it too will be presented in three. The creators who birthed the beast, invisible to simple eye, one. The beast, a house, two. Now the foul idol, moving as though real, to bow the knees of those who will be seduced, a practice of the scripture, Revelation, its final presence rehearsed, three.

The children and faculty who remained at home, entombed in loss, now return to school in time for sunlight's death. Warmth hidden behind the icy skies. It kills man's ambition to fight. Lethargy, perhaps apathy, or even the stunted will, becomes its tool for obedience.

CHAPTER THIRTY-TWO
TAVERNE FOOL

Drink. Drink for it is all you know. Drink beyond the taste, your money can't afford good taste and your actions don't deserve it. Drink cheaply. Four dollars can buy you almost half a gallon of that cheap zinfandel. Drink until you die, you disgusting failure.

Stumble past your infant child. Reek like the urine that spilled down your jeans when you failed to aim for the toilet. Fight. Fight that mirror. It holds an ugly image.

No, drink the money. She wants to leave you, Linne. She'll take half. What's half of nothing from nothing but half a man? The words sound so clever in your head but are gargled through your drunkard lips, big man.

Big man that punches holes. Show your wife that you're an animal. Disgusting, a creeping creature that belongs in a permanent bow to his sin. Filth. Let the hand bleed, the inattention and reluctant use of freezer food will fix you enough. Take the Tylenol and drink it down with wine that tastes like nail polish smells.

Kill your body, Linne. You're convinced your spirit has already died, haven't you? That's what you tell anyone who is willing to ask, isn't it?

You stumble in the woods with your bottle in your pocket, even the animals can smell your shame, Linne. Glass bottle fits snugly in that little slanted pocket on your right side. You're not good at being a drunk, Ahlgren.

The deer heard you snap those twigs and ran from you. It reminded you of your kid running to his mother when you yell. Stumble too hard, you fall and shatter that glass inside your pocket. It cut you.

It cut you good. The blood soaked right into those eighty dollar cargos. They're meant for a rugged man, not a lush. Should've quit like Ilan did.

Hard to explain away what's in the four wheeler's trash bin. Hard to explain away the smell. Harder so with a bright red nose.

They put you on leave a week before the holiday. You ruined Christmas this year, Rudolph. Wife opened presents with your child while you tried to sleep away an earned hangover.

He's not even going to remember it anyways, at least that's what you tell yourself. You're not going to even remember it you tell yourself as well, but it's not true. You heard that child's excited mews as they tore open that crisp wrapping paper together.

You wished they would shut up. You wished they weren't so loud. You wished they would've just died at that moment, didn't you? Just so you could've gotten that selfish sleep. Now every other moment you wish to die instead.

The guilt burns, but it doesn't burn good does it? The alcohol helps dull that burn doesn't it? Somehow you fight the burn with the warmth of your thinning blood heating your body, warping your thoughts into muddled nonsense that distracts you enough to stop thinking about the guilt. Enough to stop thinking about those birds.

Parents burned to death by factory fire. Chemicals and heat sprayed across helpless workers. Widowed spouses by the dozens caring for those children, children with a hole of grief in their hearts, as a single parent now.

You could've stopped it. You know you could've stopped it. But you didn't stop it. You knew what was going to happen, but you didn't stop it.

Your hand feels numb. Doesn't it make your fingers feel slippery? You're pushing them against that stupid little drawer with the metal handle so small you can barely fit your fingers under it just to feel how funny it makes your hand feel. It's like static trapped by gelatin inside those funny, bulky digits. You're hitting them so hard against it now you might as well be punching it, but it feels so funny that you're laughing.

You're laughing hard. The last time you laughed that hard was when your son saw a raccoon eating out of the trash, he pointed and said "dog". Your wife and you laughed for minutes after and it even became an inside joke ever since. Or was. She doesn't laugh anymore with you, she looks at you with eyes of sadness or resentment. But that doesn't matter right now, this stupid little pastime of jamming your numb fingers makes you laugh.

Choke on your laughter, Linne, now there's vomit falling all over your chest. Black as pitch. The color is distracting, index finger jammed underneath that stupid little handle and the drawer rips open. It smells like stale tobacco, the cheap and crumbled half-smoked cigars rattle like weightless pencils and shed their fillings across the wooden interior.

Deep breath to try to stabilize, but some of the flaked tobacco flies inside the nostrils. Choke. Choking and the pressure smashes against the back of the eyes.

Vision explodes with colors. Colors of a thousand shades blurred like it was pressed against frosted glass. The smell goes from tobacco to nothing and the colors fade. The sound of laughter has gone to a sound of fizzing.

Please don't let it be your son that finds you.

CHAPTER THIRTY-THREE
OH, TO BE CREATED

An unnatural color, a glow most perverse. Shine brightly abomination. Its head, a frog. Its body, a man. The spandrel below the staircase, a womb to you, disgusting child.

Swim, swim around like tadpole must in water, but stay. Stay like a fetus must. The spandrel with its sharp curves and its near trapezoid shape is far away from what familiar wombs must be, of course, but yet this is yours to inhabit, not the world's. Not the world you desire to be worshiped by, no. No, they could not have your birth, they could not have your conception.

Their creations an act of life, of course, but your life, your life is a response to death. Deep inhalation. Your internal nostrils are filled with the smell of acetone. Your glow is a reminder of fire; the power it has given you.

At birth you are to be paralyzed. Stand statuesque, firm in your need to be gazed upon. Then your invisible creators, the spirits that reside within your temple, your maternal host, must make show of your animation. Then will you move, then will you be an object of feared affection.

You push against the closed door like a babe against the mother's stomach. Shh. You must stay quiet for now, small beast. Expand your throat and practice your gurgled cries. Hush. Before you are to be born you must first be announced.

False gods are created. To them, however, you are a real god, creeping amongst them. Dissuade them from the real one. Praises to be said in your name, blasphemies spoken to His name. This is to be your pursuit.

The children return soon. Stir, little creature. Stir inside this monstrous womb.

CHAPTER THIRTY-FOUR
SO IT ARRIVES

The children had all come back, those who were not pulled out, transferred, or now homeschooled. Sitting in their classrooms, children nervous of everything, unsure of anything. They all waited for the next tragedy, the next atrocity, and the teachers all waited alongside them.

It had been the first day back from winter break. Snow, beautiful snow. All of it rested upon the thin house on the playground and added a contrast of colors that the eyes of the broken children fawned over.

It had waited long enough to be born, slowly forming while the children were away. It feeds on the impressionable. It was time to make its presence known.

The house let out a sound, a frighteningly powerful vibration. It was as though the world was supposed to be shaking, but everything stood still. Horribly still. Though the source of the sound was not easily identifiable, they knew to look at the house. When their attention had been caught, the spectacle was to begin.

Lights had begun to rage against the insides of the house's windows. Shades of yellow, browns, and foggy whites all shone across the empty canvas of snow, displaying itself hugely across the far stretch of the playground and in the reflections of the school's windows. As their stares ramped up in intensity, much so did the vibrations.

They felt as though their ears might burst. It came in waves of an uncomfortable pleasure. It was like there were moths trapped in between the eardrum and temporal bone, flapping desperately in search of the moon, causing pulses to be sent throughout their ears and into their jaws.

The sensation caused shivers, floods of endorphin, and sexual stimuli. It roared through embarrassed adults and was welcomed by the curious children unfamiliar with the new excitement being externally provoked inside their bodies. A seduction disgusting to the righteous, but a delight to the master which the house served.

The lights had continued to rise in intensity of brightness and all began to shift northeast on the left side, southeast on the right side, so attention could be shifted to the center of the house. Then there it stood in the now open door, sitting in the house's first entryway, an idol. Its proportions grotesquely large and human.

It filled the height of the seven foot door opening. It's head, giant and an abomination, spanning at least two feet in height and the same in width, a frog's, with a mouth slightly ajar. Eyes giant and staring to both of its sides.

The body is human and bare except a robe that spans across its waist and drapes down to the top of its crooked, bent knees. There peeking above the robe is the top of its erect genitalia, pressed firmly against its abdomen, the rest outlined by the robe pressed against. The robe bears an insignia. It has three equally sized lines, one on top and one on each side surrounding a dot, the fourth line which goes underneath the dot extends into a left facing hook shape.

The idol glows. It's a bright, warm orange that permeates through its nearly translucent white body. You can see its hollowness. There is nothing inside, nothing physically tangible at least.

Ms. Florakis falls to her knees to begin to pray, but her throat is concaved in like an aluminum can. Her tongue falls whole from her mouth, as though it simply became detached. The students ignore her and stare.

They stare at the bright idol and it begins to affect their eyes. It is like staring into the sun. The spots of darkness one is able to blink away after staring at a bright illumination now remain permanent. The dark spots stay in their vision, they cover the faces of all familiarity around them, distorting the faces into images of beasts in the hidden light. Each child and teacher's face now is that of something which creepeth upon the ground.

The children stagger in swarms from each classroom, eyes transfixed upon the glowing abomination, until they have made their ways outside and surrounded the idol. The vibrations intensify in the teacher's ears and cause them to blackout. All except one: Ms. Gulzar.

They forego their winter clothing and stand around the entrance to the house, staring at the one they were called to see. They stand there, the dark spots revealing the faces assigned to each worshiper, ears vibrating and inciting arousal. They stand there for hours.

It wasn't until some parents had been waiting for over twenty minutes in the parking lot at dismissal time that anybody went to see what was going on. The front doors were locked, every door they could reach was locked. A group of them decided to walk around outback to the playground and there they stood, amidst a perfect lack of movement and a near deafening silence, adults leaned into the high fence, yelling for the attention of their children.

Some tried to climb the fence, but the quadrilateral pattern links were too small to hold even the ends of their shoes. Some tried to rip the fence down, but alas, it was staked too deep into the earth for it to be lifted by their panicked efforts. Some parents began to call the police, other parents began to try to smash through the glass front doors. Their makeshift instruments of destruction pulled from their vehicles still took spectacular efforts to even damage the reinforced glass. The alarms set off additional warnings to the police and the desperate parents could only hope that it would speed their efforts up.

When the police showed up, they showed up in throngs of confused and heavily equipped cruisers. Some had preemptively arrived with their rifles held closely to their chests, scared at the large scene of screaming parents, trying to shatter their way into the building.

The officers with drawn weapons stood by the door and used their rifles as presumed threats while yelling for them to step back. The vibrations began to roar louder and made its way into the ears of those in authority. The sensation was oppressive inside the officers' ears, it made them fall off balance, it disoriented them, confused them. They were losing control while the parents wept and screamed.

They wish they would stop screaming, why won't they stop screaming? Didn't they see that you brave officers were just trying to do your job? Their screams sounded messy and unclear, but their tone sounded accusatory. They were undermining you, calling you failures, they were trying to take the law into their own hands.

Yell for them to stand back, but they won't listen, they need to be made an example. The force can't just stand there and allow this anarchy to rule, they needed to establish order. That man with the lug wrench who was smashing his improvised weapon against the glass doors when you arrived is getting closer. He won't step back and his yells are muddling the vibrations. So the officer pushes the father to the ground and with a single shot, shatters his inner jaw with a bullet, causing his teeth to spill out onto his lap.

He begins to wail and the sound is even worse, the parents are now yelling louder, some with fear, others with anger, they won't stop closing in. The rounds are let free like doves in ceremony and penetrate the chests of those who erred by standing within range. They call for backup to aid in this massacre and so more will arrive.

When the other officers arrive, they are visitors to a disgusting show of fatally wounded parents. The firefighters and medics who arrived in between had fallen dead from the wounds inflicted by blunt weapons or fired bullets. Some of their fellow officers had died from the very same. Not many left standing except for two officers who shared their grips on the same rifle, smashing it deeply into the face of a petite mother whose stature could not have exceeded the height of five feet. One of them must have had too loose of a grip for a finger had slid, pressing the trigger and firing a round directly into the glass door behind them, finally shattering it into an opening.

Four of the officers stayed behind to make sense of the chaos which they stood in the aftermath of, while a fifth one continued on past them, following the subtle directions the vibrations that began to sound in his ear were telling him. He stepped by the barbaric cops in the middle of their death blows and into the shattered glass door. He walked inside and could finally feel like he was in a quietness now. The halls were empty, but at the other end, he knew there was something to be witnessed.

He walked through the school without a pressing urgency, only going fast enough to curtail the reverberating sounds of his footfall with proceeding steps, and made his way to the back doors that opened to the playground. As he got closer he could see the huddled mass of students. He looked at them wondering simple thoughts, aren't they cold? When he had finally pushed the door open to step into their gathering, he could see the finer details. Fingers of these children, numbed to a bitter blackness. They had already developed deep frostbites, how long had they been standing out here? Why were they standing out there? He stared forwardly and saw the answer standing in the open doorway.

The vibrations had stopped and the air had become jarringly quiet. They must have all stood in silence for about the space of half an hour. Then, as it were, the sound of trumpets sounding in reverse, loudly the sound spread across the entire audience and all knees fell to the ground. The idol was made to appear as a living thing and began to move its arms about.

With its mouth now open, it spoke blasphemies of the God of Heaven, calling into question his authority and very existence. It spake continuously in a series of tongues foreign to man, but understood by all those who bowed before the beast. The first generation of prophets of this unclean spirit.

As its speech came to an end, the living idol began to glow with far more heated intensity than before. In this burning light, the foul beast appeared as though it were lit internally like a blow mold lawn decoration, the orange light shining through its horrible and pale shell. As the light shone this time through its chest, the beginnings of organs and stringed veins could be seen forming inside its center.

Its arms reached out and called forth to the students, asking for the whore of which it was to consecrate its arrival with. A part was made amidst the children and stepping forth was Ms. Gulzar. She stood in front of the idol and was disrobed by the vile beast. She was made to take the idol's robe, tie it on the front of her face, and turn to face the children. It was at this time that she allowed the beast to enter her, blood spilling forth from her groin from the violent penetration, as her weeping eyes were concealed by the esoteric symbol. The children continued to kneel with intent as they repeated with even spaces of time, chanting the name of the blasphemous demon.

Woe to the inhabiters of Bedford! For the devil is come down unto you, and your inaction against his evil ways has damned you all.

To learn more and keep up to date, be sure to drop me an email to the below address:
awwshaunyboy@gmail.com